Animal Miracles of the GOD Kind

Do people today still experience miracles, dreams, and visions as they did in Bible times?

Do people today still have dreams and visions of heaven including some of animals being there? Are these stories true or are they part of our imagination? I can not speak for all of them but having experienced some very, very specific revelations from God through dreams and visions, I am convinced that they can and do happen.

Animal Miracles of the God Kind includes visions and messages which I believe allow us to understand beyond this world an eternal paradise which includes the animal kingdom along with man. It also includes many inspiring true-life stories of the love and devotion between man and animals.

By Amazon Christian Best Selling Author
Dr. Mary Buddemeyer-Porter

Animal Miracles of the GOD Kind

I had the honor of reading Mary's new book, *Animal Miracles of the God Kind*. I was at first skeptical about miracles but it wasn't long until I experienced an animal miracle of my own during the time when my father was very ill and facing the end of his time on this earth. God does truly use His animal creation to teach us and to minister to us.

Mary is a wonderful person and friend. I am so grateful to this lovely lady for spending over twenty years of biblical study in God's word concentrating mainly on God's love for all creation. I came to know Mary when I went through a five-year season of pet loss. I too was told that animals did not go to heaven. I just could not bear it that they would perish after life on this earth. Thank you, Mary, for being obedient to God's calling.

Cheryl Beaverson
Michigan

I applaud you for all of your hard work and efforts that went into writing this book.

This book explains how every animal is unique in their own way and how we need to open our eyes and our minds to their purpose on this earth. The personal stories are so inspiring and heartwarming. And, scientific and biblical evidence together, bring to the reader a new message of understanding and enlightenment concerning creation. Yes, animals do go to heaven.

Susan Lacaille
Chicago, IL

Animal Miracles of the GOD Kind

by

DR. MARY BUDDEMEYER-PORTER

Amazon Christian Best Selling Author

EDEN PUBLICATIONS, LLC.
Wichita Falls, Texas

Editor: Barbara Grazdan
Contributor: Robert Clark
"The Miracles of Fido" edited by Barbara Grazdan and Karla Harris
Layout and page design by Crystal Wood
Cover Graphics/Illustration by David Fredrick

Eden Publications, LLC.
Wichita Falls, Texas
www.creatures.com
www.creaturesinheaven.com
www.petlossbooks.com
Copyright © 2010 Mary Buddemeyer-Porter

For Worldwide Distribution

ISBN 978-0-9790722-2-2

Acknowledgments

I wish to thank each person who has written stories found in *Animal Miracles of the God Kind*. I also want to extend my love and appreciation to all who love and care for all the creatures God has put in your path throughout your earthly journey.

I want to thank Beverly Clark and Sandy Stevens, who have prayed me through so many difficult situations with a special prayer that Beverly will be greatly rewarded for working with Eden Publications, LLC..

I thank Ron Porter, my faithful partner in life who has labored with me to fulfill God's mission for our work on earth.

In memory of Bob Buddemeyer, who started out with me on this wonderful journey of life co-creating the wonderful Land of Music® series and is now in heaven cheering our sons, Eden and Roman, and their families on as each completes their earthly missions for the glory of God.

In memory of Roger Fritz, who worked with me on the *Fido* book and other projects as well. His counsel is greatly missed.

A very, very special thanks to Barbara Grazdan for her wonderful and excellent editing. Without her expertise, many stories and commentary would be misunderstood and grammatically unreadable. She has dedicated many, many hours editing *Animal Miracles of the God Kind*. It is my prayer that she will be rewarded many times over for her work.

Most of all, I want to thank God for granting me this wonderful mission in life and sending all of those who have helped me in so many ways to reveal His love and eternal plans for all creation including mankind.

Table of Contents

About the Book

The purpose of my books, *Will I See Fido in Heaven?* and *Animals, Immortal Beings,* was revealed through nearly 200 scriptures from the Book of Genesis through the Book of Revelation that there is eternal life for all animals below man and the need for man to come to salvation through Jesus Christ. There are wonderful true-life animal stories in them but the focus of their mission is different from *Animal Miracles of the God Kind.*

Animal Miracles of the God Kind proposes to reveal a deeper dimension, one of Heaven and the spirit and soul of man and animals and God's love for both.

It includes numerous heart-warming stories of the love and bond between man and animal. Many of the stories in *Animal Miracles of the God Kind* give supernatural knowledge beyond this life that animals do go to Heaven with scriptural references often added for support. Some of these stories you may or may not believe, but for those who have had the unexplainable and supernatural experiences they are very real. I believe some of the stories will confirm God's ability to communicate to us that our deceased and beloved pets truly are in Heaven.

Miracles or signs and wonders are as much a part of reality as the flesh. They reveal an inanimate but very real spiritual knowing, yet scientifically unexplained part of every being. The Holy Spirit gives us a different dimension of the spectacular and unscientifically proven, yet understood experiences in dreams and visions. These dreams and visions reveal another and real dimension of life that not only does Heaven exist but that God gives us dreams and visions and speaks to us through the Holy Spirit, revealing to us that the spiritual world is as real as the physical world of flesh and blood. We, for the most part, can only see the fleshly, physical existence due to our spiritual blindness.

Do animals see into the spiritual world things we do not see? The story "A Child Blessed" is a wonderful example of the spiritual understanding of animals. It is found in *Will I See Fido In Heaven?* The story of "Hero, the Doberman and Penny, the Beagle" is another example from this book. Do children often see into the spiritual world things we adults most often can not see? The story "Angel and the Angel Fish," I believe, gives us further insight into what the innocent children of creation see. I am convinced from the dreams and visions I have experienced and ones which have been brought to me concerning children, that because of their pure and innocent spirits and souls, they can see angels and demons sometimes.

Dreams and visions are often God's ways of communicating with us giving us comfort, direction, and some understanding beyond this life. The stories and experiences within "Animal Miracles of the God Kind" reveal this avenue, one of the spiritual world, in leading mankind to look beyond the natural into a very real, eternal world of God's spirit.

The Bible says that in the end times we will have dreams and visions. Prophecies will become clear as we compare the plight of Jews throughout history concerning what the Old Testament reveals will happen before God delivers Christians and all creation below man from this world of sin. *(28) And it shall come to pass afterward, (in the last days,) that I will pour out my Spirit upon all flesh: and your sons and your daughters shall prophesy, your old men shall dream dreams, your young men shall see visions; (29) And also upon the servants and upon the handmaidens, in those days will I pour out my Spirit: (Joel 2:28-29 KJV)*

There will be more people God allows to experience Heaven and come back to tell us. There will be more visions and signs as you will see in this book of God's promise to us of a glorious and wonderful eternal life with Him and all of creation. He would not have created something had He not made it perfect.

Warning

Some dreams, visions and prophecies are not of God, however, so we do have to pray for discernment. John Wesley, recognized as the founding father of the Methodist Church, said to be sure to test the spirits to make sure they are of God.

Beloved, believe not every spirit, but try the spirits whether they are of God: because many false prophets are gone out into the world (1 John 4:1KJV)

Charles Capps in his book, *Angels,* speaks of supernatural experiences such as angels, revelations and visions. He says: God will not have angels appearing to you or have you seeing some kind of vision just so you can say, "Hey, I'm spiritual! I had a vision!"

If revelation knowledge is going to come forth in any vision or supernatural experience that God desires to give, then it will come without your seeking after it or looking for it. If you are always looking for supernatural appearances, then Satan may try to bring you satanic enlightenment.

If you are looking for a greater revelation, then your motive is not right, and it will cause you to get some kind of revelation that is definitely not of God.

True religion is Christ-centered and based on the truth of the Gospel of Jesus Christ. Don't base your faith on a vision, an angel or a revelation. Base your faith on God's Word.

For all who have never had any supernatural experiences of the God Kind, I can only say that for you to believe in them you will have to believe the Bible is the true Word of God and, add to that, faith in Him and all of His ways of communicating with us as the Bible reveals. Pray always for discernment and wisdom to understand the full meaning. We may wish for God to reveal certain things to us but normally He does that through His word and not through dreams and visions. Those experiences happen without asking when God knows we need an answer or He simply wants to bless us and let us know that He, " Our God" is real and He knows our heart. He has shown us through His word that these types of experiences are as real as what we read on the written page and see in flesh and blood. One example is Balaam and his donkey.

It was not until I had one of the critics read the manuscript of this book that she believed in the supernatural as she had never had such an experience. It was in her un-belief and questioning God that He clearly allowed her wonderful supernatural experiences. She had two other adults attest to two different wonderful and unexplainable Miracles of the God Kind. God is real and so is Heaven. There will be an increase of the supernatural through signs, wonders, dreams and visions in the last days. However, the Bible also warns us that the devil will deceive even the elect of God if we do not test the spiritual realm to see if what we have heard or seen is truly of God.

One way Satan and his demons can mislead us is through ghostly presences that we believe are our pets or people of the past who had died. Demonic spirits duplicate or counterfeit, so to speak, persons or animals that have passed on and we are lead to think that they are ones whose spirits have stayed long after their physical bodies have died.

The Bible says *to be absent from the body is to be present with the Lord.* And, *it is appointed to every man once to die and then the judgment.* King David said that he could go to his dead son (in Heaven) but his son could not come to him.

After this life is over we either go to Heaven or hell and the animals all go to Heaven. There is no coming back as another person or animal. Another deception is reincarnation.

Any supernatural experience we have has to be tested. So often we so want to see the presence of someone, or some animal, that has died. Satan is more than happy to let one of his demon spirits portray themselves as one we long to see or be with.

God gives every living being an eternal soul and spirit. So, every being has one fleshly body and one spirit given by God. When the blood within, which is the spirit of the life, ceases to flow, the physical body dies and the real person or animal, their eternal spiritual being, lives on either in Heaven or hell.

The Bible says Satan is the god of this world. He was given that position by man when Adam and Eve sinned. It is only through Jesus Christ that creation can be redeemed for eternal life with God.

As the god of this world, Satan and one third of all the angels, now fallen, are roaming to and fro to mislead us at every opportunity. Be aware of any such deception. As Christians, we have the authority to plead the blood of Jesus over any situation and rebuke Satan in the name of Jesus, and Satan and his demons have to leave. Satan tries to counterfeit everything of God but there is one thing he can not counterfeit and that is the blood of Jesus.

With this in mind, I feel assured God does sometimes allow us to see our family and animals in visions to bring us messages from time to time after they go to Heaven. I believe this book contains many such experiences which I pray will bless you and give you added faith and assurance of God's love for all He created.

Foreword

To fully understand *Animal Miracles of the God Kind* you must read Mary's books *Will I See Fido In Heaven?* and *Animals, Immortal Beings*.

I have always believed that Earth, as we know it, is the illusion and the Spirit World is the reality and truth. Eternity is forever. Life here and now is just a dressing room for all eternity. Thru God's love for all His creation, animal, man and the beauty of the earth, we have only a glimpse into the realm of Heaven.

Because Scripture says that man was created in the image of God, many theologians have interpreted that to mean that only man has a soul and spirit; however, the Holy Bible makes it clear that animals too, have an eternal soul and spirit.

You will be delighted, as I have been, to share in the research that Mary has done, proving that without a doubt, all creation here is just a shadow of God's master plan and love for the world He has created. Before meeting Mary and reading her books, listening to her music, I had grieved over my very special pets that had died. There was a hole in my heart. Now I can hardly wait to meet them at Heavens Gate, along with my family and friends. It brings a new understanding to who our God is and how much He loves all of His creation.

All animal lovers will delight in reading this book.

Beverly Treece Clark

Introduction

Biblical Facts Everyone Should Know

**The History of the Dead Sea Scrolls
and the Apocrypha Books**

The Dead Sea Scrolls

The Dead Sea Scrolls are ancient manuscripts from Palestine. The scrolls were found in caves near the northwestern shore of the Dead Sea. These scrolls are the "greatest manuscript discovery of modern times." They include all of the books of the Old Testament except Esther. Some of the books are in nearly complete form. They are the oldest known manuscripts of any books of the Bible. The scrolls are kept in the Shrine of the Books, part of the Israel Museum in Jerusalem.

The History of the Apocrypha Books

After the first edition of *Will I See Fido in Heaven?* was printed, a dear friend from California, Margaret Miller, sent me a gift of beautiful reproductions of old Bibles dating back to the 1300s. Along with these Bibles was a copy of *The Forbidden Book* by Dr. Craig Lampe, a work about the writings, translations and lives of those who scripted the early translations of the Bible. Within *The Forbidden Book* was the research on the Apocrypha Books.

Dr. Lampe says: "What we don't understand, we fear."

Dr. Craig Lampe wrote *The Forbidden Book*. It is about the great transcribers, ministers, and printers who often lost their lives for the sake of the Bible. Dr. Lampe has spent many, many years in research collecting Bibles along with his friend Johnathan including over 1,000

Bibles dating before 1800. What they were to discover was a shock to them and, I must say, to me, a Protestant, as well. I will quote what Dr. Lampe said concerning the Apocrypha Books being a Protestant himself, "What we don't understand we fear."

The "Apocrypha" are fourteen books found in the original Hebrew scriptures, along with the other thirty-nine books of the Old Testament. "Jerome" transcribed them in Latin in the 300s A.D. and named them the "Apocrypha" meaning "Hidden" Books of the Bible. In case you are a Protestant and do not know these facts you are in for a surprise:

It was not until 1885 that the Apocrypha books were removed from the Western Orthodox churches in the Protestant versions of the Bible which includes the United States and most of Europe. All Bibles for 2,000 years had the Apocrypha books in them, including the King James Bible. The Apocrypha books have always remained very much a part of all Eastern Orthodox Protestant Bibles throughout the remainder of the world.

Did you know?

1.   The Apocrypha books were in the original Hebrew Scriptures (Septuagint).

2.   They were canonized in AD 406 by the Council of Carthage.

3.   It was a crime punishable by one year in jail and a fine if they were removed from the Bible.

4.   The New Testament includes over 400 Scriptures from the Apocrypha books quoted by Jesus and the Apostles.

5.   Segments from them have been found in the Dead Sea Scrolls.

6.   The Apocrypha books are important because they are instructions for the Jewish people about a king who was to come who would be a spiritual king and not an earthly king. They have valuable prophetic messages, address evil, and the results of sin.

7.   They had been part of the Holy Bible for over 2,000 years. No one knows why in 1885 two men, Westcott and Hort, had them eliminated.

8.   There are no Scriptures in these books that suggest any of the Catholic doctrine Protestants disagree with. It was a group of Jewish, not Christian, scholars who tried to convince the scribe, Jerome who was transcribing them in Latin in the 300s that they were not in the original Hebrew Scriptures. However, that turned out to be untrue and Jerome did include them in his translation but put asterisks by them to leave doubt of their authenticity.

The Apocrypha books are valuable to all Christians. Theologians of old and founding fathers of the Lutheran, Presbyterian, Baptist and Methodist churches read from the Apocrypha books in their ministry including John Wesley, Martin Luther and John Calvin.

The Catholic Church has removed the eleventh chapter of II Esdras and the Prayer of Manasseh, and, a large portion of the 100 verses from the Book of Daniel are missing in most Bibles.

The Book of Ecclesiasticus and the Book of Sirach are two different titles of the same book depending on which Bible versions you read. I quote scriptures from the Book of Wisdom, Tobit and Ecclesiasticus.

Some of the scriptures I include in *Animal Miracles of the God Kind* came from the Apocrypha in the Protestant 1611 King James Version and the 1560 version of the Geneva Bible. I also quote from the 1609 Catholic Douay Rheims version. Another wonderful and pure translation I use comes from the Jewish version, The Holy Scriptures. Most scriptures, however, are from the more modern versions.

The word "miracles" was not found in the original translation of the Bible. The words "signs and wonders" were the terms used concerning supernatural experiences.

You will find many signs and wonders in *Animal Miracles of the God Kind*. I pray these stories and scriptures will be a blessing to all who read them.

CHAPTER 1

A Touch of Heaven on Earth

⊰ Little Pepi Porter, My Baby Girl Dog ⊱

The pain of losing my beautiful little black, silky, long-haired Cocker/Pomeranian mix baby girl still stands out as a pain that was almost more than I could bear.

My husband Ron and I found her during a stop on our way from St. Louis to attend a meeting in northern Missouri. It was a cold and rainy fall night. I'd been driving and couldn't stay awake so I pulled into a little country filling station to get some candy.

As I came out of the station, I saw two dogs all curled up under the overhang trying to stay dry. One was a little black dog with long hair and the other was a medium-sized hunting dog with white and brown fur. As I walked by them, the little black one looked up at me. I saw her eyelids didn't look quite right, but she seemed so precious and so in need of a home. When I stopped to look at her she just put her head back down as if to say, "She doesn't want me either."

I felt concerned for both dogs but knew we already had one loving beagle hound at home and wondered what we would ever do with three dogs if we rescued these two.

We drove on to northern Missouri, but I was unable to keep the image of the helpless dogs out of my mind. So, on our return to St. Louis two nights later, we stopped to see what we could do about them.

I had remembered where she was but when we got within about fifty miles of the filling station we discovered that due to flooding we would have to take about a 100 mile detour around Interstate 70. I was so upset I didn't know what to do. Finally we got back to the end of

1

the flood zone and there was a police officer standing to make sure that no one drove into the flooded area. Praise God for that officer! We pulled up to the officer and told him of a little dog we so wanted to try to reach and where it was. The officer said that the Interstate was flooded from the other side right up to that filling station but that if we took the side road we could actually get to the station from this side without driving through any flood. I couldn't believe it. I was so excited about getting there and hoping she would still be all right. As soon as we got back to the gas station I got out to see if I could find the dogs but they were not to be seen. I went inside and the young lady behind the counter said that the little black dog had wandered up one day with several other dogs. She said her brother would take the little black dog home on the weekends and bring her back to live at the station during the week. They thought she was pregnant because her stomach was swollen. The other dog belonged to a farmer and just visited the station to keep her company.

The young lady said that although her brother did take her home on weekends she would let me have the little black one. She went out in the pouring rain and called her. They had named her Precious and she came running around the corner as fast as her short little legs could carry her. I gave her a hotdog, picked her up all wet and muddy, and put her in a cardboard box in the back seat with my mother, who was riding home with us to live. We named her Pepi, and almost immediately she fell fast asleep. Mother petted her as we drove through that glorious night the remainder of the three hundred mile trip home.

We took Pepi to the vet and it turned out she had three kinds of worms and was swollen up because of them. She also had a problem with her third eyelid. It drooped over her eye, not descending correctly and the doctor had to operate on it. She was in great shape thereafter.

Dr. Steinberg said Pepi was about two years old and was a Cocker/ Pomeranian mix. She was the most precious little fur ball. She and Duffy, our beloved beagle, were best of friends and went everywhere with us. Pepi always insisted on sitting between my husband and me while Duffy slept in the back seat.

Pepi brought us complete joy for 10 years. Then one day I noticed some lumps on her. The vet felt that they might be fatty tissue and I decided to start giving her natural cure supplements in case it was cancer. She continued to live a happy normal life for another two years until one day while walking her I noticed she was getting so weak she could hardly walk. I picked her up and finished the walk holding her in my arms. As soon as I got home I called Dr. Steinberg. He told me to bring her in. He checked and her blood indicated she was in need of blood and said he would operate on her but that I needed to get some blood from the local emergency veterinarian clinic. I called my best friend Debbie and she went with me. We prayed constantly. We delivered the blood and Debbie went back home. By then it was about 2:00 in the afternoon.

I went to pick up my grandchildren from school and got home about 4 p.m. Shortly thereafter, the phone rang telling me to get to the clinic as soon as possible as Pepi was full of cancer. It would be cruel to bring her back after surgery because she would have very little time to live and would be in great pain. I immediately called my husband and told him. He wanted us to wait until he got there to let her go on to Heaven but the vet said he couldn't wait as she would be waking up any moment.

The thought of the separation and that I had somehow let her down by not being able to make her well was devastating. I took her in to the vet with her little eyes sparkling, looking at me as if to say, "Mommy, I will see you after while. I know you brought me here to get well." I did notice something when I left her. She had had gray around her mouth and some around her eyes, but that afternoon all of the hair on her face was pure black. At that time, I thought it seemed so strange. It was as if she was young again.

I held Pepi while she received the injection and it was comforting to know that I was with her until her spirit left. But, for some reason, I did not feel that she had yet gone to Heaven. I wanted to take her body home with me so I could bury her but Dr. Steinberg said he would have to keep her in a cooler all night.

It hurt so much to leave her little body in a cooler all alone. I could not go to sleep until early morning, as I could not believe the nightmare of having to let her go. All night I kept feeling Pepi was cold.

The next morning my husband, Ron, awakened saying that he'd had a dream of a little girl who was saying she was very cold and lost and didn't know where to go. He at first thought it was a child but then realized it was Pepi. Ron told her to go toward the light. God revealed through Ron what I felt in my spirit as he had no way of knowing that I kept feeling that Pepi was cold.

I did not believe it was really time for her to go and, possibly, I was trying to hold on to her spirit so to speak. But as soon as Ron told her to go toward the light, I have no doubt she went straight to Heaven.

Once a month for several months I would have a dream about Pepi, always on a Friday night. She had gone to Heaven on a Friday night just before Mother's Day. It was the third month when I heard God speak to me, saying, ***"You can hold her for a moment. She is with me in Heaven."*** I absolutely believe that for just a moment I held her again as I felt her silky black fur, though I did not see how she could be in my arms and in Heaven at the same time. Yet, I never doubted God's word that night.

In that precious moment God gave me a special gift, allowing me to hold and pet Pepi and yet be assured she was with Him. God so blessed me, allowing me that precious moment in time. I saw her just as she was when she was young, silky black with no gray around her mouth or eyes. She was again in the prime of her life. I have read and been told by others who have seen their pets after they have left that the pets appeared to be about three or four years old again, youthful and full of life.

I cried many tears over Pepi's physical death, yet I continued to praise God over and over that she was with Him. Through all of the tears I felt peace and really started visualizing her in Heaven without pain and suffering. The Bible says: *"I go to prepare a place for you, if it were not so I would have told you." (John 14:2 KJV)*

God's tender mercy is over all of His works (creation), and He gave us scriptures to reveal that truth. *(8) The LORD is gracious and compassionate forbearing, and constant in his love. (9) The LORD is good to all men, and his tender care rests upon all his creatures. (10)All thy creatures praise thee, LORD, and thy servants bless thee. (11) They talk of the glory of thy kingdom and tell of thy might, (12) they proclaim to their fellows how mighty are thy deeds, how glorious the majesty of thy kingdom. (13) Thy kingdom is an everlasting kingdom, and thy dominion stands for all generations. (Psalm 145:8-13 The New English Bible)*

⊰ Jesus Comes to Sarah ⊱

Sarah Neuman, an editor for the *Post Dispatch of St. Louis*, called me one day to write an article on the immortality of animals based on *Will I See Fido in Heaven?* During our conversation she revealed the following personal story of how Jesus comforted her after the loss of her precious dog. It is one of the most amazing stories of assurance of the Love of Jesus for both man and animals that I have ever heard.

Sarah said: My precious little dog had become terminally ill and I knew I should let her go. I called the vet and he said he would come to my home to put her to sleep. I held her and did fine until the vet picked her lifeless body up and started out the door with her. I was in such grief I fell to my knees in the middle of the room and started crying out to God to please let me know if she would be in Heaven. I was weeping uncontrollably when I felt an arm around my shoulder. *I looked to my side and there was Jesus kneeling beside me with his arm around me and just beside Jesus was my beloved baby wagging her tail and licking the face of Jesus.* I immediately started rejoicing and praising God as He had answered my prayers in a way far more real than I could have imagined.

We can rejoice in the miraculous God encounter that Sarah experienced. *My mouth shall speak the praise of the Lord; And let all flesh bless His holy name for ever and ever. (Psalm 145: 21 Jewish Holy Scriptures)*

❄{ Sparky Comes Back }❄

The story of Robin Pressnall was sent to me by a dear friend in Christ, Margaret Miller. Robin tells of her own experience about her friend Lou as she wrote in her letter telling of her loss of her precious little muttipoo, Nicholas, on May 19, 1998. The story is one of a miracle picture of God, provided at just the right time to reveal the eternal life of animals and how God uses them in times of sorrow for reassurance that all is well in Heaven.

Robin said: It was two years ago, a friend of ours, Lou, was diagnosed with breast cancer. It was too late to do much to help her. Another friend of ours, Jan, was Lou's best friend, and also a nurse. On many occasions, Jan and I would have "discussions" about whether or not animals went to Heaven. I always contended that they did, because the Bible says that there are white horses at the right hand of God...so it always seemed to me, that there would be other animals in Heaven. She always said, that animals did not have souls, therefore they could not go to Heaven. (Her strict Baptist upbringing was coming through!). As Lou became sicker and sicker, Jan stayed with her day and night. Lou finally sank into a coma and stayed there for three weeks. When she died, Jan was there. She called me the next morning to tell me that Lou had died. But she didn't tell me the rest of the story for several weeks. It seems that on the night Lou died, she awoke suddenly from the coma! ***Her eyes sprang open, and she exclaimed, "Sparky!!"*** And then just as suddenly…she died. None of her family knew who "Sparky" was. Not her husband of 45 years, nor her grown children…no one. One day, a couple of weeks later, Jan got a call from Lou's family, asking her to come over. It seemed they had something important to show her. It was an old black and white picture…of a little girl, and a German Shepherd. ***On the back was hand written in faded ink…Lou…age 10…and Sparky.***

From the Messianic and Visionary Recitals in the "Dead Sea Scrolls Uncovered" we read from Ezekiel 8:3 in which the author is working under the inspiration of Ezekiel's vision of the new Temple or the Temple of the end of days referred to and extended into the ideal picture of Jerusalem. (To the reader: These are fragments so some words will be missing and other words are divided in parentheses.) The archangel Michael ascended to the Highest Heaven then spoke the Angels of God *(2) he said 'I found troops of fire there… (3) {Behold,} there were nine mountains, two to the eas[t and two to the north and two to the west and two} (4) {to the so}uth. There I beheld Gabriel the Angel… I said to him, (5)'… and you rendered the vision comprehensible.' Then he said to me… (6) It is written in my book that the Great One, the Eternal Lord…(7) the sons of Ham to the sons of Shem. Now behold, the Great One, the Eternal Lord… (8) when …tears from … (9) Now behold, a city will be built for the Name of the Great One, [the Eternal Lord] … [And no] (10) evil shall be committed in the presence of the Great One, [the Eternal] Lord …(11) Then the Great One, the Eternal Lord, will remember His creation [for the purpose of Good]… [Blessing and honor and praise] (12) [be to] the Great One, the Eternal Lord. To Him belongs Mercy and to Him belongs…*

⊰ She Knew Me ⊱

Don Hall wrote, after reading my *Fido* book, concerning an experience he had had when he and his wife had to let their little Muffin go to Heaven. God speaks when we least expect it and when we most need it.

Don says: I have just finished reading your wonderful book; it has changed my life and has given me a better and different view of the creatures and the Lord himself. When I read the part where you didn't go but had your son take Duffy, your beagle of 17 years, to be put to sleep, it broke my heart because my wife and I had almost the same experience with Muffin. She was 17 and we couldn't bear to see her put to sleep so we left her with the doctor and the nurse and went into the next room and prayed. Today, I broke down thinking how I had left her at that moment. I was crying and talking to the Lord and as I told the Lord, "Lord, she didn't know anyone when she slipped into eternity." My heart leaped for joy at his answer. ***He said, "She knew me."***

I learned after not being with my beagle Duffy when he went on to Heaven that I would never leave my precious pets in their final moments on earth and wanted to make sure that they knew I was right there telling them I loved them and would see them in Heaven soon. But, as Don said, God was with them. God says in the Bible*: "Are not five sparrows sold for two copper coins? And not one of them is forgotten before God."(Luke 12:6 NKJV)*

In Matthew we read:*.." Are not two sparrows sold for a farthing? And one of them shall not fall to the ground without your Father" (Matthew 10:29 KJV).*

The New King James Version: says "Are not two sparrows sold for a copper coin? And not one of them falls to the ground apart from your Father's will." (Matthew 10:29 NKJV).

I have used this verse in my books but it was not until I read Don's story that I realized that God truly is there when every

single creature, even the sparrow, a creature that is of such little value in the eyes of man, dies.

The following is the rest of the story from both the Good News Bible and the 1611 King James Bible *(4) I tell you, my friends do not be afraid of those who kill the body but cannot afterward do anything worse. (5) I will show you whom to fear: fear God, who, after killing, has the authority to throw into hell. Believe me, he is the one you must fear! (6) Aren't five sparrows sold for two pennies? Yet not one sparrow is forgotten by God." (Luke 12:4-6 Good News Bible)*

The 1611 Authorized King James Bible, Luke 12:4-6 written in the old English style and spelling says*: (4) And I say vnto you my friends, Bee not afraid of them that kill the body, and after that, haue no more that they can doe. (5)But I wil forewarne you whom you shall feare: Feare him, which after he hath killed, hath power to cast into hell, yea, I say vnto you, Feare him. (6)Are not fiue sparrows solde for two farthings and not one of them is forgotten before God? (Luke 12:4-6 1611 King James Bible).*

◦⊰ Hero the Doberman and Penny the Beagle ⊱◦

I went to Osage Beach, Missouri, to the new Dogwood non-kill animal shelter for a book signing. At the book signing Dr. John E. Reinhold a retired veterinarian and father of the head of the shelter shared an amazing story about his two dogs unlike any I have ever heard. This wonderful story will let you look at the animal world in an entirely different way. I asked my dear friend Sheila Boyd, a great editor to write and edit the story for me.

As told to Sheila Boyd by Dr. John E. Reinhold, DVM, President of Board of Directors, Dogwood Animal shelter, President of Camdenton, Missouri, United Methodist Church Council.

Having been a veterinarian for 39 years, Dr. John Reinhold has seen many extraordinary things happen with animals, but what his wife, Judy, and he experienced in 1990 surpassed all their understanding.

Their Beagle, Penny and their Doberman, Hero, were truly life partners as they did everything together for the eight years Hero was alive. It seemed as though when Penny tilted her head high in the air with her nose focused on something only she knew, Hero would seek out the elusive target for her and off they'd go. They were a team, and it was truly amazing to watch them play and romp on the farm with all the other animals.

At the age of eight, Hero developed a deteriorated spinal canal which led to pneumonia. His death was eminent. John and Judy realized that they couldn't watch their beloved dog live in excruciating pain for who knew how much longer? They both knew that they had to give him back to God.

Are not two sparrows sold for a farthing? And one of them shall not fall on the ground without your Father" (Matthew 10:29 KJV). On the evening of their decision, Penny and Hero were laying on the living room floor on the rug where John was going to administer the prescription for euthanasia, while Judy assisted and held the vein where he needed to insert the needle. As hard as it is for any veterinarian to put any animal to sleep, it is that much harder to make that decision for their own pets. John and Judy have never experienced an incident like this before or since, nor have they heard of anyone else, but they both witnessed what they deem a miracle from God.

At the instant of Hero's last breath, Penny's head slowly raised and her eyes saw what John and Judy can only explain as Hero's spirit leaving his body, like a balloon floating to the ceiling. Immediately Penny got up, walked through the living room and into the kitchen with her head held high looking up, then her eyes moved from the ceiling out the kitchen window. John and Judy were speechless, to say the least!. While they fully believe that animals are incredibly intelligent, knowing and sensitive, this reaffirms their beliefs to a much higher level.

You are concerned for men and animals alike" (Psalm 36:6)

For we know that when this tent we live in now is taken down - when we die and leave these bodies — we will have wonderful new bodies in Heaven, homes that will be ours forevermore, made for us by God himself, and not by human hands. How weary we grow of our present bodies...We want to slip into our new bodies so that these dying bodies will, as it were, be swallowed up by everlasting life. This is what God has prepared for us and, as a guarantee, he has given us his Holy Spirit. (2 Corinthians 5: 1, 2, 3, 4, 5)

This reaffirms God's tremendous compassion for all creatures. John and Judy have had over 100 animals, but this was the first time that God has shown His compassion for them during this very painful and difficult time. John and Judy hope and pray that those who hear this story would feel the tremendous "awe" in what they felt. They also feel that it is unfortunate that everyone who loses a beloved pet doesn't experience this incredible sight. They gave praise and thanks to God for allowing them to experience a touch of Heaven that day.

Written and Edited by Sheila Boyd. All biblical references are quoted from *The Book*, a special edition of The Living Bible published by Tyndale House Publishers, Inc.

⊰{ An Unexpected Trip }⊱

I am including a story by a dear friend, Frances Svedbeck, as a tribute to her, and to her obedience in writing "Do Animals Go To Heaven"?

Frances is now in Heaven but in her book she told the story about her wonderful dog, Koala. She lived in Oregon and we spoke by phone quite often. Our company sold her book as well. God had revealed to her through her adopted mother, who had gone on to Heaven, that Frances was to get her book published and get it to the public. Her book was published in 1994, one year before my first book came out. God had led us both to reveal to the world His wonderful truth that animals do have eternal life. Frances was a wonderful Christian. She had many dogs but one that was very special to her was Koala. Frances and her husband have three grown sons. She shared her love for God and her dogs, especially the German shepherd named Koala with me often.

Frances held Koala as her spirit departed her body. Though she had suffered through the loss of her husband and the added financial and physical burden of operating a farm, the pain of letting Koala go was almost more than Frances could endure. But Frances did have God's word in her research through Scriptures that Koala was in Heaven. From that, she gained her strength and her ability to praise God even in her tears. She was to learn, however, that God had a special blessing to give her: an understanding of the life that she and Koala would have together one day in Heaven.

I called Frances often but over a two year period I noticed that she was getting weaker. Cancer was making it harder for her to come to the phone. I told Frances I was going to pray for her healing but she said "No, don't pray for my healing. I want to go to Heaven to be with Koala and the others waiting for me." I can just picture Frances and Koala walking through the meadows of Heaven sharing their experiences on earth and their love for each other. Now, they can communicate without any barriers. This is the story as told by Frances.

On the afternoon of the sixth day following Koala's departure from this world, I decided to take a nap, since sleeping at night was not an easy accomplishment. If I had known that I would soon be seeing my little Girl-Baby in a magnificent dream, I would have danced all the way to my bed. But there was nothing in my thoughts to indicate such a wonderful experience awaited me. All I sought was a little rest for my weary soul.

I suddenly found myself sitting in an easy chair, at one end of a very long, exquisitely furnished room. I observed, curiously, a shoe box on the lower shelf of an end table to my right. It seemed out of place in such lavish surroundings. About fifteen feet further to my right, a man was sitting sideways in his chair at the near end of a long elegant table. Beyond him were plush couches and furnishings one might find in some European palace. The room seemed endlessly long, and yet I had the feeling it was only a small part of some immense structure.

A woman sat about twenty feet across from me. We all seemed to be waiting for we knew not what. Then suddenly a vivacious silver and black German shepherd came in and hurried over and stood with her front paws resting on the arm of the woman's chair. Startled, the woman leaned away in her seat.

I saw then that the shepherd's mouth was opened widely, and she eagerly sought someone to help her. Without hesitation I went over and, never touching her, reached my hand around her mouth, and squeezed together a clamped instrument, removing it from her mouth. For a long moment, we gazed into each other's eyes. She moved her lower jaw as though greatly relieved, then turned and disappeared from the room.

There were now several people in the room, and quite a bit of chatter. I saw a cabinet with what appeared to be two or three knobs, and almost symbolically, turned one of the knobs. The place instantly quieted. Then turning to the people, I said, "Ladies and Gentlemen, I would like your full attention. We have just witnessed a miracle here. I would like us all to pray and thank God."

When I returned to my seat, I heard a little girl's giggling laughter behind me, out beyond the room. My gaze returned then to the mysterious shoe box.

The first thing I saw when I opened my eyes was a shoe box in my closet. It was similar to the one in the dream, perhaps a little larger, and it was to my left, whereas the box in my dream had always been to my right.

I raised up on my elbow, and suddenly found myself speaking aloud... ***"You have just seen Koala as she is now in Heaven. You were permitted to remove the spring-hook from her mouth so that she can now speak."***

I had interpreted the dream, an awesome thing to do. That is something I had never before done.

It was all so incredibly wonderful; to see Missy (as Frances often called Koala), with her new fur coat; her body renewed to youthful vigor, both her ears standing up. She had always had one ear that refused to stand up. My faith was bolstered to a new high. I began praising the Lord for all His mercies to us. I remembered looking into Koala's eyes; it came to my mind that she also was now learning that it was I, Ma, whom she had seen. I felt a warm glow about me.

Animals spoke in the Bible. We know Adam and Eve were tricked by the serpent who spoke in the Garden of Eden: *Now the serpent was the most cunning of all the animals that the Lord God had made. The serpent asked the woman, "Did God really tell you not to eat from any of the trees in the garden?" (Genesis 3:1 NAB)* **They did eat the forbidden fruit and fell into sin and God had to cover them with animal skins. Their sins brought physical death upon all creation. God had created everything to live forever and that remains true for the soul and spirit as God sustains/keeps them alive; however, all fleshly bodies have to die and in a sense be re-born or renewed into perfection in Heaven.** "Your justice is like the highest mountains: your judgment, like the mighty deep; all living creatures you sustain, LORD" Psalm 36:7 NAB)

So Koala had to die physically because of the sins of man but God has now given her a new glorified body.

In the Book of Numbers the donkey of Balaam spoke when it saw the Angel of the Lord. Through a vision God gave Frances, we can understand that God had planned for man and animals to communicate in Heaven. Oh, the wonders that wait us in Heaven. My favorite song growing up was "Talk to the Animals." I would go around the farm and touch the tops of the heads of the various animals and look in their eyes and sing that song just hoping that somehow they could talk to me.

Balaam was disobedient to God. The King of the Moabites, Balak wanted Balaam to go with them to rise up against the Israelites as God said the Israelites are a blessed people. God also has said that those who curse Israel He will curse. He will cause their nations to fall. God has made that clear to all who oppose Israel even to this day. God had told Balaam not to go with the princes of Moab. He went anyway. God was very angry and used his donkey and an angel to get Balaam's attention as we learn in the Book of Numbers. *(28) And the Lord opened the mouth of the ass, and she said unto Balaam, What have I done unto thee, that thou has smitten me these three times? (29) And Balaam said unto the ass, Because thou has mocked me: I would there were a sword in mine hand, for now I would kill thee. (30) And the ass said unto Balaam, {Am} not I thine ass, upon which thou hast ridden ever since {I was} thine unto this day? Was I ever wont to do so unto thee? And he said Nay (Numbers 22: 28:30 KJV)*

❧ My Old Dog Scooter ❧

This story is told by Wendy Allen of Kalamazoo MI.

Upon occasion I believe God can allow us to have visitations from Heaven to give us great comfort about our pets in Heaven and experience a supernatural vision of seeing, hearing or feeling their presence for just a moment as a reminder that they are still very much alive.

Wendy states: I had a dog named Scooter. He was just a mutt in the eyes of most people but he was my life. I got him before I had children, so he was my baby.

I had him for 14 wonderful years. On November 19, 1997 I had to put him to sleep. That was the hardest thing that I have ever had to do in my life. I will never get over him. But I want to tell you that he is still with me. I know this because of what has happened to me. I always felt like I did the wrong thing when I had him put to sleep. He had a brain tumor and I have never forgiven myself for doing this. He started coming to me in my dreams about three months after he died. At first, he would just fade away when I would go to touch him. I would wake up crying because I didn't understand this. Then one day I was cleaning the living room and I looked up and there he was standing there smiling at me and then he was gone. I thought I must be going nuts because now I am seeing him in person.

Then I started hearing his nails coming across the kitchen floor but he wasn't there. The last dream I had was the most real. I was letting in my other two dogs at the front door. First came Daisy; then came Annie; then, came my Scooter last in the door. I am staring in amazement. He walked into the living room and climbed right into his green chair. I walked over to him thinking he was going to disappear but he started talking to me. *He told me that he did not blame me for what happened and that he is very happy and for me not to be sad anymore because he is in Heaven and he will see me there.* Then he let me touch him and kiss him and I could smell him so I knew he was real. *He said he had the best life ever with me.* He licked my hand many times and my face. And off he went wagging his tail. So I know Scooter is in Heaven. I still cry a lot but I know *I WILL SEE HIM AGAIN.*

⊰ Dad and Scooter ⊱

Wendy Allen writes: My father had passed away four years before. I was driving down the road about six months after he passed on. All of the sudden my truck filled with the scent of pipe tobacco (my father smoked a pipe) and I could feel his hand on my shoulder. *I am all right.* He told me. I do believe that my dad and Scooter are just hanging out together!

Psalm 90:4 Jewish Scriptures is the same as 89:4 in Christian Bibles. This is a Prayer of Moses the man of God. *For a thousand years in Thy sight are but as yesterday when it is past, And as a watch in the night. (Psalm 90:4 Jewish Holy Scriptures)*

⸎ The Spirit of Snoopy ⸎

My dear friend, Debbie, told me of a vision she had when her dog Snoopy went to Heaven. Debbie is a wonderful, loving, and spirit-filled Christian. When I told her that God had given me the mission of writing Christian books on the immortality of animals based on the Bible, I thought she would say I was crazy and she wouldn't want anything more to do with me but she was completely supportive. I didn't know, however, for several years after my first book came out about her experience with Snoopy.

Debbie said: Our dog Snoopy was a mix but she looked like an English setter. She was black and white. She had spots and patches of black and white with fringe on her tail and legs. She was very beautiful. My sister's dog, Lacy, had 10 or 12 puppies and most of them were black but she was the only spotted black and white one. Lacy was black with a little white on her. The puppies were at my Mom and Dad's house in Wichita, KS. When people came to look at the puppies to pick one out my Mom would always hide Snoopy. She didn't want her to leave. I was visiting from Pueblo, Colorado. Snoopy was so cute that I just had to take her home with me. Eric, my husband, and I had one problem with taking her with us, however. My Dad solved that problem by building a little cage so that we could take her home on the train. She made it just fine. She traveled everywhere with us around the country. She was very good natured and loving. She was wonderful with the kids. She passed away when we moved to St. Louis. All that I can say is that she was my best friend and I missed her so much when she left… Snoopy was in the family room when suddenly her body just fell over on the floor. I witnessed her spirit as it went out of the family room through the kitchen and out the door. She was running. She was free.

The Book of Wisdom says, *Your imperishable spirit is in everything.* *(Wisdom 12:1 NJB)*

Thou sparest all things because they are thine, our Lord and master who lovest all that lives; for thy imperishable breath is in them all. (Wisdom 21:1 The New English Bible)

⋅⊰ Tina's Short Return ⊱⋅

God blesses Linda Sue Pearson with a vision of her beloved Tina. It reveals the kind of bodies animals have in Heaven; ones we can actually feel and hold.

Linda Sue Pearson adopted a dog named Tina in 1997. She was a white four year old retired greyhound. Linda adopted her at an Adopt-a-Greyhound Program. Two months later she adopted a five year old male, named Ike. Tina and Ike became inseparable. But in 2000 Linda noticed Tina had a swollen lymph node on the right side of her neck. She had a fever and no appetite. After being tested for numerous diseases Linda took her to a specialist who finally diagnosed her with lymphoma cancer. Linda was given a few options. One was chemotherapy. The success rate was good and it was possible for her to live one or two more years. Even though it was costly, Tina began therapy and within a few days Tina was back to her old self. One month later, however, she went into the ER never to return home. The Doctor did all possible for Tina but her liver and kidneys started shutting down and Linda had to let her go. The grief was almost unbearable. Linda had spoken to me by phone and I assured her, her precious Tina was in Heaven but that did not take away the pain or for that matter, give her assurance that Tina was in fact in Heaven. Two days later Linda's roommate brought home another greyhound. He was a newly retired black male. His name was Tyson. Her roommate retired early due to sore ankles but about 2:30 a.m. Tyson was pacing the floor and seemed a little nervous in his new home. Since we didn't have a backyard, I asked my roommate to walk him. I fell back asleep quickly and then all of a sudden I awoke. I sat up in bed and saw in my comforter the perfect shape of Tina sleeping on her left side. I looked on the floor and saw Ike sleeping in his usual place on the floor and there was no sign of Tyson or my friend in the room. They were still on their walk. I then realized this was Tina on the bed. I started petting her. I looked around my room again and, I thought to myself, I know what I am seeing and I am petting my comforter. I then pulled my hand away from the comforter and my hand began to tingle. I fell back to sleep not to awake until morning. When I awoke, I remembered everything. I felt God had blessed me with such a special gift. I felt so much better and couldn't wait to get to work to share my story with my friends.

(19) The Lord hath established His throne in the Heavens; And His kingdom ruleth over all.(20) Bless the Lord, ye angels of His, Ye mighty in strength, that fulfill His word, Hearkening unto the voice of His word. (21) Bless the Lord, all ye His hosts; Ye ministers of His, that do His pleasure. (22) Bless the Lord, all ye His works, In all places of His dominion; Bless the Lord, O my soul. (Psalm 103:19-22 Jewish Holy Scriptures)

❧ Pretzel Speaks ❧

Bobbie Sundrud from California has had three Heavenly messages giving her great peace as God revealed that her pets are in Heaven.

Bobbie states: These visions gave me incredible peace and I never did have to grieve the passing of these wonderful dogs, because I was so comforted by the visions. I am a believer of Christ and believe He gave me a wonderful gift – the assurance that my dogs, all of them, will be waiting for me in Heaven!

One day after a day of teaching school, I was sitting in the kitchen and I saw a vision behind my head. It was Pretzel, a terrier-poodle mix. He was old by then. I saw him in a meadow of flowers. The colors were vivid. His fur was gently blowing in the breeze and he looked young and healthy and alert. I received a message from him in my mind—it was nothing out loud, but he said to the effect ***"I wanted you to know I've died, but its okay, everything is fine now. I don't need you to grieve, I'm happy."*** Then the vision faded. I had him when I was a little girl. I immediately called my mom who lives about 60 miles away. I had no idea he was ill. She verified that an hour before the vision they had him put to sleep. He had had epilepsy for many years, but this time he went into a seizure and didn't come out of it. The vet could do nothing and after about 12 hours they had to let him go.

There are many verses in the Bible that remind us that what God created in the beginning will last throughout all eternity whether it is man, animal, or the remainder of creation, but it will all be created anew just as the original Garden of Eden. God said he knew us before we were in our mother's womb and no doubt the same is true of all creatures. *That which has been made, the same continueth: the things that shall be, have already been: and God restoreth that which is past. (Ecclesiastes 3:15 Douay Rheims Version)*

The NAB version says: *What now is has already been; what is to be, already is, and God restores what would otherwise be displaced.(Ecclesiastes 3:15 NAB)*

⊷{ Alfie is Fine }⊶

Bobbie's second vision was about her dog, Alfie. It occurred about three years after Pretzel went to Heaven.

Bobbie says: I was also in the kitchen when I got my second vision. It was of Alfie's head. He was a dachshund-terrier mix and was getting very old. Again I got the same type of message that he had died and was fine now. He also looked young and healthy. I called my mom again and she said Alfie had contracted parvo and the vet couldn't save him. This was when the parvo epidemic hit in the 70s and there was no vaccine for it.

⋗{ Lady's Long Stay }⋖

Bobbie's vision of Lady happened in 2002.

Bobbie states: Lady was and is a golden retriever. She was about 17 years old when we had to let her body go as she was in a lot of pain. The day after her passing I "saw" her by my chair where I was sitting. She was not visible to the eye, but her presence (her aura?) was so strong I knew she was standing there. She "looked" young and healthy and vibrant. Over the following weeks, I sensed her presence often, many times a day, to the point that I often found myself holding the door open so she could come with me (I knew she really didn't need the door opened, but it was a reflex to her being there) and I often talked to her. About three months after her passing I brought home a puppy. Our family had so much fun with our new family member and often I would "see" Lady standing by watching and laughing and she would be "saying" to me (without actual words), ***That puppy is sure a handful! She's going to keep you busy!*** I could tell Lady was happy we had a new puppy to love.

Then, about six months after her passing, I had a vivid dream—the kind you know has a message for you and you remember the dream your whole life because it was more than a dream, like a vision. The dream was that I was hiking with Lady in the hills. She was healthy and energetic and she was mostly running loose by my side, but then I would notice she had left me. I was disturbed and started looking for her, but she wasn't around. I backtracked and saw a path going down the hill. I followed the path to a clear blue lake that was shimmering in this magnificent light. Around the lake was a beautiful large meadow. I looked around and realized that there were lots of dogs, and people playing with those dogs. In addition to playing ball and Frisbee, the dogs were also swimming in the lake and sleeping in this Heavenly sunlight. It was a beautiful sight. I saw Lady playing ball with someone. I called her and she happily returned to me. I greeted her and we left, going up the path and continuing our walk. A while later I realized she was gone again, but this time I knew she was at the lake. I retraced my steps and went down the path and again found her playing at the lake. Once again she happily returned to me and we continued our walk, but soon she was missing again. This time I went back to the top of the path and called her and she came happily running to me with her tail in the air.

The next day at work I thought about the dream all morning. I had had a couple of similar vision-like, vivid dreams before, and they always had a message. Then it hit me. The lake was Heaven. Lady was happy to stay with me, but she also was happy in Heaven. If I needed her in my life she would stay with me, but she really belonged in Heaven now. I felt able to tell Lady that I loved her in my life, but it was time she went to Heaven and let my new puppy take over the job of being my companion. I have only sensed Lady a couple of times since I released her to move on. And my puppy is the light of my life now.

From the Dead Sea Scrolls Uncovered is a segment titled "The Splendour of the Spirits" It speaks so clearly of the fact that God is creating everything anew, young, happy and joyful. Remember these are just as they were translated so read the words ignoring the markings. *Segment 2 The Splendour of the Spirits*

Fragment 1 (9)...and all the servants of Ho{liness...} (10) in the Perfection of th{eir} works...(11) in {their} wond{rous} Temples... (12) {a}ll {their} servant{s...} (13) Your Holiness in the habitat{ion of...} Fragment 2 (1)...them, and they shall bless Your Holy Name with blessing{s...(2) and they shall bless} You, all creatures of flesh in unison, whom {You} have creat{ed...(3) be}asts and birds and reptiles and the fish of the seas, and all... (4) {Y}ou have created them all anew... Fragment 3 (13)... The Holy Spirit {sett}led upon His Messiah...

Dead Sea Scrolls Uncovered were the Dead Sea Scrolls written over 2,000 year ago and discovered starting in 1947 by Bedouin boys, it is believed, who explored many caves in the Middle east around Jerusalem. You can identify biblical scriptures which come from these scrolls. These specific fragments read much like some of the Psalms and the Book of Revelation.

Text translated © Robert Eisenman and Michael Wise 1992

⊸≼ The Heavens Shook ≽⊷

A relative of a writer who wishes to be kept unknown wrote of this unusual experience. It makes one stop and think about what we are doing in making decisions about the animals in our care and if we could have done something different as guardians of our pets.

There was a family member who had rescued an abused dog when she was first married but the dog snapped at kids and was very fearful. She thought she could love him out of his trauma but after several years he was still aggressive towards children. When she became pregnant she decided to put the dog to sleep before the baby was born. She took it to the pound and went home. A couple of hours later, she experienced severe shaking and emotional agony. She later determined that was the time the dog was actually put to sleep.

Though this is not an uplifting story, possibly it is a sign from God that we need to stop and really consider what we are doing and why. Think of other alternatives to be care takers for those God sent us to love and provide for whether they are people or animals. The Book of Romans, Romans 8:18-22 tells us that all of creation below man suffers because of our sins yet they will also gain entrance into Heaven. *(18) In my opinion whatever we may have to go through now is less than nothing compared with the magnificent future God has in store for us. The whole creation is on tiptoe to see the wonderful sight of the sons of God coming into their own. The world of creation cannot as yet see reality, not because it chooses to be blind, but because in God's purpose it has been so limited-yet it has been given hope. And the hope is that in the end the whole of created life will be rescued from the tyranny of change and decay, and have its share in that magnificent liberty which can only belong to the children of God!(22). It is plain to anyone with eyes to see that at the present time all created life groans in a sort of universal travail. And it is plain, too, that we who have a foretaste of the Spirit are in a state of painful tension, while we wait for the redemption of our bodies which will mean that we have realized our full sonship in him. We were saved by this hope, and let us remember that hope always means waiting for something that we do not yet see. For whoever hopes when he can see? But if we hope for something we cannot see, then we must settle down to wait for it in patience. (Romans 8: 18-22, The New Testament in Modern English Student Edition J.B.)*

Matthew Henry's commentary on Romans 8:19-22 says: *(19) That must needs be a great, a transcendent glory, which all the creatures are so earnestly expecting and longing for. By the creature here we understand the whole frame of nature, the whole creation. The sense of the apostle in these four verses we may take in the following observations: (1) There is a present vanity to which the creature, by reason of the sin of man, is made subject, v 20. When man sinned, the ground was cursed for man's sake, and with it all the creatures. Under the bondage of corruption, v.21. The creation is sullied and stained, much of the beauty of the world gone. And it is not the least part of their bondage that they are used, or abused rather, by men as instruments of sin. And this not willingly, not of their own choice. All the creatures desire their own perfection. When they are made instruments of sin it is not willingly. They are thus captivated, not for any sin of their own, but for man's sin: By reason of him who hath subjected the same. And this yoke (poor creatures) they bear in hope that it will not be so always. We have reason to pity the poor creatures that for our sin have become subject to vanity. (2) The creatures groan and travail in pain together under this vanity and corruption, v.22. Sin is a burden to the whole creation. There is a general outcry of the whole creation against the sin of man. (3) The creature shall be delivered from this* *bondage into the glorious liberty of the children of God (v. 21)—they shall not more be subject to vanity and corruption. This lower world shall be renewed: when there will be new Heavens there will be a new earth. (4) The creature doth therefore earnestly expect the manifestation of the children of God, v. 19. Now the saints are God's hidden ones, the wheat seems lost in a heap of chaff; but then they shall be manifested. The children of God shall appear in their own colours. And this redemption of the creature is reserved till then. This the whole creation longs for; and it may serve as a reason why now a good man should be merciful to his beast. (Matthew Henry's commentary on Romans 8:19-22)*

Matthew Henry's Commentary was originally written for the most part almost 300 years ago. Matthew Henry was a Calvinist born in Wales in 1662. He was ordained in London in 1687 and pastored a Presbyterian congregation in Chester and at Hickney in London. He passed away in 1714 after he had completed the Old Testament and the first part of the New Testament. However, likeminded writers completed the remainder of Matthew Henry's Commentary including the Book of Romans. It was then published it in 1896.

⋅≪ Amazing Grace Goes to Heaven ≫⋅

Shawn and Julie Brady lost their gorgeous and special little girl, a Labrador retriever named "Amazing Grace." God allowed Grace to communicate from Heaven and for Julie it was in a very recognizable way.

Julie writes: It was sudden and without warning. On Monday night March 13, she was playful and acting perfect. On the following morning she was severely ill. We rushed her to the vet and we were told she had a "simple" case of gastroenteritis. They did blood work and kept her overnight to watch. I got a call the next day, less then 24 hours later, and was told that baby Grace had passed away. The autopsy showed nothing nor did any of the blood work, x-rays or other tests.

I was devastated. This was my special dog. We breed and show labs. But Grace was special, like the shy little child that clings to its mother, which was me in this case. How could this happen I thought, it was so sudden! I felt guilty, as though I should have seen something was wrong. Grace was so young and strong; death came like a thief in the night.

Later that afternoon while I was alone in my home still reeling from the shock of her passing, I heard a funny garbled sound. I thought to myself, I must have been losing it. Then I heard it again. I walked over to this basket of stuffed toys that we keep for the dogs and this little stuffed sheep that if squeezed would say "Happy Easter...baaa baaaaa" repeated over and over. I about fell over! This was Grace's favorite toy; she would come in and take every toy out of the basket to find the sheep and then she would mouth it over and over again making it talk.

But the story is so unusual because three weeks ago my husband stepped on her toy accidentally and crushed the mechanism that made it talk.

I picked the toy up and tried to make it work myself. Guess what, it was still broken and would not work for me at all. I opened it up and it was cracked and very broken. I walked away and it said "Happy Easter...baaa baaaa" about five more times. It was as if Grace was still in the room with me. I thought to myself that I don't dare be superstitious! But this was REAL and I called my husband so he could hear it. I prayed and I believe it was Gracie saying goodbye to me and giving me comfort. Since last Tuesday, March 15, the toy has been silent, not a single noise. God allowed Grace to "speak" to me in her own way, something I would understand. Praise the Lord!

Psalm 66 so beautifully speaks of God's greatness and the praises of all of his works (Creation) to Him. *(1)Shout unto God, all the earth; (2) Sing praises unto the glory of His name; Make His praise* *glorious. (3) Say unto God; 'How tremendous is Thy work! Through the greatness of Thy power shall Thine enemies dwindle away before Thee. (4) All the earth shall worship Thee, And shall sing praises unto thee; They shall sing praises to Thy name. (Psalm 66:1-4 Jewish Holy Scriptures)*

CHAPTER 2

Love, Pain, and Understanding

⊰ My Dear Mr. Blue ⊱

Our dog Mr. Blue came into my life when I was teaching music in a private Christian school in St. Louis, MO. It was Halloween night and a large, gentle young hound with white and brown fur and beautiful blue eyes had followed some kids and gotten lost. He came to a house with a German Shepherd and the family kept him for the night, but their shepherd didn't like him and they said they were going to take him to the dog pound if someone didn't take him.

Naturally, I had to try to rescue him. For several evenings I drove around the entire neighborhood and posted signs but no one claimed him. So he came to be our baby and he was a most wonderful, loving dog. He was so gentle with our two little dogs, Pepi and Angel, our cocker spaniel.

I was convinced Mr. Blue, as we named him, could read my mind. Every time I got ready to go someplace he would jump on our bed and put his head on Ron's pillow. I tried tricking him by not taking my purse, not putting on a coat or doing any of the things one would normally do if they were leaving, but I could not fool him.

When Mr. Blue was about eight he developed lumps on both of his sides but they were not malignant. I decided that we should have them removed anyway. I must say here that I had a check in my spirit when I made this decision and have always regretted it. The vet operated on both sides at the same time and the incisions were large.

It was then we discovered that Mr. Blue's blood would not clot. With two large incisions, he could not heal, even with a blood transfusion. There were medications that would make the blood clot, but we didn't know of them and neither did the doctor. We discovered

28

a chiropractor who knew how to get him natural medication, but it was too late.

Mr. Blue came home, but he had lost so much blood it was hard for him to breathe. In the middle of the night I asked God to somehow show me if Mr. Blue was suffering. I then went to get a heating pad from a back bedroom closet. As I reached in the closet I cut myself very badly on a piece of glass and became extremely sick. I thought I would faint it was so painful. I remembered what I had asked God to show me. I feel God was showing me just how much pain Mr. Blue was in, and I knew then I had to let him go.

All the next day Ron had hoped the sun would shine so Mr. Blue could be allowed to lie out on the patio one last time, but it had rained all day without stopping. Dr. Steinberg came to our home that evening and we held Mr. Blue while his spirit left this earth. However, just after Mr. Blue's spirit left and Ron was walking the doctor to his car, the clouds parted in the west and the sun came through and there was a perfect path with no clouds-just the sun beams streaming down toward earth in a perfectly blue sky making a perfect path for his spirit to enter the loving arms of his creator in Heaven. Ron came running back in the house and got me: so, together we looked up in the sky to witness his passage. God had made a path for Mr. Blue to pass through and go on to Heaven and we stood there in wonderment knowing that all was well with Mr. Blue and the Lord of Lords.

I did ask God if I could see Mr. Blue some time and a few months later I had a vision that our little Pepi had brought him back for just a glimpse. I already knew without any doubt that Mr. Blue was in Heaven, but God had allowed me that blessing and I am most grateful for the short vision of Mr. Blue. The parting of the clouds which had been overhead all day long reminded me of the new Heaven and the new earth and also of knowing that one day I will see my beloved Mr. Blue with his

beautiful blue eyes smiling at me. I will then have no more tears and get to be with Jesus my Lord and Savior, the restorer of all life below man including my gentle, trusting and loving **Mr. Blue as Revelation 21:7 says.** *(1) And I saw a new Heaven and a new earth: for the first Heaven and the first earth were passed away; and there was no more sea. (2) And I John saw the holy city, New Jerusalem, coming down from God out of Heaven, prepared as a bride adorned for her husband. (3) And I heard a great voice out of Heaven saying, Behold, the tabernacle of God {is} with men, and he will dwell with them, and they shall be his people, and God himself shall be with them, {and be} their God. (4) And God shall wipe away all tears from their eyes; and there shall be no more death, neither sorrow, nor crying, neither shall there be any more pain: for the former things are passed away. (5) And he that sat upon the throne said, Behold, I make all things new. And he said unto me, Write: for these words are true and faithful. (6) And he said unto me, It is done. I am the Alpha and Omega, the beginning and the end. I will give unto him that is athirst of the fountain of the water of life freely. (7) He that overcometh shall inherit all things; and I will be his God, and he shall be my son. (Revelation 21:1-7 KJV)*

Then I heard all the living things in creation-everything that lives in Heaven, and on earth and under the earth, and in the sea, crying: To the One seated on the throne and to the Lamb, be all praise, honor, glory and power, for ever and ever. (Revelation 5:13 NJB)

⊰⊱ Top Gun Saves a Soul ⊰⊱

An attorney and sports fitness doctor, Larry, called to inquire about publishing his book on animal immortality. First he shared with me the incredible, heartwarming story of his life with his dog, Top Gun. He had presented an actual case to a judge and jury that animals do go to Heaven, a most unique idea. The jury was made up of Christians, non-Christians, and an atheist. I was most gratified with the outcome of the trial.

Larry went to a shelter away from his town and though it was closing time he felt strongly that he needed to go there. As he walked in the door he spotted a German shepherd about nine months old who hobbled over to him. It was hiding in the corner and had never approached anyone before due to sheer fright. It had been there for almost two weeks and was to be put down the next day. He saw it was limping, scared, and had a badly injured eye. The dog had been badly mistreated but for the first time since it had been at the shelter, it approached someone. He instantly knew this was the dog for him. Larry named him Top Gun and he became a beautiful healthy dog. Top Gun and Larry shared many wonderful and happy years together. After he passed, the doctor was desperate as he missed Top Gun so much and his priest had said animals don't have souls and do not go to Heaven. He was devastated with the answer but it led him on a journey to find out for himself if there was any hope of seeing Top Gun in Heaven. His search led him to Frances Svedbeck's book, *Do Animals Go to Heaven?* and *Will I See Fido in Heaven?* He also became friends with a minister who gave him assurance that animals went to Heaven. Through this loss, however, Larry grew closer to the Lord and Top Gun inspired him to have an actual jury trial on the subject of the soul and spirit of animals. By the way, the verdict was that animals do have a soul and spirit and do go to Heaven.

Ecclesiasticus 40 says: *(8) [Such things happen] unto all flesh, both man and beast and that is seven fold more upon sinners (9) Death and bloodshed, strife and sword, calamities, famine, tribulation and the scourages; (10) these things are created for the wicked and for their sakes came the flood.(11) All things that are of the earth return to the earth again, and that which is in the waters doeth return to the sea.(12) all briberie and iniutrice [injustice] shall be blotted out but true dealing [fidelity] shall endure forever. (Ecclesiasticus 40:8-12 1611 King James Bible)*

God will punish the wicked and He will also preserve forever in Heaven all the innocent both man and beast.

The timing of Larry going to that shelter that evening was so of God. And due to Larry's trial by jury, I have included some

scriptures on the subject of the soul and spirit of animals. You will find a full understanding of the soul and spirit in Chapter 5, "The Intelligence of Animals" and even more clearly understood in Chapter 2 of my book *Animals, Immortal Beings*. The evidence of their soul and spirit, their intelligence and the symbol of their innocent, sacrificial blood will amaze you.

Genesis 1 speaks of the soul of all animals: *(30) "And to every beast of the earth, and to every foul of the air, and to everything that creepeth upon the earth, wherein there is a living soul, I have given every green herb for food.' And it was so". (31)And God saw everything that He had made, and, behold, it was very good*—- (Genesis 1:30 -31 Jewish *Holy Scriptures*)

Genesis 1:22 in the 1611 version of the King James Version says*: All in whose nosethrils was the breath of life, of all that was in the dry land died. (Genesis 1:22 the 1611 King James Bible)* Breath of life means spirit.

The original King James Version of the Bible spelled many words like they sounded and some could not be translated letter for letter thus the word "nosethrils" meaning nostrils was the spelling of that time.

Psalm 104 speaks of the spirit of both man and animals. *(28)That thou givest them they gather: thou openest thine hand, they are filled with good. (29) Thou hidest thy face, they are troubled: thou taketh away their breath, they die, and return to their dust. (30) Thou sendest forth thy spirit, they are created: and thou renewest the face of the earth. (31) The glory of the LORD shall endure for ever: the LORD shall rejoice in his works. (Psalm 104: 28-31 KJV)*

(28) You open wide your hand to feed them and they are satisfied with your bountiful provision. (29) but if you turn away from them, then all is lost. And when you gather up their breath, (spirit) they die and turn again to dust. (Psalm: 104:28-29 Jewish Holy Scriptures) Psalm: 104:28 though 29 tells us that God creates every creature, man and animals and takes their

(spirit) breath back when they die and when He sends forth His spirit new creatures are created to renew the face of the earth.

God's Revelation of the Soul

Television Evangelist Jesse Duplantis talks about his visit to Heaven in "Close Encounters of the God Kind" God revealed to Jessie when his mother died what happens concerning the spirit.

When one is born God breathes the breath of the spirit of life into them. **Jessie goes on to say:**" When someone dies, the opposite occurs. God is there to receive that breath of life back to Himself. When God breathes out, things come alive. When He inhales, that life goes back into Him."

"God made man from the dust of the ground and breathed into his nostrils the breath of life; and man became a living soul". (Genesis 2:7, Jewish Holy Scriptures)

"and to every beast of the earth, and to every fowl of the air, and to every thing that creepeth upon the earth, wherein there is a living soul, [I have given] every green herb for food.' And it was so". (Genesis 1:20 Jewish Holy Scriptures)

Job 34:14-15 is in agreement with Psalm 104:14-15 and with the revelation God gave Jessie Duplantis. *(14) If he were to recall his spirit, to concentrate his breath back to himself, (15) all flesh would instantly perish and all people would return to dust. (Job 34: 14-15 NJB)*

Jesse did not intend for his understanding and revelation from God concerning the life-breath to be used in explaining birth and death in any way other than concerning humans. However, Jesse, having seen animals in Heaven, is very aware that animals, too, go to Heaven so the comparison is a fair one and has scriptural backup as evidenced.

The Book of Wisdom also speaks of the souls including that of the animal kingdom. *"But thou spareth all: for they are thine, O Lord, which are the lover of soules." (Wisdom 11:23 The 1560 edition of the Geneva Bible)*

And levy a tribute unto the Lord of the men of war which went out to battle: one soul of five hundred, both of the persons, and of the beeves, and of the asses, and of the sheep (Numbers 31:28 KJV)

◄§ Little Missy §►

This story of love between a man and a stray kitten comes from Roger Dean Kiser.

Roger was an orphan and one who loved animals. His early life was one of rejection and abuse from adults in the orphanage but he found love in the warmth and companionship of animals. For the first few years of his youth, each pet met with untimely deaths leaving him lonely and heartbroken. That pain Roger turned in to a blessing for numerous animals desperate to be saved and in need of intense care and devotion. Few people would consider going to such lengths to save a creature such as Little Missy. Roger touched the life of this little girl if only for a moment in time, yet one that will last for an eternity.

Roger says: It was very relaxing getting away from the house for a change. My wife, Judy, and I had decided to spend five days with our grandkids at a local campground, about 15 miles from our home in Brunswick, Georgia.

The second day we were there I ran a large steel spike though my right hand. It took about twelve stitches to close the wound. But worse than that, were the six hours of waiting in the emergency room lobby to be treated.

After returning to the campsite, I found that I was really unable to do much of anything with the kids. Most of the next five days I just sat by myself as everyone fished, played volleyball and cards.

On Thanksgiving Day, we deep-fried two large turkeys It was the first time in my life that I had eaten Thanksgiving dinner outside. I must say that it was very enjoyable. At dusk, we started a large fire.

Everyone grabbed a lawn chair and sat around for hours talking, and roasting marshmallows. About twelve a.m. we decided to hit the sack.

Early the next morning we were up breaking down the campsite. I stood to the side trying to stay out of the way. My hand was still very sore and there was very little I could do that would be helpful. As I stood, I noticed a black pickup truck driving very slowly by the bathroom. I watched as the passenger threw a brown paper bag at the garbage can, missing it. When they drove away, I walked over to pick up the bag. When I picked it up, it was rather heavy. I opened the bag and saw a small kitten inside.

"Well, hello there, Little Missy," I said to the small female kitten, as I lifted her out of the bag.

I looked down the road to see if I could get the license tag number of the truck but it had already left the camping area. The kitten did not look well at all. It was dirty and looked as though it had not eaten for quite some time.

After we returned home, I tried to telephone all three vets located in our town. Being the Thanksgiving holiday, none were available until Monday morning.

I took the small kitten to the kitchen sink and tried to wash it off with a clean wet washrag. Then I tried to feed it something, but it was just too weak. So I kept it in my lap all that evening as I watched television. About ten o'clock I decided to go to bed. I laid the small kitten down beside my pillow, turned out the light and climbed into the bed. She pulled herself up next to my face as tightly as she could. All the while, she was curling herself tighter and tighter into a small ball of fur. Then she settled down and bundled up next to my ear.

I did not move a muscle as she tried to clean herself. Once in a while I would hear a faint "meow." After she was done, I carefully reached over and ran my fingers across her little head, causing her inner motor to make a purring sound.

Over the next few minutes her motor became less and less frequent.

"I love you, Little Missy," I whispered to her, as I carefully moved my finger back and forth against her ear.

At that very moment her purring stopped completely and her tiny head fell limp in my hand. I picked her up gently and carried her into my office where I laid her down in a shoebox on top of my computer desk. I turned around and saw Judy standing in the office doorway.

"Is she doing okay?" she asked me. I stuck out my hand, motioning for her to please go away, that I could not speak to anyone right then. I sat in my office for more than an hour, wondering how people could be so cruel to such an innocent little creature.

I left "Little Missy" on my desk until the next morning. I then went out to the flowerbed where our other two cats are buried and prepared a special place for her.

I am not sure what the feeling is that comes over me when something is unloved and discarded. Maybe it's all the years of me being raised as an orphan. Maybe it is all the terrible things that I too suffered as a young boy, at the hands of adults. Maybe it's the years of going hungry, being kicked, hit, and even thrown away. I really do not know. Maybe I will never know.

I do know this for sure. Every living thing on this earth should be cared for. No human being or animals should ever leave the face of this earth without having been given a chance to serve its useful purpose. I hope that when "Little Missy" left this earth last Friday night the last thing she remembered was the love shown to her by something known as a human being.

The Book of Proverbs says: *A good man is concerned for the welfare of his animals, but even the kindness of godless men is cruel. (Proverbs 12:10 TLB)*

✥ Mr. Knox Makes a Call: "The Dog Named Three" ✥

This e-mail for the creatures.com newsletter was from D. D. Heart. It is one of great compassion and sacrifice. I so admire D.D. Heart and Mr. Knox for saving this wonderful dog.

D.D Heart wrote: It was September 13, 1999. I got a call from my neighbor, Mr. Knox, who lives up the road. Twenty minutes earlier, I had heard a gunshot.

Mr. Knox informed me that there was a dog lying in his yard, and there was blood all over the place. His leg seemed to be in very bad shape, and would I come up?

Now my first thought was, "I am in horse rescue, I am not a vet. What can I do? I don't need this emotional torture." I went up anyway.

When I arrived, I found what appeared to be a Chow mix. He certainly had the blue on his tongue. I noticed this as I approached because he was panting heavily. My emotions were all tangled. I wished that call never came. I knelt down by the dog and slowly reached for him. His tail was wagging a mile a minute. He didn't appear to be in shock or vicious, just thirsty and exhausted. He accepted my hand and I gently moved it across his back toward his injured leg. He rolled slightly to his good side as if to say, "Look at what happened. Can you fix it?" I was aghast at what I found.

The left rear leg from the hock down was a bloody tangled mess. The entire bone was exposed. The foot pad dangled by a strand of filthy flesh. My heart raced. This was the worst injury I had ever been this close to.

My neighbor called the dog control officer. He came and suggested euthanasia. I dismissed his suggestion and he left. This dog was not ready to die. He was clearly asking for help. Mr. Knox brought out a clean dish towel which I wrapped around the dog's mangled leg. He didn't even whimper. We offered him some water, which he gingerly lapped. After a few minutes of discussing his future, we gently scooped him up and put him in the back of Mr. Knox's pickup. His daughter got in with the dog. We arrived at the vet's office in about 10 minutes. The vet suggested that we amputate, but I insisted that she try and save it. She tried. Forty-eight hours later, the wound went toxic and we were back at the vet's for the amputation surgery. I wondered what quality his life would have with only three legs. I know of lots of people who have three-legged dogs, so I found a way to deal with it. I also knew right then that the dog would live out his days with me. It was apparent that this dog was neglected and hungry. I would not try to find his owner. I had come to respect his bravery and good nature. He never whimpered from the pain, not even once.

Knowing I have twelve other animals to care for, my vet let me make payments on his surgery.

Mr. Knox contributed. I don't regret his phone call anymore. I named him "Three" and he lives with me. He spends most of his time in my office or out on his run. He is very happy and very sweet. If there ever was a mean bone in him, it was removed with his leg.

Many are afraid to help an injured dog of this breed or any animal that has been injured but for those who do, a special crown will surely be theirs when they get to Heaven. Certainly Mr. Knox and D. D. Heart are two.

Chapter 9 of the book of Wisdom tells of our responsibilities over creation. *(1) God of our ancestors, Lord of mercy, who by your word have made the universe, (2) and in your wisdom have fitted human beings to rule the creatures that you have made, (3) to govern the world in holiness and saving justice and in honesty of soul to dispense fair judgment. (Wisdom 9:1-3 NJB)*

·€{ The Cat Man }€·

Roger Dean Kiser happened to be in the right place at the right time and the multiple blessings that occurred from this divine appointment are found only in a fairy tale. Roger has been known as "The Cat Man" due to his rescue of and love for cats.

Roger says: I love to fish. There is nothing more relaxing than being high in the mountains breathing in that fresh cool air.

My favorite fishing spot is a lake near a little four-building, one-gas-station town. It is located high in the mountains of California and is three hours from my home. As soon as the winter snow melts each year I load my fishing gear into the station wagon and head out for a day of trout fishing.

Many years ago during one of my trips, I crossed a small dam that had been built to create a beautiful mountain lake. I pulled over to the side and began to unload my fishing poles. Suddenly, I heard a gunshot ring out, whistling as it flew over my head. I was quite surprised to hear someone shooting a firearm as this was a restricted area and no hunting was allowed. Besides, in all my years fishing the area, it was the very first time that I had ever come across anyone except a few logging trucks passing by.

I ducked down behind my automobile and looked around to see if I could spot anyone.

"Bam, bam!" Another two shots were fired.

"Zing!" rang the bullets as they hit against the large boulders. Still I could see no one.

Then four young men came walking down the dirt road. One raised his rifle and fired off a shot. A cat ran across the road and into the bushes.

"Hey! What the heck are you doing?" I asked them as they approached me. "This is not a hunting area."

"Just shooting at a darn cat," said the larger boy. Slowly another of the boys raised his rifle and fired at the cat, hidden behind the large rock.

"Come on guys. Why kill something for no reason?" I asked.

"What's the cat worth to you?" asked one of the boys.

"How about ten dollars?" I said.

"Bam!" Another shot in the cat's direction.

"How about a hundred dollars?"

"That's what it's going to take," said the largest of the four boys as he took another shot in the cat's direction.

For weeks I had been saving money to buy some type of used boat and motor so I would not have to fish from the bank. I had about one hundred and ten dollars in my wallet and about twenty dollars in my pocket.

"Okay, I'll give you a hundred dollars for the cat. Just do not kill it. Please!" I said.

I pulled out my wallet, took the money out of the secret compartment, and laid it on the hood of the brown station wagon. The four boys walked up and looked at the money.

A very serious look came over their faces. The older boy reached down, picked up the money and put it into his jean pocket. As the boys disappeared around the bend of the road, I began to look for the cat. Several minutes later, the boys drove past me in an old pickup truck, and headed back up the mountain toward town.

It took over an hour to get the cat to trust me enough to catch it. I petted her for five minutes or so, put her into my vehicle along with my fishing gear and drove back up the mountain to the little store.

I asked the owner if he knew if anyone in the area had lost a cat. He walked out to my vehicle and looked at the cat. He told me that the old man who lived next door had lost his cat about a week ago. The old man was very upset because it was his wife's cat and she had died several months before. The cat was all he had left.

The owner of the store went to the telephone and made a call. When he returned, he poured us a hot cup of coffee and we talked for about ten minutes. I heard the door open behind me and I turned around. A gray-haired man, all hunched over, who looked to be at least one-hundred years old, slowly made his way to the corner. He sat down in a rocking chair but did not say a word.

"It's his cat," the owner told me.

The elderly man tapped his walking cane on the floor three times. The owner came over from behind the counter and walked over to where the old man was sitting. The old man whispered something to the owner and then handed him a piece of paper. The owner took him by the arm, helped him up, and they walked outside to the station wagon.

I watched through the window as the old man reached in, picked up the cat and hugged it to his chest. Then they walked to a mobile home next door and went inside.

Several minutes later, the store owner came back.

"I had best be hitting the road," I told him.

"There's a reward for finding the cat," the store owner said.

"I don't want a reward," I replied; but the man held out a piece of paper and I took it from him.

I opened the folded paper and saw that it was a personal check made out to "cash" written for two thousand, five hundred dollars. I raised my eyebrows in surprise.

"Don't worry. That check's no good. Old man's been off his rocker since his wife died," said the store owner.

I folded the check in half and tossed it on the counter so that he could throw it away. Then something inside me told me to keep the check. I picked it up and placed it in my shirt pocket.

"I guess only an idiot would think that a cat is worth paying that kind of money for," he said, as he laughed aloud.

"Yeah, I know. Only an idiot would think like that." I was laughing too.

I walked out the door, got into my station wagon and drove home. The boys and their guns had made me decide to postpone my fishing trip until another time.

When I arrived home my wife handed me a note a friend had dropped by. The note said he knew a man who would sell him a boat on a monthly payment plan. I telephoned him and was discussing the boat. I asked how much he wanted for it.

"Twenty-five hundred dollars, three thousand if I have to finance for you," he told me.

I told him that I would telephone him back in about an hour. I took the check out of my pocket and telephoned my bank. I told them the story and asked if there was a way to find out if the check was good. I gave them the numbers off the check and I waited for them to call me back. Ten minutes later the call came in.

"Mr. Kiser, the check is good," said the woman, laughing.

"What's so funny?" I asked her.

"Well, when I called the bank to ask if the check would clear the gentleman there laughed. He told me that the old man who gave it to you is extremely wealthy. He owns most of the logging companies that operate in that area of California."

And, that wasn't the only surprise. That evening I drove over to see the boat, motor, and trailer that were for sale. When he removed the tarp the boat was like new. It was a great deal; I knew I wanted it. However, when I saw the boat's name I decided—right there and then—that it was meant to be. Painted on the back of the boat were the words "The Cat Man."

(24) For the creation, being at the service to you, its Creator, tautens to punish the wicked and slackens for the benefit for those who trust in you. (Wisdom 16:24 NJB)

⋙ Destined to Be Mine ⋘

From swivtjcerna@earthlink.net, this story is included in the Creatures.com newsletter. It is one of divine intervention. It reminds me of the apostle Paul in his escape from prison.

Caesar's owner writes: I had a Golden Retriever named "Caesar." He has since passed away. He was the offspring of another Retriever that I owned named "Lady." I was living in California and had just moved into a new house and, unfortunately, found that we did not have enough space for both dogs. I was heartbroken but it wasn't up to me to make this decision. Since we had just moved to the area and we didn't know anybody to give him to, we had to take Caesar to the pound with the hopes that he would be adopted right away . He was only 2-3 years old and a beautiful all blond Golden Retriever. After we dropped him off, a week passed and I was feeling depressed over the whole thing, thinking that I would never see him again.

I was attending a relative's party in the same town where the dog was impounded. It was late at night when I left and the street lights gave off an eerie glow as the whole area was foggy. I got into my car and noticed this shadow walking down the middle of the street. I swear it was just like a Steven King movie. I said to myself, "What in the world is this dog doing in the middle of this lonely street?" I rolled down the window and noticed that he looked exactly like my dog that I had dropped off at the pound a week earlier. I called his name, "Here, Caesar." He looked at me right away but stood there in the middle of the road not moving, just looking at me. I then called his name, again, in a softer, more recognizable voice and he came right over to the car wagging his tail! I thought, "WOW, this dog is an omen or something." I knew right then that he was "destined to be mine." Since that night so many years ago, I vowed never to put my dog or any animal up for adoption unless it was a dire emergency. Caesar lived a long and loving life with us until he passed away of old age. At that time, I cried my eyes out but I will always remember how sweet, protective and independent he was. Caesar was kind of strange, the kind of dog that seemed to always have something on his mind, like another entity living in a dog's shell. He was special and I have never had a dog like him nor think I ever will again. I am glad I found him that eerie foggy night.

In loving memory of my Golden Retriever "CAESAR."

(5) your steadfast love, O Lord, extends to the Heavens, your faithfulness to the clouds: (6) Your righteousness is like the mighty mountains, your judgments are like the great deep; you save humans and animals alike, O Lord.(Psalm 36:5-6 The New Oxford Anointed Bible)

❦ Sydney and Me ❧

Richard DeCarlo loves animals, especially dogs, and spends much of his time in prayer interceding for the suffering of God's innocent non-human creatures that deserve so much better in this world.

Richard writes: Star was the second of my two dogs. She was a beautiful German Shepherd. My first, a lab mix named Boots had passed away in July 2004 after a difficult two-year struggle with cancer. He fought for as long as he was able and I spent every moment in this fight along with him. Eventually the Lord took him home. Star and I grieved immensely over his departure. He was my first born. I watched him being born, and was with him for his very last breath.

For nearly four years it remained Star and me. She was very instrumental in my recovery from the loss of Boots, as I was for her. She became a very important nucleus in my life. It was almost as if it were the two of us against the world. I included her in nearly every aspect of my life, even Civil War reenacting which she loved. I had a special shabraque (a Civil War saddle blanket), made for her she so she could participate in parades with the unit. She was the hit at every event we attended.

Late in 2007 I noticed she was becoming more easily fatigued on our daily walks. By that time she was twelve years of age, so I took it easy with her, assuming it to be age-related. We still maintained at least a short walk every day, however. In April she had her vet appointment and he even concurred with me it was most likely she was just feeling her age, but other than that she appeared to be in good health. He gave me some pain medication to give her only when she required it.

Suddenly one evening in May I could see her breathing had become extremely labored, and she developed a cough. The following day, she was showing signs of a fever so I iced her down and took her to the animal hospital. They kept her for the night, gave her IVs, stabilized her fever, and gave her units of plasma. I picked her up first thing the following morning, rushed her to my vet who informed me he would treat her aggressively. At noon he called and urged me to get to the office immediately. I broke every traffic rule in the book trying to get to his office but by the time I arrived she had already expired by only a few minutes. She died, and I died along with her as I saw her lying so lifeless on the table. That was May 21, a day which I would love to forget but, unfortunately, will long remember. The most difficult part of it all is that I never was able to say my final goodbye to her and this haunts me even to this writing. The pain of her sudden departure was so difficult for me to handle, I required the help of my family priest and a psychologist. Without them I would truly have been in big trouble with myself. Next, it was a visit to my family doctor for antidepressants and anti-anxiety pills. Also, a good friend of mine gave me the book, *Will I See Fido in Heaven?* I sat outside on my front porch on a cool May evening and read it in its entirety that day. That was the first sign of any uplifting I had had in days. The book confirmed to me that scripture does tell us just how important the animal kingdom really is to God. Scripture I never knew existed before, now were the most important scriptures in the world to me. All that was written in Mary's book I confirmed with a Catholic priest and his response was, "It all makes perfectly good sense to me. It was inspired by the Holy Spirit." Little by little I began to pick myself up off the floor and immersed myself totally in Jesus Christ. It was church every day. I have a goal for Heaven now.

July 4 brought another blow to the summer of 2008. My dear friend and neighbor (only 44 years old) died of a brain aneurysm in her home. She had helped me through the loss of Star. I purchased a newspaper to see where all the final arrangements were for her funeral. That paper was to prove far more important in another way. It would sit on my table for over a week before I noticed it again. I remember one thing my priest told me during one of our conversations about bringing a rescued dog into my home. When he first mentioned it, it was of little significance as Star was very much still in my heart. Now, at least for posterity's sake, I looked in the classified section for rescue dogs and there was one that stood out. It was a rescued German shepherd. I decided to call the number and inquire about it as I had never been exposed to a rescued dog. The foster parents were very pleasant but told me I was third on the waiting list. If the first two potential owners did not adopt her I could be interviewed for her. They called to see if I wanted to see her and that her name was Sydney. We chose a location where we could all meet. When she arrived I could immediately see she was a most gentle giant without a harmful bone in her body, but still I was third on the list. When they told me the story behind her life, tears came to my eyes as I wondered how any human being could be so cruel. Six years of the most absolute horrors of hell for her life. When they went to rescue her she was chained outside, weighed only 50 pounds, and covered head to toe with fleas and bruises. When I told them the story of Star and showed them pictures of her in her Civil War uniform it became a moment most endearing to them too. A few days later they called me and asked if I was still interested in Sydney as they felt as though this pairing was preordained, and that they had excluded the other potentials that evening we met but wanted to be certain and polite. They felt I had the necessary ingredients to work with Sydney properly and kindly.

I took her into my home on July 17, 2008. After the foster parents said their final good-byes, we sat and watched Pope Benedict XVI arrive in Sydney, Australia for World Youth Days. It was so strange that the Pope arrived in Sydney the same day I brought my new companion, Sydney, home to live with me. In fact, it occurred at almost the exact moment, on such a holy event. How delighted I was! I am firmly convinced this unity between the two of us was preordained by God to mend both our broken hearts. This is why she is so special to me.

Her foster parents had worked hard to overcome all of her fears and I so appreciated their love for her. It took time but she has learned to trust and love me.

When I needed her most she has been here. My brother, only 48 years of age, died of cancer in September 2008. This has grieved me greatly. When I arrived home after burying my brother, she was there to greet and comfort me with a gentle wagging tail and precious kisses. I know she knew my pain. I truly believe this is the work of our Lord. He heard my cries, saw my tears, and heard her cries and saw her tears as well. Our Lord knew what to do.

I look forward to the time when I can introduce her to both Boots and Star as their new sister, and the four of us can dwell in God's most perfect eternal paradise where no tears of sadness will ever need to be shed again.

The Apocrypha Book of Wisdom says that God did not make death. He has never wanted to destroy the living but man sinned and corrupted the world and God had no choice. Satan brought death to all of the living. We all must die physically. However, Satan can not kill or have any part of the spirit and soul of the righteous man or non-human creatures as all creation below man

is righteous. **I have read many, many stories of doctors, ministers, lay people and children who have seen Heaven. Many record going to hell. With the exception of the worms that Scripture mentions going in and out of the bodies of those in hell, there has never been one who saw any animals in hell, yet many who have seen them in Heaven.** *(7) For the spirit of the Lord fills the world, and that which holds everything together knows every word said. (12) do not court death by the errors of your ways, nor invite destruction through the work of your hands. (13) For God did not make Death, he takes no pleasure in destroying the living. (14) To exist-for this he created all things; the creatures of the world have health in them, in them is no fatal poison, and Hades has no power over the world: (15) for uprightness is immortal. (16) But the godless call for Death with deed and word, counting him friend, they wear themselves out for him; with him they made a pact worthy as they are to belong to him. (Wisdom 1: 7, 12-16 NJB)*

⋈⊰ The White Dove ⊱⋈

June Listoe had a most mysterious and wonderful experience with a white dove.

June says: One Saturday morning I sat on our deck, drinking my morning coffee and listening to the city sounds. For days I had heard a dove that sounded like it couldn't get its vocal lessons right. I never could see this bird; however, I was sure it was a dove. I envisioned all the little doves lined up for their voice lessons and one couldn't get the coo just right. I had been sitting on the deck about an hour when I heard this unusual coo again. Looking up, directly in front of me, I saw a beautiful white dove. We never had white doves in this part of the state, only gray mourning doves. This lovely bird was snow white with a black band or collar around its neck that looked like the Lord had taken a paint brush of black and circled its neck. It sat quietly looking at me and I couldn't move. I didn't even want to blink for fear it would flutter away. Finally, I slowly got up and moved away toward the porch door. The bird fluttered through the branches of the tree almost parallel to my movements and seemed to stare deep into my eyes. I could only stand motionless, almost afraid to breathe, in complete awe mesmerized by this lovely bird.

I spent the entire day on the deck and when I moved I did so slowly and quietly so as not to startle or frighten this bird. I'm sure it must have escaped from the aviary however I will never know that for certain. I was a working woman so I was away from 6:30 am until 4:00 pm each week day. Every week day afternoon, during the entire summer, this lovely dove would flutter into the tree next to the deck as soon as I arrived home from work. Each week-end, the dove would stay around my yard the entire day, as I worked in the flower beds, mowed and edged. I gave him the name of Breezy because of his soft and gentle fluttering. He would allow me to walk up to within about two feet and then he would hop back a little. I never pushed to get closer as he seemed to be very happy just to be near. There was almost a bonding taking place. I would look for him and he wouldn't be visible. Then, I would look around and he was suddenly there.

Toward fall I worried if he would know to fly south as so many of the birds had started their migration. Breezy lingered. One October Saturday Breezy fluttered down to the fence post near me, then up to the roof edge then back down to the fence post. He seemed uneasy. He was back and forth for almost an hour. He flew to the feeder and lingered there for such a long time. Then, up to the roof edge he fluttered, looked down at me, flew over the house much like a low flying aviator, and with more strength and speed than I had ever witnessed from Breezy before, he headed southwest. I never saw Breezy again; and, I never hear the coo of a turtle dove that it doesn't bring a tear to my eye. I have told my family that when I pass away I want to have a dove etched on my headstone.

Numerous scriptures use doves as a Christian symbol for specific reasons. Possibly, the dove was a symbol for June as

well. Genesis 8:12 mentions the dove three times when reading the scripture referring to Noah and the Ark. In this passage three times the Dove is sent out of the ark to see if the land was dry enough for all aboard to leave the ark. A pair of mourning doves or pigeons was the offering Mary and Joseph took to the temple when Jesus was dedicated to the Lord just after his birth. The mourning dove has a very significant symbolic meaning. It seems to cry or mourn each morning and evening for creation. I have always wondered why I feel a bit sad when I hear its mournful coo. God and His son, Jesus, mourned and still mourn for our sins. Jesus came from the glories of a perfect Heaven and went to the pit of hell dying on the cross in agonizing pain for our sins. No doubt he is still mourning in Heaven in agony for us to turn from our evil ways as he has already paid the price for our redemption. *The time came for Joseph and Mary to perform the ceremony of purification (23) as it is written in the law of the Lord: "Every first-born male is to be dedicated to the Lord." (24) They also went to offer a sacrifice of a pair of doves or two young pigeons, as required by the law of the Lord. (Luke 2:22 TEV)*

I am sending you out like sheep among wolves. "Therefore be as shrewd as snakes and as innocent as doves." (Matthew 10:16 NIV)

When, Jesus was baptized, while he was praying, Heaven was opened, and the Holy Spirit came down upon him in bodily form like a dove. (Luke 3:21-22 TEV)

◄§ The Mysterious Goldfinch]§►

Cheryl Beaverson told the story of a mysterious visitor, the Mysterious Goldfinch, appearing on Maundy Thursday. Its visits left Cheryl almost speechless.

There was a very special visitor during Holy Week of 2009. My father had been quite ill for some time. It was Tuesday evening of Holy Week that I learned my dad had inoperable cancer. That, we learned, was why he had not been able to keep anything on his stomach for so long. So that evening he was transported from Lewes, DE to the University of Maryland in Baltimore for life sustaining treatment.

On Wednesday morning as I walked out of the house to get into my car to drive to Baltimore, all the birds that were eating from and around all the feeders flew off as they have always done in years past. At that particular moment, a thought flashed through my mind: "Gee, I just wish that they would trust me and not fly away when I come outside." I went about my business that day.

The next day, Thursday (Maundy Thursday), my sister was on her way up from Delaware to stay at my house so we could visit our dad together. That evening the most amazing thing happened. My husband Mike had put up a huge post and on top of that post we had placed our purple martin house the previous weekend. This special day he was installing wrought iron hooks to hang feeders from the newly installed bird house post. He was hammering and using a drill while hanging the hooks. I came out to watch him from our deck and he told me to watch the little goldfinch just two feet from him eating from a thistle seed sock. He told me that he was able to walk up to the bird and pet and touch it. I, of course, was doubtful and asked him to show me. He did, and the little finch stayed on the sock and allowed him to touch it. Of course, I needed to see if it would allow me to do the same and, much to my amazement, I was thrilled to be petting this beautiful creature. Later, I went into the house to get clean water for the bird bath. Meanwhile, the goldfinch had flown to our pine tree just a couple of feet away from my husband. Then, the little goldfinch flew up and sat on the hood of his sweatshirt. My sister was witness to this.

Next, the bird hopped over to Mike's shoulder, then to the sock feeder again. Friday morning (Good Friday) my sister awoke and I heard her go outside. She told me that the goldfinch was sitting on the ground sleeping under the sock feeder so she went out and it hopped up in her hand and then to the feeder. I came out and once again it allowed me to touch it. I told my sister that I had hoped it was not ill. Twice it flew down to the bird bath that was next to both of us and drank water then flew back to the feeder. Then the finch flew up in the pine tree for a few minutes then flew to the motion sensor light on the back of our house next to the deck. Both my sister and I were standing on the deck watching the bird and it took flight under the roof of the deck right between my sister and me and flew away. As it left I knew in my soul it was goodbye and I was sure I would never see it again, but on April 24 it was back. This time it would not let me pet it but my husband sat down on the ground and it hopped up behind him then through his legs and sat on his shoe for some time before flying up to the bird feeder.

I don't know when it will be back or if it is around to stay. It does not hang out with the other finches but stays by itself and it seems to be very healthy. One thing I do know: the wish I had that Wednesday morning of Holy Week wanting the finches to trust me enough not to fly away every time I come outside was answered in a very personal and amazing way the very next day. Maybe God does hear our simple pleas even when we don't expect an answer. Maybe He just wants us to trust Him like that little finch did. Does God have more amazing experiences for me to encounter with the little Goldfinch in this life; or, is my family really getting a taste of what life will be like in Heaven?

The Song of Solomon in Chapter 2 verse 12 says: *The flowers appear on the earth; the time of singing of the birds is come, and the voice of the turtle (turtle dove) is heard in our land: (2:12 The Song of Solomon KJV)*

Matthew Henry's commentary explains: The little birds, which all the winter lie hid in their nests and scarcely live, when the spring returns forget all the calamities of the winter, and to the best of their capacity chant forth the praise of their Creator. Doubtless he who understands the birds when they call (Ps. 147.9) takes notice of those who sing for joy.(Psalm *5:11) The cooing of the doves is heard in our land,* which is one of the season birds mentioned in Jer. 8:7 that observe the time of their coming and the time of their singing, and so shame us who do not understand the times, nor sing in singing time.

Solomon in his Song of Solomon found in the Old Testament is speaking in Chapter 2 of the time when Christ reveals himself in a most loving and trusting way, through the innocence of creation. This scripture brings the message that, just as the birds of the air, we are to praise God in all things, through all our pain and in all of our joys.

⊰{ The Pretty One }⊱

Roger Dean Kiser had numerous encounters with animals. This story will no doubt really touch your heart. If we could all look at all man and creatures as "Pretty Ones," the way Roger, his wife and a special grandmother did, the world would be a much better place to live.

Roger says: It had been a very long night. Our black Cocker Spaniel, Precious, was having a difficult delivery. I lay on the floor beside her large four-foot square cage watching her every movement, and waiting just in case I had to rush her to the veterinarian.

After six hours the puppies started to appear. The firstborn was black and white. The second and third puppies were tan and brown in color. The fourth and fifth were also spotted black and white. "One, two, three, four, five," I counted to myself. I walked down the hallway to wake my wife Judy and tell her that everything was fine.

As we walked back down the hallway and into the spare bedroom, I noticed a sixth puppy had been born but was lying all by itself over to the side of the cage. I picked up the small puppy and laid it on top of the large pile of puppies which were whining and trying to nurse on the mother. Precious, immediately, pushed the small puppy away from the rest of the group. She refused to recognize it as a member of her family.

"Something's wrong," said Judy.

I reached over and picked up the puppy. My heart sank inside my chest when I saw the little puppy had a cleft lip and palate and could not close its little mouth. I decided right then and there that if there was any way to save this animal I was going to give it my best shot.

I took the puppy to the vet and was told nothing could be done unless we were willing to spend about a thousand dollars to try and correct the defect. He told us that the puppy would die mainly because it could not suckle. After returning home, Judy and I decided that we could not afford to spend that kind of money. At least, we needed to get some type of assurance from the vet that the puppy had a chance to live. However, that did not stop me from purchasing a syringe and feeding the puppy by hand. I did that every day and night every two hours for more then ten days. The little puppy survived and learned to eat on his own as long as it was soft canned food.

The fifth week I placed an ad in the newspaper and within a week we had people interested in all of the pups, except the one with the deformity. Late one afternoon I went to the store to pick up a few groceries. Upon returning, I happened to see the retired schoolteacher who lived across the street from us waving at me. She had read in the paper that we had puppies and was wondering if she might get one for her grandson and his family. I told her all the puppies had found homes but I would keep my eyes open for anyone else who might have an available cocker spaniel. I also mentioned that if anyone should change their mind I would let her know. Within days, new families had picked up all but one of the puppies. I was left with one brown and tan cocker, as well as the smaller puppy with the cleft lip and palate.

Two days passed without me hearing anything from the gentleman who had been promised the tan and brown pup. I telephoned the schoolteacher and told her I had one puppy left and that she was welcome to come and look at it. She advised me that she was going to pick up her grandson and would come over at about eight o'clock that evening.

That night at around seven-thirty, Judy and I were eating supper when we heard a knock on the front door. When I opened the door, the man who had wanted the tan and brown pup was standing there. We walked inside and took care of the adoption details then I handed him the puppy. Judy and I did not know what we would do or say when the teacher showed up with her grandson. At exactly eight o'clock the doorbell rang. I opened the door and there was the schoolteacher with her grandson standing behind her. I explained to her the man had come for the puppy after all and there were no puppies left. "I'm sorry, Jeffery. They found homes for all the puppies," she told her grandson.

Just at that moment the small puppy left in the bedroom began to yelp.

"My puppy! My puppy!" yelled the little boy as he ran out from behind her grandmother.

I almost fell over when I noticed that the small child also had a cleft lip and palate. The boy ran past me as fast as he could down the hallway to where the puppy was still yelping. When the three of us made it to the bedroom the small boy was holding the puppy in his arms. He looked up at his grandmother and said, "Look Grandma, they found homes for all the puppies except the pretty one and he looks just like me."

The schoolteacher turned to us, "Is this the puppy that's available?"

"Yes," I answered. "That puppy is available."

The little boy who was now hugging the puppy chimed in, "My grandmother told me these kinds of puppies are very expensive and that I have to take really good care of it."

The grandmother opened her purse but I reached over and pushed her hand back down into her purse so that she could not pull her wallet out. "How much do you think that puppy is worth?" I asked the boy. "About a dollar?"

"No. This puppy is very, very expensive," he replied.

"More than a dollar?" I asked.

"I'm afraid so," said his grandmother.

The boy stood there pressing the small puppy against his cheek. "We could not possibly take less then two dollars for this puppy," Judy said squeezing my hand.

The schoolteacher took out two dollars and handed it to the young boy.

"It's your dog now, Jeffery. You pay the man."

Still holding the puppy tightly, the boy proudly handed me the money. Any worries I'd had about the puppy's future were gone.

The image of the little boy and his matching pup stays with me still. I think it must be a wonderful feeling for any young person to look in the mirror and see nothing except "the pretty one."

We tend not to look upon God's creation the way He does. All is perfect whose heart is right. How pretty is all creation the Book of Ecclesiasticus says: *(22) How lovely, all his works, how dazzling to the eye! (23) they all live and last for ever, and, whatever the circumstances, all obey (25)* *one thing complements the excellence of another. Who could ever grow tired of gazing at his glory? (Ecclesiasticus 42:22-23, 25 NJB)*

⊸{ Roy Hayes and His Dog, Chance }⊷

Roy Hayes grew up at Boys Ranch in Texas after being rejected by his own family. The story of his life and the love for his dog, Chance, reveals a wonderful truth of a second chance for both of them.

Boys Ranch Alum Becomes Dog's Best Friend. Roy Hayes loves animals. During the past five years, he has rescued countless dogs and cats by removing them from danger and finding them good homes. One of those homes is his own, where he currently has four dogs, four cats, and two cockatiels.

Two years ago, Roy, who is employed at Cal Farley's Campus Support Center in Amarillo, was on his way to work when he saw a puppy playing near a busy street. Roy immediately stopped and retrieved the puppy. Upon closer inspection, he noticed that the puppy's eyes were swollen. A visit to the veterinarian revealed that the six-month old Alaskan malamute had severe corneal damage that was probably the result of a malicious act. One eye was completely without vision and the other only had 30 percent sight. Roy adopted the puppy, named him Chance, and nursed him back to health. A local television news program produced a brief story on Chance. The puppy also won first place two times in the local Society of the Prevention of Cruelty to Animals (SPCA) Mutt-Fest competition.

Like Chance, Roy was given a second chance when he was young. His mother passed away when he was only ten days old. A short time later his father remarried. "I did not have a close relationship with my father and stepmother," Roy said. "We weren't close. I think I was in the way." The constant turmoil in the home led the family to seek placement.

Roy was 13 when he arrived at Boys Ranch. "I was excited, nervous, and I did not know what to expect," he said. "I will never forget the day my dad drove me to the Boys Ranch office in Amarillo. Cal Farley came out to greet me. He shook my hand and said, "Welcome to Boys Ranch." That's something I will never forget.

While at the Ranch, Roy was involved in drama, sports, and the chapel choir. He participated in the building trades program and enjoyed riding in the annual Rodeo. "I rode bulls, although I did not consider myself a cowboy," he said. "I had many opportunities to do things that I would never have participated in if I had lived at home."

Roy has many fond memories of living at Boys Ranch, especially of the many celebrities who visited the Ranch, such as television and movie stars Roy Rogers and Dale Evans, Ken Curtis (Festus in "Gunsmoke") and Frank Sutton (Sergeant Carter in "Gomer Pyle"), singers Tennessee Ernie Ford and Glen Campbell, radio personality Paul Harvey and Dallas Cowboys Coach Tom Landry.

Roy considered Cal Farley his father and his passing in 1967 was the saddest day of his life.

Roy graduated from Boys Ranch High School in 1971 and joined the Army several years later. He came back to Cal Farley's in 1999 as a staff member, where he currently works in the Development Department.

Roy associates his "rescue" by Cal Farley and Boys Ranch with his rescue of Chance. He feels that they both were given a "second chance for success."

"I think I relate to Chance, seeing what he has been through as an abused dog," Roy said, "I can relate his story to my own life."

"Boys Ranch was the best thing that ever happened to me. Boys Ranch helped me become a better person, a more caring person. If it wasn't for the Ranch, there is no telling where I would be." **Without Roy, Chance probably would not have had a second chance.**

It is such a comfort to know that God preserveth all that He has created and even the angels worship Him. Roy and Chance will be in Heaven together as Nehemiah states. *(6) "Thou, even thou, are Lord Alone; thou hast made Heaven, the Heaven of Heavens, with all their host, the earth, and all things that are therein, the seas, and all that is therein, and thou preservest them all; and the host of Heaven worshippeth thee" (Nehemiah 9:6 KJV)*

⁂ Pastor Hayford and Ginger ⁂

Dr. Jack Hayford, pastor of Church on the Way in Van Nuys, California heard from God quite unexpectedly.

Pastor Hayford was in his study when the family dog, Ginger, came in. He was annoyed at her presence. He had tried repeatedly to communicate with her, but could find no response or intelligence in her personality, unaware that a previous owner had mistreated her. (He attributed her listlessness to stupidity.) That is, until God unexpectedly spoke to him: ***"Why do you hit the dog? Do not take lightly My concern for Ginger"*** was the message. Dr. Hayford put great effort into reaching out to her, so that she and the pastor became very good friends.

(89) For ever, O LORD, Thy word standeth fast in Heaven. (90) Thou faithfulness is unto all generations; Thou hast established the earth, and it standeth. (91) They stand this day according to Thine ordinances; For all things are Thy servants. (Psalm 119:89-91 Jewish Holy Scriptures)

Matthew Henry's commentary explains these scriptures: *All creatures are, in their places, and according to their capacities, useful to their Creator, and fulfill the purpose of their creation; and shall man be the only rebel, the only revolter from his allegiance, and the only unprofitable burden of the earth?*

The Inhumanity toward Animals.

Ann Marie Rogers said God had revealed to her through three different visions that the animals would be in Heaven.

Ann Marie states: I have been an animal person all of my life and a Christian for most of it. I believe God called me to help them in any way I can because I know that He loves his creation. I am now using your Fido book as a Christian witness for other people in the animal rescue field in Michigan. We deal with so many unwanted animals on a daily basis that it is hard not to become cynical and really not like people much. Unfortunately, we have to euthanize many of these poor unwanted dogs and cats and although it is difficult, I know that they will all be with the Lord.

Ann Marie Rogers Asks, "Don't You Love Them?"

I have a very strong bond with animals and always have. Sometimes I feel closer to them than I do my own species. I have worked in the animal rescue field all of my life. I started volunteering in shelters when I was old enough to do so and then managed several different types of animal rescue organizations. I am also a Christian, having given my heart to the Lord in high school. I always felt that God called me to help animals. I've always believed that animals do go to Heaven despite the fact that many Christians believe they do not. However, I would often get angry with God when seeing the cruelty of man toward animal life. I have seen an awful lot of it to be sure.

One particular day I was praying to God and asking Him why He let this horrible suffering go on with His animals, who are so innocent and at the mercy of man. "Don't you love them?" I asked the Lord, tears streaming down my face. Not expecting an answer, I continued to cry feeling so saddened and disheartened by what I had seen that day at the shelter. In the next moment, to my astonishment and joy, the Lord spoke to me as plainly and sweetly as could be. ***He said, "Do you think that you love them more than I? I created them. Of course I love them!"***

When the Lord spoke those words to me I was elated. Yet, I knew I had to apologize to the Lord as it divinely came to my understanding that the poor animals had fallen under the curse along with man. They had to suffer along with mankind. After all, look what Jesus, God's own son, had to suffer on the cross. The suffering of man and animals alike does not mean that God does not love us or does not love the animals. He loves us all dearly and has a place for us, His people, <u>and</u> His animals beyond this life on earth.

The book of Psalms says: *(8) "The Lord is gracious and merciful: patient and plenteous in mercy. (9) The Lord is sweet to all: and his tender mercies are over all his works". (10) Let all thy works, O Lord, praise thee: and let thy saints bless thee. (Psalm 144:8-10 the 1609 Douay Rheims Bible)*

✤ Cinnamon ✤

From the Life and Times of Roger Dean Kiser comes a story about his kitten, Cinnamon, and his gallant effort to save her.

Roger says: I left California about 13 years ago and moved to Brunswick, Georgia. Since that time, hardly a day goes by that I do not think about returning to fish for striped bass in the beautiful California Delta.

I, like many other people, can not afford a very elaborate vacation. My Social Security disability check, together with Judy's job as a waitress, will not allow us to head off to Rome or other fancy places such as that. However, we had managed to put back a little money and my dream of again fishing in the California Delta waters was finally coming true.

The round trip ticket would cost us less then $400 and two days of fishing would cost about $100 per day. In addition, Judy and I were invited to stay (at no charge) in the home of my best friend, Danny, who was in need of a liver transplant. With our round trip airline tickets in hand and $400 in cash, off we flew to sunny California.

The first day of our vacation was spent with Dan and Lois. We talked, laughed, and made up for lost time in our friendship.

Dan and Lois live right on the edge of a very poor area, known to most as the dreaded "Airport District." It is not a very good neighborhood and if you are unknown your personal safety was something you had to be very careful about.

Nevertheless, on Tuesday morning, I was up early and decided to take a stroll around the old neighborhood.

This was the same area where my former in-laws had lived before their deaths. I noticed that not much had changed since I left some years ago. The young teenage kids were still cursing and fighting with each other as their individual gangs trotted down the street to see what they could steal from the local corner markets.

I slowly walked down the edge of the street until I got to the corner of Connie Way. I looked at the large water filled holes aligning the half-paved, pot-ridden roadway filled with trash and mud just as it had been thirteen years earlier. Halfway down the block, I saw the small shack-looking house where my in-laws had once lived. As I looked farther down the street I could see ten or fifteen old broken-down junk cars lining the roadway as well as tons of used worthless old tires, among the large piles of trash, crushed tin cans and broken glass bottles. It was like looking at a war zone where someone had dropped an atomic bomb. It was a place where nothing would ever change for a thousand years or more. There was absolutely no color for the eye to see except a light white gray. Everything looked dead and totally barren of life.

I jumped as I felt something rub against my leg. When I looked down I saw a small cinnamon colored cat rubbing back and forth against me. I could hardly believe my eyes when I saw the cat's leg was severely injured. I picked the animal up in my arms carried it back to Danny's house and gave it bowls of food and water. I watched as she ate the food, gulping every bite as though she had not eaten or drunk in days.

The small cat had a broken leg which was swollen, and it was actually walking on the stub while dragging its entire foot behind as it traveled along.

I immediately called a veterinarian and explained the situation. I was told they would not take stray cats unless there was someone who would take full responsibility for payment of the treatment.

After visiting with another veterinarian and agreeing to pay a $25 examination fee, the cat was examined. We were told that the cat's foot was broken and that its leg had almost been twisted completely off. Amputation of the entire leg from the shoulder down was the only recourse. We were also told the injury must have happened at least a week or two before as the infection had spread into the shoulder. He told us the charge for removing the entire leg would run about one thousand dollars.

Unable to pay the high fee, Judy and I took the cat back to our room. We tried to make it as comfortable as possible through the night. The next morning I walked down to the corner store where I learned that earlier in the week four young boys had twisted the cat's leg until it broke, then they smashed its foot with an old car starter. They shot it in the back of the neck with a pellet gun and buried it still half-alive.

For hours Judy and I stayed on the telephone trying to find a vet to help us save the animal, but to no avail. Danny finally came into our room and told us it was a hopeless case and we should just have the cat put to sleep. However, I just could not do that.

"Dan, if I ever accomplish anything in my life, I will save at least one thing from the Airport District," I told him.

Danny looked at me with tears in his eyes and said, "Roger, that is why we have been friends for so many years. You just never give up when it comes to fixing something that is broken or hurt."

Well, by the end of the day a surgeon at the Modesto Spay and Neuter Clinic agreed to amputate Cinnamon's leg at their cost, which totaled $377.84.

Judy and I gave up our fishing trip and used the money toward Cinnamon's medical expenses. Sonny's Real Pit Bar BQ threw in $50. Our friend, Sharen Jackson, though she had bills because of breast cancer surgery, threw in $130, and my son, Roger, pitched in another $100.

The wonderful people at Delta Airlines refused to accept the $75 fee it normally charges for pets to travel. They insisted that Cinnamon fly home with Judy and me free.

Cinnamon now lives here with us at our home in Brunswick, Georgia. As I sit writing this story, Judy is in the bedroom crying her eyes out. Judy stood silently watching Cinnamon as she used the litter box for the first time in her life. There stood Cinnamon, all alone, trying to cover her business with a now invisible leg..

Here was an innocent little animal that had never hurt anyone. She had her leg broken, almost torn away, and now amputated. Shot in the head with a pellet gun and then buried alive by four people who call themselves human beings. In spite of all of her suffering, Cinnamon still had the heart to hobble up to a strange man standing on the street corner, in a place that could only be known as "a war zone," and rub against his leg to let him know that she still loves "all" human beings.

It is not Cinnamon or the people mentioned in this story that are the heroes here. The true hero in this story is "the spirit of goodness" and "the spirit of kindness" shown by the people who reached out to help an innocent cat. It's a wonderful, wonderful feeling that lives deep in the hearts of most good, kind, and decent people; a special feeling that makes an "honest to goodness hero" appear when a real hero is needed.

The story of Cinnamon speaks of the goodness of Roger, not the cruelty of the wicked both he and Cinnamon had to face. The Book of Jeremiah asks: *How long will our land be dry, and the grass in every field be withered? Animals and birds are dying because of the wickedness of our people, people who say, 'God doesn't see what we are doing'" (Jeremiah 12:4 Good News Bible)*

CHAPTER 3

Creations Praise to God

⊰{ Even the Sparrows Praise God }⊱

September 13, 1998 I was asked to speak at the Blessing of the Animals at Noah's Garden Pet Cemetery in Detroit, Michigan. It was a beautiful warm Sunday morning before I was to speak that I was invited to an outdoor service at Cascade Christian Church. It was within walking distance of Noah's Garden Pet Cemetery.

I sat under a beautiful blue sky with billowing white clouds overhead listening to a wonderful sermon. During the service, as in most churches, we sang a number of songs, but as the second song was sung something awe inspiring happened. The song was about all creation praising God. As we sang, I looked up at a wondrous sight. A small flock of birds was circling the congregation and singing at the top of its lungs. They circled and sang during the entire song. But upon the last pitch of that joyous song, the birds flew off never to be seen again.

I sat there amazed that I would witness such a spectacular Godly event. I was reminded of St. Francis talking to the birds upon several occasions and the birds singing in Solomon's temple. It was in a very small way a glimpse of heaven where both man and beast will praise God endlessly one day.

The Book of Daniel originally had 100 verses in Chapter 3. However, most Bibles do not include all of these verses as they are mainly praise verses of all creation spoken by Shadrach, Meshach, and Abednego, the three who escaped death after being thrown in the fiery furnace for not praying to Nebuchadnezzar. *"Bless the Lord, all birds of the air; sing praise to him and highly exalt him forever"* (Daniel- The 1609 Douay Rheims Bible)

All Creation Praises God

Many ask me if I believe animals can speak in heaven. I believe they do. Balaam's donkey spoke to Balaam and a snake spoke to Eve before sin entered the world in the Garden of Eden. I don't believe we will need the same type of speech to communicate in heaven. Mentally, our thoughts, I believe, will be understood and they will be pure and sinless thoughts in heaven as we will all be without sin there so we will not mind if others can read our minds, so to speak.

As for the animals, the Bible says they praise Him. The book of Psalms says they praise God and the Book of Revelation says that all creation will praise Him in heaven. Praising is a kind of prayer. The following scriptures are from the books of Daniel, Psalms and Revelation. *O ye whales, and all that move in the waters, bless the Lord: praise and exalt him above all for ever.(Daniel 3:79 Douay Rheims Bible)*

O all ye fowels of the air, bless the Lord: Praise and exalt him above all for ever. (Daniel 3:80 Douay Rheims)

"Bless the Lord, all his works in all places of his dominion: "Bless the Lord, O my soul" (Psalm 103:22 KJV)

"And every creature which is in heaven, and on the earth, and under the earth, and such as are in the sea, and all that are in them, heard I saying, Blessing, and honour, and glory, and power, be unto him that sitteth upon the throne, and unto the Lamb for ever and ever." (Revelation 5:13 KJV)

Praise God in All Things

God's promise is this: each one of us has our own mansion in heaven and in our mansion we will find all that we have loved on earth. Pepi is with my parents and Duffy and the other pets I have had and I know my mansion is being built near my family so we will have an eternal celebration one day.

It is not good to be sad over the earthly things or to grieve too much over our pets. We have so much to do to help make a better life for others here on earth. When we praise God in all things the pain starts to go away.

I am so thankful for a message written by Mrs. Evelyn Roberts, the wife of evangelist Oral Roberts. She shared her grief and recovery after their daughter had been killed in a plane crash.

Evelyn Roberts says: My daughter was young and just recently married when she and her husband were tragically killed in a plane crash. The death was absolutely devastating. I would wake up and could hardly get out of bed from grief.

This went on for a number of weeks until one morning the Lord brought to mind the scripture *Praise God in all things*. I started to praise God even though my heart was breaking and within a short time I began to have peace.

In remembrance of Evelyn Roberts' teaching, I started doing the same thing concerning Pepi and have now learned to do this with all of my pets and family members when they go to heaven. The Book of Psalms 148 says: *(5) Let every created thing give praise to the LORD, for he issued his command, and they came into being. (6) He established them forever and forever. His orders will never be revoked. (Psalm 148:5-6 TLB)*

⊰ Smoky Mountain Rescue ⊱

Tina Houska has been a dear friend of mine for many years and I know her heart for Jesus and for His creation. I didn't know her husband cared so deeply for animals. This story gave me great joy.

Tina said: We spent a week in the Smoky Mountains this summer. It was a nine hour drive from St. Louis to the Smokies. While we were there two stray dogs came to our cabin. They were very skinny from malnutrition. We knew they needed food badly so we bought dog food to give to them while we were there. Everyday when we came back to our cabin, there they were waiting, hungry and thirsty. The week went by and we had no way to bring them home. The nine hour trip back home was very long and sad as we kept thinking about the dogs and what would happen to them but we had to get back to work.

Once home, my husband could not get the dogs out of his mind. Three days later he told me he had to go get them. "It was an "Eight Below" thing" is what he told me. I could not argue with that. He left and drove nine hours to retrieve the dogs just hoping that after the long trip they would still be there. Sure enough, it was as if they were waiting, just praying that somehow we would come back and get them. They needed no persuasion. They jumped right into the truck as if their prayers had been answered and made the nine hour trip home sleeping inside the cab.

We took them to the vet right away. They had no chips in them. They had whip and hook worms which can be fatal to dogs when they are not taken care of. Usually dogs get them from eating raw meat or small rodents. We wormed them and had them spayed and neutered and got them all their shots.

The two are doing very well and living large in our home with our other rescue dog and cat. We are very thankful for the opportunity to give the two dogs a good home and, no doubt, they are even more thankful that we love and care for them in their forever home.

I know Tina and her husband do not have a lot of money so it was a huge financial sacrifice for them to rescue and get the dogs back to health. *GREAT is the Lord, and greatly to be praised in the city of our God, in the mountain of his holiness (Psalm 48:1 KJV)*

CHAPTER 4

The Intelligence of Animals

There are many experiments which have been conducted on the intelligence of various species of animals. Almost every animal has far more intelligence then we have given them credit for. When I look at my dogs knowing that their intelligence ranks as that of the average three year old child to one ten years of age or older, it makes me think what life would be like if I had to depend on another species to care for me without any verbal language to communicate my needs, or, hands to be able to show or write down my thoughts and show my intelligence and understanding. I have observed two seeing-eye dogs do things they had never been trained for and go places with very little instruction. In fact, no instruction at all, in one case, in order to avoid danger to their master. Many animals have to make decisions on their own for the protection of their human companions. The elephant and crows I wrote about in *Animals, Immortal Beings* give you a glimpse of their intelligence and their sense of humor as well as of their pain when losing one of their own. The word "instinct" so often found in the Bible when referring to animals means "God given intelligence." It is one word for years we have mistakenly believed to mean acting in a robot form of brainless activity. Possibly, if man had more instinct we would have more understanding and compassion for all of God's creation. It is the animals who have to figure out what we want from them, our thoughts and verbal commands. Most try so hard to obey.

The Importance of the Blood

The mystery of understanding how important the blood is in connection to the soul (mind) and body of everything from the sacrifice of animals in the Old Testament times to the final sacrifice of Jesus Christ today is explained by Reverend David Allen Lewis in *Mysteries of the Bible Now Revealed.*

Rev. Lewis reveals the importance of the Blood of all creation and the sign within it concerning salvation. This is scientific evidence which brings great joy and understanding concerning the sacrificial animals and their relationship to the Blood of Jesus as well as the sign of salvation within every living organism.

Under the sign of salvation is the lifeblood of all living things.

In Leviticus 17:14 we are told, *"For the life of the flesh is in the blood; and I have given it to you upon the alter to make an atonement for your souls: for it is the blood that maketh an atonement for the soul." (Leviticus 17:14 KJV)*

The life of every creature is in the blood. That is why I have told the people of Israel never to eat or drink it for the life of any bird or animal is in the blood. So whoever eats or drinks blood must be cut off. (Leviticus 17:14 TLB)

For it is the life of all flesh. It's blood sustains its life. Therefore I said to the children of Israel, 'You shall not eat the blood of any flesh, for the life of all flesh is its blood. Whoever eats it shall be cut off.' (Leviticus 17:14 NKJV)

Deuteronomy 12:23 says, *"Only be sure that thou eat not the blood: for the blood is the life; and thou mayest not eat the life with the flesh." (Deuteronomy 12:23 KVY)*

Before Jesus Christ made his ultimate and everlasting sacrifice for us on the Cross of Calvary, the blood of animals was required as a sacrifice for the sins of the people. No longer is the blood of lambs or goats or bulls required for the salvation of our souls, for Jesus-the lamb of God-made the final blood sacrifice for the sins of the world.

We can not live without blood. It carries carbon dioxide through the body from the cells to be released by exhaling. The blood exchanges carbon dioxide for oxygen and is then carried to the cells of the body. It is truly life-giving oxygen that allows the cells to metabolize food to sustain us. It is the red blood cells which are the carriers of both oxygen to the cells and carbon dioxide away from them to be exhaled.

The blood is the only organ in the body that is liquid. It invades every cell in the body. It brings nourishment and fights disease and carries out the waste of the body. It is the life giving force that keeps the body alive. It is the spirit of the breath of life.

Keep in mind what Reverend Jesse Duplantis said about God breathing the breath of life into the living and when He exhales He takes the life breath/spirit of that being back to Himself and the physical body dies. The life breath or spirit of life is in the blood.

Not only people but the blood of all vertebrate and invertebrate animals depend on this same system of oxygen/carbon dioxide transfer to exist. Surely, the Bible is correct when it states that *"the life of the flesh is in the blood"* *(Leviticus 17:11)*

It is the hemoglobin, the author says, that contains the "sign" of the redemptive power of blood. Hemoglobin is a compound formed by the protein globulin, joined together with an organo-metallic compound, hematin. The metal portion of the hematin is an atom of iron, held within the compound of a porphyrin complex. It is this structure which forms the hidden "sign" of the redemptive power of the blood which flows through our veins. **IT IS A CROSS.**

When God created animals and man, He knew that it would be only through the shedding of the blood of Jesus Christ that our redemption would come. He placed the sign of that shed blood, the cross of Calvary, within the very life-blood of His creation.

How amazing that God sent His son to shed his blood for the salvation of mankind and even to redeem/restore creation below man back to God. Before Jesus came God had to use the innocent blood of animals to cover our sins.

What about Plants? Another very interesting fact.

Plants do not have blood but they do have chlorophyll depending on light for photosynthesis. The chlorophyll molecule is similar to hemoglobin in our blood. In the center of the molecule as in the center of hemoglobin in blood, the center of the structure of chlorophyll also **FORMS A CROSS.**

How wonderful that God has placed a sign of salvation within every living thing of creation.

All creation is amazing from man, animals, plants, the earth, and, the Heavens. They are all an unbelievable wonderment of God.

Without a soul and a spirit, animals could not think, make decisions, love, hurt, or feel pain as these inanimate elements are located in the soul. And the soul can not be found within the fleshly body of any animal or person. We know that according to Leviticus 17:14 that it is the blood that is the atonement for the soul. The soul is the essence, the eternal being of all creation. The word "soul" has been translated in many Bibles to say "being" or "living being" rather then soul. Soul in its original translation from Hebrew is "Psyche" and translated from Greek is pronounced "Nephesh." Living soul is translated, "Nephesh chayah."

Numerous scriptures speak of animals having a soul, such as in Job 12:10, Numbers 31:28, Revelation 16:3, Genesis 1:30 (The Holy Scriptures Jewish Bible, Wisdom 11:27and others.)

Genesis 9:8-18, the original Douay Rheims translation from 1609, mentions four times that animals below man have a soul and also includes them in the eternal covenant that God made with Noah. The original translation of Noah (Noe) was:

(8) And God spake unto Noe, and he said to his sons with him, saying, And I, behold, I established my covenant with you, and with your seed after you;

(10). And with every living soul that is with you, as well in all birds as in cattle and beasts of the earth, that are come forth out of the ark, and in all the beasts of the earth.

(11). I will establish my covenant with you, and all flesh shall be no more destroyed with the waters of a flood, neither shall there be from henceforth a flood to waste the earth.

(12). And God said: This is the sign of the covenant which I give between me and you, and to every living soul that is with you, for perpetual generations.

(14). And when I shall cover the sky with clouds, my bow shall appear in the clouds: And I will remember my covenant with you, and with every living soul that beareth flesh: and there shall no more be waters of a flood to destroy all flesh.

(16). And the bow shall be in the clouds, and I shall see it, and shall remember the everlasting covenant, that was made between God and every living soul of all flesh which is upon the earth. (Genesis 9: 8 10-12, 14, 16, 1609 Douay Rheims Bible)

God made an eternal covenant with both man and the animals. This is significant as it is a promise from God for all creation.

Also, the Jewish Holy Scriptures Genesis 7:15 says: *Pairs of all creatures that have the breath of life in them came to Noah and went into the ark. (Genesis 7:15)* **"Breath of life" in original translation means "spirit."**

And Genesis 7:22: *All in whose nostrils was the breath of the spirit of life, whatsoever was in the dry land died. (Genesis 7:22)*

(29) After this the Lord looked upon the earth, and filled it with his blessing.

(30) With all manor of living things that thee couered (looked upon) the fact thereof, and they shall returne to it againe. (Ecclesiasticus 16:29-30. The 1611 version of the Authorized King James Bible)

The Douay Rheims 1609 version, Ecclesiasticus 16:30 and 31 reads: *(30) After this God looked upon the earth, and filled with his goods. (31) The soul of every living thing hath shewn forth before the face thereof, and into it they return again. (Ecclesiasticus 16:30 and 31 Douay Rheims Bible)*

Ecclesiastes 3:21 asked *"who knows if or whether the spirit of man goes upward and the spirit of the animals goes downward." (Ecclesiastes 3:21)*

Biblical evidence dictates that not all of the spirits of mankind go to Heaven yet that the spirits of all the animals do. Why does Solomon even speak of this subject in his writing of the book of Ecclesiastes? Actually of all of the Books of the Bible, this is the only Book that speaks from a human view of life not from God's point of view. Solomon's purpose as being the wisest man ever born debates the issue which prompts us to use our intelligence to reason and seek Godly wisdom to find answers to the question of immortality, and the rewards of living a Godly life according to the Bible. The fact is Solomon has previously answered this question in Ecclesiastes, Chapter 3, prior to this troubling debate which seems to confuse and divide people even today.

God breathed the spirit of life into every being and it became flesh.

The word "Spirit" is translated from the word "ruach" in Hebrew and means "wind, breath-the living power of God's will at work," the "breath of life" or the "breath of the spirit of life." Thus, when you read ***breath of life*** in the Bible it is actually referring to their spirit whether it applies to man or animals as stated in Genesis 7:22 from the Hebrew/Jewish Holy Scriptures.

The animal's spirit comes from God the same as ours does. Their recognition of spiritual beings, which is evident from the story of Balaam's donkey and from the book ***Angels on Assignment***, in which Reverend Buck's dog, Queenie, recognized the angels who would come to visit before Reverend Buck knew they were there. This indicates the spiritual side of animals just as the story of Jesus sending a legion of demon spirits into the herd of swine concluding that evil spirits can be sent by man into innocent animals.

God breathes His spirit into every living being. Animals remain spiritually connected with God. Yet, they have a distorted nature due to the fall of man who presently has dominion over them. A child is not conscious of sin, nor is an animal. Their souls and spirits are pure and innocent. They are not spiritually blinded by sin. It is when and if a person mentally reaches the age of accountability that their soul/mind becomes conscious of sin. They then have the free will to reject or accept Jesus. Animals do not need to choose. Man's control over them is ended when their spirit is released to go back to God.

⊰{ And Rammo Will Lead }⊱

This is a wonderful story of a seeing-eye ram guide for a blind cow. It comes from Mary Hurt of Willard, Missouri owner of Whisper, a Guernsey cow and Rammo, a male Rambouillet sheep. The story was printed in the Springfield News-Leader by Susan Wade. Springfield, MO.

On an 80-acre farm east of Ash Grove, Missouri, Whisper and Rammo affectionately nuzzle and butt heads. The two are inseparable.

A closer look and you know why.

Whisper, a Guernsey cow, is blind. But what she doesn't see, Rammo, a four-year-old male Rambouillet sheep, is Whisper's eyes, if you will. Rammo has watched out for Whisper since the cow was born two years ago, said the animals' owner, Mary Hurt.

"He seemed to realize she was blind and he started leading her around."

Rammo nudges the cow away when she's about to run into something, and spends hours at Whisper's left side while the two munch grass.

Even after two years, the Hurt family and their friends shake their heads in wonder at the friendship.

"Nobody ever believes it," Mary Hurt said. "They think we're pulling their leg."

It's easy to see why Whisper needs Rammo, but why does Rammo need Whisper? The answer is a mystery.

Stacy Hamilton, dairy specialist at the University of Missouri extension center, said rams tend to be loners and are not especially nurturing. Rammo is an exception. He spends more time with Whisper than he does with four other sheep on the Hurt Farm.

And Whisper is with Rammo more than she's with the other cattle.

Whisper, named for her quiet moo, roams the entire 80-acre farm. She's a good milker, usually producing 3½ to 4 gallons of milk a day.

There's something else about Whisper–she likes to play with kids. The cow chases Mary Hurt's six children and tries to get in on the action when they play volleyball in the field behind the house.

When Rammo's not around, family members yell out, "Gate!" when they see her heading for trouble. The cow stops; then, slowly walks in a circle until she gets her bearings.

Many people would have let Whisper die when she was born, but Corey Hurt couldn't do that.

Two years ago, Mary Hurt's 20-year-old son picked up and carried home the newborn calf from a neighbor's field where she was born.

Because her blind left eye never grew and the right eye was also blind, the farmer who owned her was going to leave her in the field to die.

"I've just always liked animals," Corey Hurt said. "You would not go out and let them die. There wasn't anything wrong with her except she was blind."

The Hurts say Whisper isn't any trouble, especially with Rammo taking care of her. "I think really that animals are smarter than we give them credit for," Mary Hurt said.

Whisper has now gone to Heaven, relieving Rammo of his duties as a seeing-eye ram. It is so "of God" to have taken Whisper

to Heaven first. *(6) Go to the ant, thou sluggard; consider her ways and be wise: (7) Which having no guide, overseer, or ruler, (8) provideth her meat in the summer, and gathereth her food in the harvest. (Proverbs 6:6-8KJV)* **An ant has intelligence so how could we not expect for the ram and cow to have more wisdom and along with it a love and companionship beyond our understanding. Yet scripture says as for the cruel and thoughtless man who was going to leave the little calf in the pasture to starve to death:** *Stupid men will start being wise when wild donkeys are born tame. (Job 11:12 GNB)*

Ben Barnett preached on the subject of animals both in reference to their symbolic meaning found in the Bible and to the true fallen nature of animals as we know them.

He found 130 references to animals in the Bible and 33% of them were about sheep while over 20% referred to a serpent. Sheep were one of the main animal sacrifices in the Old Testament. They were sacrificed by the Jews to cover the sins of man until the Messiah came. Normally the reference to the serpent symbolizes Satan and his demons. Genesis, Chapter 3, sets the stage for the Old Serpent, the devil.

Jesus said a good shepherd will lay down his life for his sheep. That is what the real shepherds did often in the Old Testament times. They loved their sheep and the sheep loved them just as we love our pets today. And Jesus, often represented as the good shepherd, laid down his life for all humanity. He died sinless for the sins of man. Sheep were innocent/sinless creatures whose blood was used to cover the sins of man until Jesus came and died once and for all to take away the sins of humanity if the people would confess their sins and accept Jesus as their Lord and Savior.

The Bible also says that "the sheep hear my voice and comes but the voice of a stranger they will not answer." This is referring to Jesus, as those who know him as their personal savior recognize the things of God and how to be obedient to his will for our lives.

This is a wonderful representation also of shepherds and their flocks. It was the custom of the shepherd to take their sheep to a large fenced in area guarded by a sheep guard. Sheep from many herds were put together in a large holding area. When the shepherd came to get his sheep, usually the next morning, as they would be placed in a holding area over night, the shepherd would call for them. Only his herd of sheep would come. And the sheep would enter only through the gate they were led through. They did not try to enter any other way, they could not enter any other way, just as we can not enter Heaven any way but through Jesus Christ as he said, *"I am the way, the truth and the life: no man cometh unto the Father, but by me"* (John 14:6 KJV)

⊷⊰ Action Jackson and the Little White Mouse ⊱⊶

This happened as I was completing this book and seems to amaze all that I tell the story to. Does it have to do with intelligence, a spiritual sense, or did Jackson have other intentions?

I was sitting at the computer working on *Animal Miracles of the God Kind* when I noticed my son Roman's cat, Jackson, whom I have been babysitting for the past six months, had brought an unexpected gift to me. Jackson was a beautiful long-haired yellow cat known for bringing in dead mice, moles, rats, and birds upon occasion to show me just how diligent he was in caring out his earthly mission. We have a doggy door for all of the dogs, and Jackson used it as well to come in and out, but this day was quite unusual. I normally do not notice him, but for some reason, as he walked past my side on the way through the office I saw something white coming out of his mouth and it was easily recognizable as a white mouse. Ron was here helping and I said rather frantically, please grab Jackson and try to get the mouse. Ron went over to Jackson and he simply let Ron have the mouse. It was completely unharmed. There was not a tooth mark of any kind on "JJ," as we called him (short for Jackson Jr..), but as Ron held JJ it was obvious that he was under quite a lot of stress and highly traumatized from the ordeal. Ron had brought me a new, very tall trash can with a swinging top so for a time JJ was placed in it for safe keeping while I tried to find a home for him. Everyone told me to let him out in the field somewhere but being a white mouse I didn't see how he would have a chance as he would be easily spotted by a predator. I then came to realize that JJ was not at all afraid of people or even having animals stare at him through his new glass house. He loved to play on the wheel and other items purchased for his comfort and enjoyment. He was out all hours of the day and night. He came out, especially, when there was any food put in his bowl and would come right to my hand to get it. As he popped in and out of his various tunnels our dog Sally, the German shepherd, would sit and watch him sometimes for an hour or two at a time.

So, along with five dogs there was also a white mouse. But as I am finishing the writing, my precious Jackson, just one year old, has disappeared. I pray continuously that he is safe and will return. JJ also went to Heaven from some kind of allergy the vets could not treat.

This experience did bring to mind Isaiah 11:6-9 where the wolf shall dwell with the lamb. Some day Jackson and JJ will be playing together in Heaven as they would have in Paradise before man sinned. The Book of Isaiah tells us what it will be like when we get to Heaven. Even those of the human race and of the animal's world who were enemies on earth will be friends in Heaven. *(6) The wolf also shall dwell with the lamb, and the leopard shall lie down with the kid; and the calf and the young lion and the fatling together: and a little child shall lead them. (7)And the cow and the bear shall feed; their young ones shall lie down together: and the lion shall eat straw like the ox. (8) And the suckling child shall play on the hole of the asp and the weaned child shall put his hand on the cockatrice's den. (9) They shall not hurt nor destroy in all my holy* *mountain: for the earth shall be full of the knowledge of the Lord, as the waters cover the sea. (Isaiah 11:6-9 KJV)*

⊰{ Hero Dog Saves a Baby's Life }⊱

The following story is from the *News & Views* (International Association of Pet Cemeteries magazine). I was given permission to share this wonderful story for which I am so grateful.

Member J. Fennel states: "Our Golden Retriever did something truly heroic and amazing! On November 1, 1996, our seven-week-old daughter was in her bassinet in our living room for a nap for about an hour. Roxanne, our then two-year-old dog, was snuggled up on the floor taking a nap near the baby. I was washing dishes only a couple of steps away. Roxie began to come to me, then go to the baby, and run back and forth between us. After about thirty seconds, she began to get more excited and kept rubbing her nose on my leg and running through the house. I went into the living room to check the baby and to my horror, our new baby had stopped breathing. I picked her up and shook her gently and she caught her breath. We took her immediately to the hospital where she stayed under observation for two days. She was found to have slight asthma and today is a very healthy three-and-a-half year old. Roxie is now five and a very important part of our family. I feel in my heart that Roxie saved our daughter's life. Thank goodness we had her because I don't know if I would have gone and checked on her again. Roxie will always be my hero, and our daughter always says, "Roxie, you are my best friend!"

The Book of Job says: *(7) You have only to ask the cattle, for them to instruct you and the birds of the sky for them to inform you. (8) The creeping things of earth will give you lessons, and the fish of the sea provide you an explanation: (9) there is not one such creature but will know that the hand of God has arranged things like this! (10) In his hand is the soul of every living thing and the breath of every human being! (Job 12:7-10 NJB)*

⚜ A Horse Named Shane ⚜

The following tribute to a horse named Shane is from Cathy Kennedy, Egg Harbor Township, New Jersey as she writes in the Creature Feature of Eden Publications.

Cathy writes: I recently had to put my horse to sleep. I got him on December 21, 1971 for Christmas from my family. Everyone chipped in. I saw an ad in the local paper for pleasure horses for sale so we went. It was feeding time when we arrived and they all came running in from the corral. After they were done, they went back out and in came this skinny chestnut gelding with a white stripe down his face. He was looking for his dinner but to no avail. I fell in love with him at first sight. We loaded him on the trailer and brought him to our barn.

Then, 28 years later, after the greatest trail rides and the times when I just needed to talk, he's gone and I find myself lost. I know in time the hurt will stop or subside a little. In all those years, we moved him to at least six or seven barns until we bought our house. We went through a lot together including a husband who was very jealous of him. At one point, I had to sleep in his stall! Sometimes I thought he really understood what I was saying. Maybe he did.

The last eight years of his life were spent at our house in my backyard. I guess he was just like an old dog. He would shake hands, give kisses, count, and drink soda out of a can. He would follow me around like a puppy and wanted to spend every minute with me. Shane could undo any lock on a stall door and undo clips on stall gates. I could go on forever about all our trail rides but then I would have to write a book.

I named him Shane because it means "God's Greatest Gift." That's what I have written on his tombstone. It was the hardest thing I have ever had to do, putting him down, but I know it was best for him. Shane, if you're listening, I love you and miss you but I know I will be riding you again in the end. So until then, run free.

Just as Jesus will ride a white horse out of Heaven with all his chosen saints to take the earth back from Satan and rule the earth, Cathy will get to ride Shane again one day. The book of Revelation says: *(11) Now I saw Heaven opened, and behold, a white horse. And He who sat on him was called Faithful and True, and in righteousness He judges and makes war. (12) His eyes were like a flame of fire, and on His head were many crowns. He had a name written that no one knew except Himself. (13) He was clothed with a robe dipped in blood, and His name is called The Word of God. (14) And the armies in Heaven, clothed in fine linen, white and clean, followed Him on white horses. (15) Now out of His mouth goes a sharp sword that with it He should strike the nations. And He Himself will rule them with a rod of iron. He Himself treads the winepress of the fierceness and wrath of Almighty God. (16) And He has on His robe and on His thigh a name written: KING OF KINGS AND LORD OF LORDS. (Revelation 19:11-16 NKJV)*

❧ Scarlet Saves Her Kittens ❧

Only a few years ago, a cat named Scarlet made headlines around the world.

Scarlet risked her life to re-enter a burning building FIVE TIMES to rescue her tiny kittens one by one. Even through her eyes were blistered shut and her paws were burned, the cat did not rest until she had retrieved all of her babies, tenderly touching each one with her nose to make sure they were safe.

How often do we think about the love animals have for their babies and families. What must it be like to have your babies taken away from you every time you have them?

❧ Smokey and her Babies ❧

June Listoe told the story of a mother cat who had to learn to trust. It is so painful to find an animal that simply can't trust us to help them. If only they knew our hearts.

June writes: While living on the West Coast, a beautiful smoky gray cat rather adopted my yard as its haven. We had dogs that did not take kindly to cats but for some reason they tolerated Smokey. Smokey, however, was very, very independent and would not let anyone get close to her. I put food out on the patio for her, even though she would bristle and hiss if I even approached her.

Before long it was evident that Smokey was in a family way. The children and I watched her pregnancy progress and often remarked about how her kittens would look and where she might go to deliver her babies. As time went on I realized I had not seen Smokey for several days and would watch out my kitchen window hoping for a glimpse of her, but she was not to be seen.

Early Sunday morning I walked out on the patio, the California sun was warm and comforting and I stood quietly listening to the morning sounds and watching the busy humming birds. My family was still asleep and I wanted to absorb the tranquility of this lovely morning. I walked down to the dog run, petted and hugged them, then turned and strolled back toward the patio. I stopped, thinking I heard a meow, looked around and saw nothing. I shook my head and decided I must have just had Smokey on my mind and was hearing things. I took a few more steps and again thought I heard a meow. Looking around I saw Smokey spring out of the bed of ivy next to the fence. She started toward me, meowing every step, and it was evident that she had given birth.

I spoke to her, congratulating her on her new family, how happy I was to see her, etc., all the time amazed that she had even approached me. I turned and started toward the patio door and she came running alongside! I stopped, spoke to her again, and when I took about three steps forward she darted right in front of me. Again I stopped and this time said to her "Smokey, are you trying to tell me something?" She had started back toward the ivy bed and I followed. As I looked across the ivy there didn't seem to be a leaf disturbed but Smokey knew where she was going. Into the ivy she jumped and there were four wee little kittens in a hollowed-out nest of leaves. Suddenly, I could see what she was so distressed about, two of the kittens seemed attached and when she tried to nurse, one was not able to reach her for food.

I carefully reached in and found the cords of two kittens had become wrapped around a tiny, tiny twig making it impossible for them to snuggle up to Smokey when feeding. I knew I had to get them separated and I could not do that in their current nest. I started toward the house and Smokey was with me every step. I went inside and found an old bath towel, manicure scissors and rubbing alcohol. I knew I was to become a midwife that Sunday morning. I went back outside to a waiting Smokey and we gathered up the kittens and took them into the family room.

This wild, independent and usually defiant Smokey was a frightened but trusting mother, needing help. I snipped the little cords from around the twig separating the kittens, placed them all in the bath towel under a bench in the family room. There they nested for several weeks, growing, trusting, being nurtured and in the shelter of our home that Smokey had always viewed with suspicion.

Psalm 104 speaks of God wisdom in making creation: *How many are your works, O Lord! In wisdom you have made them all, the earth is full of your creatures (Psalm 104:24 NIV)*

◄⦗ Brat Calf Digs a Hole ⦘►

The story comes from John and Michele Helfrich of Justin, Texas. It is an amazing story. As I read this story, I realized all of the wonderful relationships I could have had growing up if I had just spent more time with the various farm animals we had.

Michele writes: We were weaning one of our longhorn heifers and had Brat calf in a paddock (a small enclosed area near the barn). The water line to the barn runs underneath the paddock, and one day it broke—water was bubbling up like a spring. My husband spent most of the day digging to find the hole in the pipe. The pipe is about four feet underground and he didn't know where the hole might be. Before he found the hole, he had dug up a long trench about five feet long and four and a half feet deep.

While he dug, our heifer kept an eye on him and would occasionally go and stand by him and watch. She also watched while he fixed the pipe. He came inside after fixing the break and had supper. John then went back out to fill in the ditch. He started to shovel in the dirt and was soon amazed to find that the heifer was helping him. She started pushing at the dirt with her head and horns, shoving in the dirt. He would shovel and she would push in dirt beside him. After he had shoveled for a while, he jumped in the ditch to pack down the dirt. The heifer jumped in with him and stomped her feet, and then she jumped out when he did and commenced to shovel in dirt again with her head.

I watched the heifer for an hour. I have never seen anything like it and wouldn't believe it if someone told me. We always knew she was special, but had no idea just how special she truly is. The heifer, by the way, is now a cow with a baby of her own. She still lives here and I doubt we will ever sell her. Her name is Tupelo Honey (also known as "Brat Calf").

God made all His creatures in wisdom and with wisdom. *(24) For Wisdom is quicker to move than any motion; she is so pure, she pervades and permeates all things. (25) She is a breath of the power of God, pure emanation of the glory of the Almighty; so nothing impure can find its way into her. (26) For she is a reflection of the eternal light, untarnished mirror of God's active power, and image of his goodness. (Wisdom 7:24-25 NJB)*

(Emanation means to flow out of, to proceed out of, as Wisdom flowing out of God). Throughout all Bibles the feminine vernacular is always used when speaking of Wisdom.

❧ Lady Saves a Man ❧

Jill Wiss sent this story for our creatures.com newsletter.

Who can doubt the intelligent actions and desperation of Lady in trying to communicate to one human being, without the ability to talk, of the danger another human family member was in.

Jill states: We recently lost our 13-year-old mixed breed dog, Lady. She was a wonderful friend to everyone in our family. She died within a week of being diagnosed with acute kidney disease. We miss her terribly. I write this story in her memory.

Lady was a very special little dog. She was only about ten months old when we were busy getting ready for a long car trip. I was in the house with Lady packing and preparing for the trip. My husband was outside in the garage, or so I thought. Lady was very easy to train and fairly obedient. She knew she was not permitted to jump on the furniture, and for the most part we had no trouble with her obeying. As I was about to go up to the second floor and take a shower, Lady started to bark, ran into our living room, and jumped on the couch as she peered out the window. After scolding her for jumping on my good couch, I put her back in the kitchen.

Once again, as I attempted to go up to the second floor to take a shower, Lady ran into the living room, up on the couch and barked and barked. Angry, I put her behind the gate in the kitchen. She continued to bark. As I started up the stairs, I heard a faint call for help. The town workers were sawing tree branches about a block away so I could hardly hear that call for help. Lady was now scratching at our back door trying to get outside. I opened the door and called to my husband. With that, Lady bolted by me and ran to our car which was parked on the street. She stood by the back of the car barking. My husband had crawled into the trunk to secure the spare tire and make room for our luggage. (Our trunk door automatically closes electronically.) When he was securing the tire, he shook the car and the trunk door closed before he could get out.

If it wasn't for that sweet little dog persistently barking and jumping on the couch, I would have gone upstairs to take my shower, blow-dry my hair, etc. I wouldn't have had a clue where my husband was and would have probably assumed he went to the store.

Lady saved my husband that day and continued to be a loyal, faithful companion to all of us through the years. She was truly a gift from God.

An insightful scripture from Job says: *Who endowed the ibis with wisdom and gave the cock his intelligence? (Job 38:36 NJB)*

⊰⊱ Goldie Saves Her Best Friend ⊰⊱

Reverend John Edwards tells a wonderful story about his golden retriever Goldie and their daughter Kelli's little dachshund, Peanut.

This is truly a story of sacrifice, intelligence, and the love of one wonderful Golden Retriever for her little pal Peanut, the dachshund.

Reverend John Edwards said: My family was living in Greenville, Texas, on a three-acre tract of land before I went into the ministry. We love horses and dogs and had both on our land. I was working for a local machine shop company at the time. Goldie, the Golden Retriever, was known as a mothering dog who cared for anything that needed help. Goldie and Peanut, the dachshund, were free to roam over the land and went hunting often but this time they did not come back and four days had gone by. We were desperately concerned that something had happened to them.

After work on the fourth evening, I went to sit on the porch and happened to look down the highway and thought I saw Goldie. She would stop for a bit then start to walk again. I was so excited that it might be her I jumped in the truck and drove to where she was. Goldie had been carrying the little dachshund in her mouth. Little Peanut had been shot seven times with a shot gun and Goldie knew the only hope was to get her back home so she could possibly be saved.

The vets were closed by then and I had to wait until the next morning when the vet office opened at 9:00 a.m. so I took Peanut with me to work and laid her on the bench. My boss, Mr. Riches, an Englishman and the owner of the business, came in and saw her lying there and I said that I had to wait until the veterinary clinic was open to take her. With that, my boss picked her up and said he would be back. In about two hours he came back and told me I could pick little Peanut up the next day. I said I didn't know whether I could afford to pay for her operation but the boss told me not to worry. It had already been taken care of.

And to have an even more compassionate and sacrificial ending to the story. John said: I had to trim the horses' hooves. Horses' hooves grow just as our finger nails grow and they must be trimmed or they will grow so long they will crack and split. It will then be very painful for the horse to walk. Dogs love to chew on the hooves as it is very nutritious for them. Since little Peanut was all bandaged up and laying on the porch he could not get around so Goldie brought the pieces of the hooves to him to chew on.

God is so good and so faithful to those who truly love Him with all of their hearts and John Edwards certainly does that. John is one of the most wonderful and straight forward men of God I have ever known. He preaches salvation and the need to love and trust our Heavenly father. Reverend Edwards loves animals so, naturally, God sent me to the right church when the crew and I moved to Texas. *(57) All ye works of the Lord, bless the Lord: praise and exalt him above all for ever. (81) O all beasts and cattle, bless the Lord: praise and exalt him above all for ever.*

(89) O give thanks to the Lord, because he is good: because his mercy endureth for ever and ever. (Daniel 3:57,81,89 The Douay Rheims Bible)

⊶{ Calvin Brings a Daffodil }⊷

This story was sent to me by Rachel through Lois Ballinger about her dog, Calvin.

Animals must feel the pain and sorrow we go through. My childhood dog, Tipsy, did.

Rachel said: My mother died recently and since she was very close to me, I was very upset. One day I was sitting outside, thinking about the wonderful times I had with my mother and how I will miss her. My dog was lying in front of me in the summer sun. He was sun tanning when he looked up at me with his dark brown eyes. Calvin is a crossbreed between a husky and a black lab and has the eyes of a caring and deeply thoughtful dog. He is very friendly and I love him dearly.

He looked up at me and saw that I was very miserable. When he got up I thought he was going further out in the yard to sleep there. When he came back about two minutes later he had brought me back a daffodil that he had found lying in the garden. He placed it by my feet and put his head on my foot. From then on, I have felt more at peace about my mother's death. Now I know that dogs are never really clueless of our feelings. Calvin is my helping hand when I am down in the dumps and he can always cheer me up with his thoughtful ways.

The Book of Ecclesiastes 3:11 says we don't understand or have the wisdom to know all of Gods works. We get so caught up in our own worldly concerns and only occasionally do we recognize the precious gift of love and sympathy we are given by God's most innocent and precious creatures. *God has made everything beautiful for its own time. He has planted eternity in the human heart, but even so, people cannot see the whole scope of God's work from beginning to end. (Ecclesiastes 3:11 The New Living Translation)*

❧ Does Shawnee Understand? ❧

This story is from Marge Smelser of St. Louis, MO.

Marge says: Several times we have stopped by the Ladue Animal Shelter to pick up "marked" animals. It seems that on every "animal rescue run" (as I like to call it) one of the sweethearts tugs especially hard on our hearts and he/she becomes a permanent family member! Others have been nursed back to physical or mental health and find their way to a new home via PetSmart. We've come to accept this as our calling for this time of our lives. There's never a dull day—as you well know! One of our rescue babies is named Shawnee and to her a name means everything.

On a typical winter evening I watch television and on this particular evening several years ago I was sitting in my Queen Anne recliner. Shawnee was sitting on my lap, sleeping, as always and I was crocheting with the television on for background noise.

This evening we were watching "Touched by an Angel." The episode was about a wealthy and successful CPA who wanted to win God's favor by giving monetary gifts to the poor. However, his heart wasn't in the right place. He didn't feel satisfaction from his gifts; things started going wrong for him; so he decided that there wasn't anything to this "God and good works" idea. (Remember that Shawnee is sleeping by my side.) The actor pointedly yells: "There is no God!" Immediately, Shawnee barks, still asleep, as if he had a bad dream! He's never done this before in the ten years that we've known him. Toward the end of the show, it happens again! The actor screams: "There is no God." Shawnee, still asleep, barks as though he is upset! Since then, he hasn't barked in his sleep. This certainly gives one food for thought!

(30) Let all the earth tremble before him. The world is firmly established and cannot be shaken. (31) Let the Heavens be glad, and let the earth rejoice! Tell all the nations that the LORD is king. (32) Let the sea and everything in it shout his praise! Let the fields and their crops burst forth with joy! (33) Let the trees of the

forest rustle with praise before the LORD! For he is coming to judge the earth. (1 Chronicles 16:30-33 TLB) **The earth and all on and in it are righteous. They are rejoicing. It is man that is the sinner and will be judged for their sins. It is man that has to fear the judgement.**

A Lesson from the Geese

This was from a speech given by Angeles Arrien at the 1991 Organizational Development Network and based on the work of Milton Olson. It is a story you may have heard or know about as it is common knowledge that geese work together when they fly to save their energy and, in case of injury, to help and protect each other. They form life partnerships with their mates which is a great lesson for us as well.

Fact 1: As each goose flaps its wings it creates an uplift for the birds that follow. By flying in a "V" formation the whole flock adds 71% greater flying range than if each bird flew alone.

Fact 2: When a goose falls out of formation, it suddenly feels the drag and resistance of flying alone. It quickly moves back into formation to take advantage of the lifting power of the bird immediately in front of it.

Fact 3: When the lead goose tires, it rotates back into the formation and another goose flies to the point position.

Fact 4: The geese flying in formation honk to encourage those up front to keep up their speed.

Fact 5: When a goose gets sick, wounded or shot down, two geese drop out of formation and follow it down to help and protect it. They stay with it until it dies or is able to fly again. Then, they launch out with another formation to catch up with the flock.

There is great wisdom and work ethic given animals for survival through companionship and partnerships. *(24) "There be four things which are little upon the earth, but they are exceeding wise: (25) The* *ants are a people not strong, yet they prepare their meat in the summer; (26)The conies (small rabbit like animals) are but a feeble folk, yet make they their homes in the rocks; (27)The locusts have no king, yet go their forth all of them by bands (28) The spider taketh hold with her hands, and is in the King's palaces (Proverbs 30:24-28 KJV)*

⊰ The Stray Dog ⊱

Charles Spurgeon (1834-1892) was a noted British Baptist minister. He was one of the most recognizable and popular ministers of his time. He told of a story of a stray dog who once befriended him.

He states: I recollect using, with very considerable effect in the Tabernacle, an incident that occurred in my own garden. There was a dog which was in the habit of coming through the fence and scratching in my flower-beds, to the manifest spoiling of the Gardener's toil and temper. Walking in the garden one Saturday afternoon and preparing my sermon for the following day, I saw the four-footed creature, rather a scurvy specimen, by-the-by, and having a walking-stick in my hand, I threw it at him with all my might, at the same time giving him some good advice about going home.

Now, what should my canine friend do but turn round, pick up the stick in his mouth, bring it, and lay it down at my feet, wagging his tail all the while in expectation of my thanks and kind words! Of course, you do not suppose that I kicked him, or threw the stick at him any more. I felt quite ashamed of myself, and told that he was welcome to stay as long as he liked, and to come as often as he pleased.

There was an instance of the power of non-resistance, submission, patience, and trust, in overcoming even righteous anger.

How often we don't look beyond our selfishness, or, simply blinded by ignorance, see the need, love, and spiritual side of God's creatures that try desperately to befriend us. Yet when we

do, we are lead to a love of the spiritual realm that forever changes us. *"Thine incorruptible spirit is in all things"*. *(Wisdom 12:1 The 1611 King James Bible)*

"For your imperishable spirit is in everything". *(Wisdom 12:1 NJB)*

The Perfect Love Story

If you want to hear the perfect love story, learn about the life of the eagle. They have a courtship period before they make a life-long commitment to each other. However, it is the female who chooses her mate and for good reason. They understand love differently than we humans, it seems. Theirs starts out as a practical love for the survival of their young then develops into a lifelong endearing love.

Eagles take their marriage vows for life. But first the male has to prove himself worthy of being able to care for the eaglets. The female and male eagle who is courting her will fly far up into the air; then she will drop a twig. He has to fly down and catch it. She will then get a larger and heavier twig and drop it for him to catch. This continues on until he has proven himself worthy to be her life mate and be able to catch a baby eaglet should it fall from the nest. If he cannot catch all of the twigs she drops, she rejects him and awaits a stronger man to fly into her life.

Once the female is satisfied he is the one for her, they start a courtship high in the sky, singing a love song to each other, flying in large circles, dipping down and performing spellbinding maneuvers one could not imagine unless they observed them with their own eyes. (Their final courtship results in mating to bring their first baby into the world.) They stay married for a lifetime, and each day the male will bring a little gift for his mate, such as a green twig. They fly together, raise their babies together, and continually act affectionate toward each other throughout their life. It is truly a love story made in Heaven.

The Book of Ecclesiasticus 1611 version of the King James Bible, the New Jerusalem Bibles, and The New English Bible speak about all creatures going in pairs, male and female, just as we find in the book of Genesis. *(22) How lovely, all his works, how dazzling to the eye! (23) They all live and last for ever, and, whatever the circumstances, all obey. (24) All things go in pairs, by opposites, he has not made anything imperfect: (25) one thing complements the excellence of another. Who could ever grow tired of gazing at his glory? (Ecclesiasticus 42:22-25 NJB)*

The 1611 King James Bible is more difficult to read as the words are written more as they sound and in the style of that time. Sometimes the word (he) appears as "he" and sometimes as "hee." *King James version: Glory of God in Nature. (21) Hee hath garnished the excellent workes of his wisdome, and hee is from everlasting to everlasting, unto him may nothing be added, neither can he be diminished, and he hath no need of any counseller. (22) O how desireable are all his workes: and that a man may see even to a sparke. [to the eye] (23) All these things live and remaine forever, for all (bses), and they are all obedient. (24) All things are double one against another: [go in pairs] and hee hath made nothing imperfect. (25) One thing establisheth the good of another: and who shalbe filled with beholding his glory: (Ecclesiasticus 42: 21-25 The 1611 King James Bible)*

(21)He has set in order the masterpieces of his wisdom, he who is from eternity to eternity; nothing can be added, nothing taken away, and he needs no one to give him advice. (22) How beautiful is all he has made, down to the smallest spark that can be seen! (23) His works endure, all of them active for ever and all responsive to their various purposes. (24) All things go in pairs, one the opposite of the other; he has made nothing incomplete. (25) One thing supplements the virtues of another. Who could ever contemplate his glory enough? (Ecclesiasticus 42:21-25 TNEB)

⊷⊱{ Duke Knew When to Jump }⊰⊷

My daughter–in-law Lisa lives in Wichita Falls, Texas. Lisa met Duke in a most unusual way. He was street smart, no doubt, and he also had the intelligence to recognize help when his life depended on it.

Lisa reports: I was driving down the street in Wichita Falls on a rainy day when I noticed a large German shepherd mix dog running for his life. The dog catchers were after him. I had to do something so I just stopped the car opened the door and Duke made a mad dash and jumped in.

I brought him home. He was dirty and skinny from having very little to eat and he looked fairly old. Apparently, he looked much older than he was because he was in such poor health, malnourished and unkempt. My husband Eden said we could keep him as he thought Duke, as we named him, was in the final stages of his life. It turned out that Duke was actually a very young dog, and, unfortunately for Eden but fortunately for Duke, his stay was going to be many years.

Duke had two other dogs to keep him company in his back yard. He lived a life of luxury. He was a dog with plenty of food to eat, water to drink, and friends to play with. He did love to chase cars. And, when he would get out of our wooden fenced-in yard, by digging under or finding a weak board he would be off and running. Unfortunately, the mailman hit him during one of his escape runs. No doubt Duke went right to Heaven and, as Eden said, he died doing what he loved best to do and that was chase cars.

The book of Psalms reminds us that all of creation does live and last forever. So is there a possibility that Duke is chasing chariots in Heaven? *(7)Thy righteousness is like the mighty mountains; Thy judgments are like the great deep, Man and beast Thou preservest, O Lord.(8) How precious is Thy loving-kindness, O God! (Psalm 36:7-8 Jewish Holy Scriptures)*

The Intelligence of the Bee
From *Heaven and the Angels* by H.A. Baker

How often do we stop to think how bees and spiders and ants and other such creatures work to make a living and do it in perfect harmony with their own kind? The honey bee is a wonderful example.

The honey bee knows, without being taught, how to build, with the least wax, a cell that will hold the largest possible amount of honey. This hexagonal cell is of such perfect geometrical measurements that men could not improve the plan, and, yet the bees, untaught, working in unison and perfect co-operation, build this perfect cell in the dark. This is knowledge without instruction. This is perfect co-operation. A whole swarm of bees doing intricate work puzzles the minds of men. And, they do it all in the dark without any language we humans can detect. **H.A. Baker goes on to explain that in Heaven the family of God works together in much the same way.**

All wisdom comes from God and He measures it out to all of His creation. The book of Ecclesiasticus Douay Rheims 1609 edition explains it. *(1) All wisdom is from the Lord, and hath always been with him, and is before all time. (4) Wisdom has been created before all things, and the understanding of prudence from everlasting. (6) To whom hath the root of wisdom been revealed and who hath known her wise counsels? (8) There is one most high Creator Almighty, and a powerful king, and greatly to be feared, who sitteth upon his throne, and is the God of dominion. (9). He created her in the Holy Ghost, and saw her, and numbered her, and measured her. (10) And he poured her out upon all his works (creation) and upon all flesh according to his gift, and hath given her to them that love him. (Ecclesiasticus1:1, 4, 6-10 1609 Douay Rheims Bible)*

The book, *Heaven and the Angels* by H.A. Baker, records many visions and revelations of Heaven. In Chapter 9, it speaks

of the soul and the spirit of all creation as Reverend Baker states:
Scientists know that this "intuitive" sense we call instinct is found in all
the natural creation in humanely unexplainable measure. The homing
pigeon instinctively flies to its home. Robins return at the right season
to build their nests, each type of bird their own unique style of nest.
The humming birds work in pairs building their minute nests. Ants
and bees work in colonies, or swarms in perfect co-operation in caring
for their young and in doing their own perfect little bit in life without
being taught.

Every living creature in Heaven possesses this intuitive knowledge,
according to his capacity and position in God's economy. In redeemed
man this intuition increases as development enlarges the capacity and
the need for it.

*(1)Then Jonah prayed unto the Lord his God out of the fish's belly, (2)And
said, I cried by reason of mine affliction unto the Lord, and he heard me; out of the
belly of hell cried I, and thou heardest my voice …(10) And the Lord spake unto
the fish, and it vomited out Jonah upon the dry land (Jonah 2:1-2, 10 KJV)*

❧ Lady Jane ❧

**Sandra Curcy of Matawan, NJ shares the story of a Muscovy
duck she named Lady Jane.**

Sandra says: She was the smallest and the daintiest of the Muscovy
ducks and her name was Lady Jane. Nothing else distinguished her
from the other ducks on the place. For all the three years of her life,
she came with the rest of the flock every morning and evening to be
fed. I always talked to them and they let me know by "hissing" and
neck movements (which is how they talk) that they were hungry NOW
and would I please hurry it up a little.

Early one especially clear spring morning, I came out of the house
and found Lady Jane sitting on an old tree stump near the grapevine.
She jumped down as soon as she saw me and came closer, "talking." I

greeted her. "How are you this morning, Lady?" Being a mere human, I thought she was telling me how hungry she was. As I walked to the barn, she waddled in front of me, stopping now and then to look at me and "talk." She led me into the barn and stopped. Again she turned, looked at me and "spoke." She was standing in front of a nest of hay and feathers filled with eggs. We stood together looking at the nest and I said to her, "What a beautiful nest, Lady. You certainly are going to have a large family," and started my chores.

Each morning after that, she would be waiting to lead me to the barn, stopping, turning to look at me and "talking" as we walked. As before, she would lead me to her nest and I would admire it.

One day, there seemed to be fewer eggs in the nest and I asked her what was happening. She just turned and looked at me. The next day, I was sure the nest was less crowded and I finally understood what she had been trying to tell me all along!

She continued to wait for me every morning, leading me to the barn and her nest but, inevitably, there came the day I found an empty nest. She never waited for me again. I had let poor Lady Jane down— I did not help to save her eggs.

A short time later, she was missing from the flock that greeted me at feeding time. I searched and searched, but could not find her, until the dog persisted in trying to climb a certain hollow, old tree that grew close to the house. Lady Jane had taken matters into her own hands! Inside the trunk of that old tree, about ten feet off the ground was Lady and the beautiful family that she had hatched.

How she found this spot, ten feet up, inside the tree still puzzles me for I have never seen a Muscovy duck fly (I never could catch Lady going into or coming out of that hollow tree) and Lady Jane, along with the rest of the chickens and ducks, stayed close to the barn which is nowhere near the old tree!

Lady Jane knew the deadline. God gave her the understanding to be prepared as Ecclesiasticus 39 tells us. *(33) The works of the Lord are all good, when the time is right, he gives whatever is needed. (34) You must not say, "This is worse than that," for, sooner or later, everything proves its worth.(35) So now, sing with all your heart and voice, and bless the name of the Lord! (Ecclesiasticus 39:33-35 NJB)*

⊰{ Sweet Pea and Bean }⊱

This story comes from Elizabeth Fay. She has a God-given love for rabbits, especially those in great need. What Elizabeth has observed over the years concerning the love and care rabbits offer each other will give you great insight into the minds and hearts of one species of God's innocent creatures.

Sweet Pea's world was completely dark and totally silent. The poor little tan-colored Holland Lop (bunny) was dumped at the shelter at the end of her life. How broken hearted she must have been and scared beyond comprehension, at the strange scents and different feel of what she sat on, as she waited to be labeled "un-adoptable" and sent off to be euthanized. Why did someone keep her for 8-10 years and now abandon her? God had better plans for Sweet Pea. Shelly is the vet tech who rescues those like Sweet Pea on death row for no fault of their own. She tries to find them loving forever homes and she knows I'll take the most severely handicapped.

I had a widower bunny also known as my caregiver bunny, Bean. He immediately took to this blind, deaf little girl, showing her all around. Where the food is, the water, the litter box with hay and the pen which was now "their" home (when not making the most of their rabbit-free-run-time). There were times when even a caregiver needs a little relief from their responsibilities. That's when I would tend to Sweet Pea's chronic ear abscesses. It's also when I learned this little senior citizen had been blessed by our creator with just enough tenacity to recover and move on from the hurt and fear of being abandoned at a time she needed her humans the most.

With the loving devotion from Bean and a new sense of security, she almost doubled her life to a ripe old age of 14 years. This is almost unheard of even for Holland Lops, considering she had multiple medical problems, including periodic seizures.

I would wrap her up in a baby blanket and cradle her in my arm when giving her medication or cleaning her ears. I'd make click-clicks with my teeth while resting my chin on her forehead so she could feel the vibrations. Bunnies make click-click noises when they are happy. When she was tired of playing the role of my little bunny baby, she would tenaciously thrust her chin up under mine and that meant, "enough already." She wanted to be put down so she could find Bean. She did this by following the scent of his path. If Bean had doubled back she would become frustrated and start thumping for Bean to come and find her. And he always would. Sweet Pea learned that whenever my scent was getting stronger it meant I was handing out treats, so to make sure she didn't get passed over, she'd immediately sit up like a prairie dog with her front feet in the begging position. Sometimes, I just wanted to close the curtain or open the window, and there she'd be sitting right up begging. That sight was so precious I couldn't resist giving her a small diced piece of dried pineapple.

One day Bean and Sweet Pea were taken to the vet and five large African parrots came in for beak, nail and wing trims. What an event that was for all three of us. The parrots had no intentions of complying with the purpose of their appointment and proceeded to voice their opinions—very, very loudly. One took off running out of the exam room and down the hall with the vet assistant in quick pursuit. Bean was scared out of his wits. I kept reassuring him I would not let those big birds get him. The decibel at which these five parrots squawked was deafening. Even I momentarily lost my hearing. But, there was little Sweet Pea, sitting on the exam table in the adjoining room munching on her baby carrot, completely oblivious to the incredible volume of noise around her.

It was not until it was time for Sweet Pea to go back to our creator that I understood the significance of that day.

Sweet Pea's seizures began to occur more and more frequently. Following one rather lengthy seizure she had trouble positioning her hind legs under her in order to get up to the food dish. She wasn't about to let a little inconvenience detour her. If it meant she had to scoot her bottom half then she'd just keep at it until she got where she wanted to go. Soon it was necessary for me to feed her baby food with a syringe and give her fluids under her skin as she no longer had any muscle tone.

I carried her around like a baby, loving her and imagining her with Jesus crossing a bridge with a small stream leading to a beautiful green grassy area. I knew it was getting close to time for her to go and I didn't want her to suffer. In my mind's eye, I would speak to her of how her legs would again be strong and flexible. She would hear the click-clicks of other bunnies awaiting her in Heaven. She would see a little white bunny with big black eyes that was her beloved Bean coming to join her also one day; and, finally me, as in Heaven she would now be able to see and hear us.

As time went on I prayed and prayed for Jesus to call Sweet Pea home while she was resting peacefully but he didn't. I was really upset with God that she had to suffer.

Then completely unexpected, I suddenly knew why we'd gone through that day at the vets with the deafening noise of those five African parrots. I would understand that what I now was witnessing was nothing short of a miracle. God had shown me that Sweet Pea was totally and utterly deaf and there was no doubt about it. It was also significant that Sweet Pea was a lop bunny, meaning the ears are longer than an up-eared rabbit and lop ears hang down all the time. Sweet Pea had just lifted her right ear up over her head and turned it to a corner in the living room. She held it there as if hearing more than one word. In my mind, I thought, is Jesus calling her?

But she didn't go, and the seizures kept coming. Then it happened again, she lifted her right ear straight up over her head and turned it to the same corner of the living room. I believe Jesus, creator of all life, was indeed calling her home to be made new again. It was hard for me to fathom that as much as Bean and I loved her, Jesus loved her even more, but after all, it was He who created her soul to especially bond with ours. From where she rallied the strength is a mystery to me, but she managed, to one last time, tenaciously thrust her little chin under mine, because she knew I loved it when she did.

I'd watched my dear bunny "hear" and "listen" two times to someone I couldn't see. Time kept passing and then Sweet Pea cried out in pain. I believe a blood vessel broke in her head and she was finally free from that sick little "living space suit" that housed her soul while she was on earth.

I reasoned with the Lord and I believe He answered my cries as I said: "Why did she have to die in pain? Why didn't you just call her home?"

I was reminded that she needed the pain to let go. She needed the pain for me to let her go. She had had a wonderful life with Bean and me and she didn't want to leave. We loved her so much. But now she has no more pain. It was then a warm peace came over me.

Though I cried and grieved over her parting, I again thought of the two times when I witnessed seeing the deaf lop lift her ear up over her head, as if listening to a sound or voice coming from the ceiling in the living room. She had heard something I couldn't (and now I understood the significance of being at the vet the same day and time as were those five very loud African parrots).

Shortly after Sweet Pea went on ahead of us to Heaven, God had another little Sweetie Pea awaiting us. Her name is Li'l Sara. She is another little Holland lop, blind in one eye and quickly losing the sight in her other eye. She had fur missing from her face and her eye ducts were closed due to scar tissue and her tears ran down her face, scorching off the fur. She was undernourished and her coat was thin and coarse. I put her in the pen with Bean and she immediately sidled up alongside him and stretched out all four legs, as if to say, "Oh yeah, these digs will do nicely," and she was already smitten with Bean. He instinctively knew to groom the tears from her face before any more fur could be scorched off.

Li'l Sara quickly gained weight and her winter coat came in thick with a beautiful sheen to it. She is like a fuzzy medium brown teddy bear. The fur grew back, restoring her face to the distinctive roundedness of a lop's head.

What would I do without Bean? God had given him a caregiver spirit to nurture and love Sweet Pea and now he had Li'l Sara to care for. He surely knew I needed him in order to heal another little hurting soul.

The Book of Genesis gives us so much information concerning God's creation and how He blessed all creatures and provided for them and said that they were good. It also said that man was to be in charge of the animals just as Elizabeth has been for bunnies. *(20) The God commanded, "Let the water be filled with many kinds of living beings (souls), and let the air be filled with birds."(21) So God created the great sea monsters, all kinds of creatures that live in the water, and all kinds of birds. And God was pleased with what he saw (22) He blessed them all and told the creatures that live in the water to reproduce and to fill the sea, and he told the birds to increase in number. (24) Then God commanded, "Let the earth reproduce all kinds of animal life: domestic and wild, large and small" — and it was done. (25) So God made them all, and he was pleased with what he saw.*

(27) So God created human beings, making them to be like himself. He created them male and female, (28-29) blessed them, and said, have many children—I am putting you in charge of the fish, the birds, and all the wild animals.—I am providing fruit and grain for you to eat. (30) But for all the wild animals and for all the birds I have provided grass and leafy plants for Food"—and it was done. (31) God looked at everything he had made, and he was very pleased. (Genesis 1:20-31 Good News New English Version – some paraphrased).

CHAPTER 5

Miracle Healings

⊰ My Dog Fan ⊱

Janet H. Kerr of Dacula, Georgia writes of two miracles which happened to her dog, Fancy, called "Fan" for short. The love Janet showed for Fan in a time of crisis and her pleading with God brought healing where it didn't look possible.

Janet said: In December of 1993 I went up to Animal Control in Gwinnett County in Georgia to look over the "treasures" up there. I chose Fancy and the friend in the next enclosure. I really needed two more dogs with nine I already had at home. I was not sure why I was up there, but there I was. Still can't fathom that. She and Frida jumped in the car and quietly came home with me, along with Fan's kennel cough virus she never disclosed until we were home. Very nice! Generously the virus trotted through six more of my original pack. After croaking and hacking, all were again well in ten days. There was lots of noise, but not deadly.

A year later Fan disobediently ran into a grove of trees and while we went home, she wouldn't budge— just barked and barked. She finally gave up when I came up to her and started to follow me home as I grumpily "read the riot act" to her. We were crossing the street near home when a lady going to work came over the hill. I signaled to Fan to get off the street and she did the opposite. The car didn't even try to stop as it closed on her. Seeing the inevitable, I yelled at top volume, "Stop!" She then put on her brakes, but Fan was hit. She yelped. I ran to her and signaled the car to go on. You could see Fan had tire marks over her hips, scratches on her right front leg, skinned down to the bone and a broken tooth tip. She couldn't move. I carefully dragged her to the road side and began talking sadly to her. Her mouth bled a little and then stopped. I asked the Lord to please save her but I was consumed with sadness that she might be leaving me. I told her I enjoyed her so much. I didn't go into scolding at all. I didn't feel anger at the lady—not then, anyway. I had to concentrate on Fan completely.

I took my left hand and turned it palm up, spread out my fingers slightly, and began to stroke her with the lightest touch possible. About the second stroke, her pupils, which were huge (in shock), began to contract again until they were back to normal. In a few minutes she seemed strong enough to move and stand. She slowly limped home under her own power. She climbed the steps to the kitchen and lay down on the doggy bed under the table. She went to sleep. I decided to wait and see since she was a terrified bundle of nerves in the car after going to the vet and back months before for inoculations. She should have had a broken pelvis with that car running over her back, but it wasn't. Neither was her skinned leg broken. When I thought about it later I was so thankful something had kept that car from killing her. She got well on her own and is bouncing about even now.

Ask and it will be given to you, seek and you will find; knock and the door will be opened to you. (Matthew 7:7 NAB)

✧{ **Fan Gets Healed Again** }✧

The second miracle occurred in September of 1997. I noticed a pink spot on Fan's nose in her whiskers. Then it grew into a pink lump and five days later turned black and grew more. It was growing into an ugly mass.

That did it! I remember getting more than a little angry. For me, disease is from the devil. Jesus spoke to diseases, so I did too. Every day I would "read the riot act" in a firm voice telling it to go. I wasn't tolerating any more cancer cells in my pups after losing Scooby Duke and Samo to this stuff. It began to disappear and was gone before the week was up. It's still gone.

Janet spoke to the problem and it left. It is not God bringing illness and disease upon the earthly bodies, but the old devil who wants no more then to kill, steal, and destroy both man and beast.

The thief cometh not but for to steal, and to kill, and to destroy: I am come that they might have life, and that they might have it more abundantly. (John 10:10 KJV)

⊰{ Rusty's Miracle Healing }⊱

Cassandra Browning, a young lady from Ohio, wrote me about her dog Rusty. This is a true story about a young girl who loves God and knows the power we have when we put our complete faith in Him. God still heals today and He doesn't stop at healing just people. Reverend John Wesley, the founder of the Methodist church, found that out when God healed him and his horse at the same time. Now Cassandra tells us about God's healing power for her dog, Rusty.

Cassandra writes: My name is Cassie. I go to Solid Rock Church in Monroe, Ohio. My pastor, Lawrence Bishop, told me to tell you about my testimony on how God has healed my dog.

The vet thought that my Yorkshire terrier, Rusty, had a pancreatic tumor because his insulin level was far too high and his glucose level was much too low. The vet referred us to another vet to get an ultrasound done.

God, however, came to me in a dream and told me that Rusty is healed. Saturday night, January 12, God woke my mom up at 3:00 AM and she looked up and said, "God, give me a sign that Rusty is healed" and then she fell back to sleep. That same night I had a dream that a spirit was working around the house. We didn't know what it was and then it went and laid down in my mom's bed. It looked just like her. My mom and I (holding Rusty) walked over and asked, **"Who are you?"** God rose up out of her and said, **"I am God."**

'I asked, **"Can we ask you a question?"** He said, **"Yes."** I asked, **"Will you heal Rusty?"**

He stretched out his arm toward Rusty and said **"He is healed,"** and this healing just poured all over Rusty. We could see it coming down inside of him. When my mom and I looked back up, God had disappeared.

When I told my mom about the dream I had she began to cry and tell me that she asked God for a sign that Rusty is healed. We believe that God healed Rusty at that very moment and that nothing was going to show up on the ultrasound.

When we took Rusty to get the ultrasound that Wednesday morning they did not find anything on the ultrasound! Thank God! The vet said that all of Rusty's organs look good (even his pancreas). The vet doesn't understand why Rusty does not have the symptoms of the tumor when his insulin is so high.

She said it shouldn't be that high (I have faith that God has made it normal now. He doesn't show the symptoms of a tumor because he doesn't have a tumor). The vet is running another blood test to check his insulin levels and glucose levels. She said that it is completely inappropriate for his insulin levels to be that high. She believes there may be a tumor that she couldn't see with the ultrasound, but I know that there isn't a tumor.

God told me that Rusty is healed and that's what I am believing! God is not a liar.

Yesterday at church, a man walked up to me and told me, **"I don't know what you're dealing with but God told me to come over to you and tell you that it is almost over and that everything is going to be okay."** That was more confirmation to me that God has indeed healed Rusty completely! Thank you, Jesus!

I know that God is working in this situation and that Rusty's insulin levels and glucose levels are back to normal. I believe that Dr. Schrader (the vet that did the ultrasound) will get the results back this week from the blood test and see that Rusty's insulin is down to normal and his glucose is up to normal. She may not understand it, but it's true. She said that looking through all of his records it doesn't make any logical sense that he would be completely healthy. But isn't that how our great God works? Some things we aren't supposed to understand. We are supposed to just trust Him. He works everything out.

My mom and I keep thanking God. He has worked a miracle in our lives. I can't praise and thank God enough for healing Rusty! He is so awesome! *"By his stripes ye were healed." (1 Peter 2:24 KJV)*

"For the spirit of the Lord hath filled the whole world and that, which containeth all things, that knowledge of the voice." (God) *(Wisdom 1:7 1609 Douay Rheims Bible)*

Psalm 144 reminds us: *(9) The Lord is sweet to all: and his tender mercies are over all his works. (10) Let all thy works, O Lord, praise thee: and let thy saints bless thee. (Psalm 144:9-10) The 1609 Douay Rheims Bible)*

❧{ John Wesley and His Horse }❧

I have had many ask if we can pray for healing for our pets just as we do for people and can they be healed? I have no doubt animals can be healed through prayer and faith. There are those who would agree with me, both lay people and those in the ministry such as the noted minister John Wesley.

Reverend John Wesley, in the 1700s, wrote a theology or a method to teach and preach the gospel. It became known as the "method" or guidelines for him and his fellow ministers as they spread the gospel throughout much of Europe and the United States. This "method," established to spread the gospel, was the foundation of the formation of the Methodist church.

Wesley rode his horse going from one church to another as that was the main mode of transportation in the 1700s in reaching people all over England. One day while riding from town to town he developed a very bad headache. His horse was limping as well. Wesley remembered that God said to ask for our needs to be met.

He wrote: "My horse was very lame yet I rode seven miles having a bad headache. Then it occurred to me to ask God for the healing and (what I here state is the naked fact; let every man account for it as he sees good.) I then thought, 'Cannot God heal either man or beast, by any means, or without any?' Immediately my weariness and headache ceased, and my horse's lameness in the same instant. Nor did he halt any more either that day or the next. A very odd accident this also!"

You would have to know the tremendous faith John Wesley had in his heavenly father and the mission that he was so faithfully fulfilling to understand God's total compassion for him and his horse. John Wesley desired that every man, woman and child would come to salvation. He rode horse-back many thousands of miles during his lifetime preaching all over the United Kingdom and, for a short time, in America as well, to carry that message. He had numerous instances when preaching in the pastures, under trees, and in the roadways where the animals such as horses and birds would come near when he was preaching as if to listen quietly. They would then walk or fly away after the sermons were over. Wesley preached wherever anyone would listen to him. His listeners ranged from small groups of people to large church congregations. He believed in fasting and he required all who were preaching with him to fast every Friday and pray.

Remember Jonah, the guy who got swallowed by a whale for disobeying God. God told him to warn the people of Nineveh but he didn't want to. Well, after Jonah repented while inside the big fish, God gave him a second chance. After the fish spit him out, he went to the king of Nineveh and delivered the message from God. The king took action and required the people to fast and pray and wear sackcloth. Even the animals had to fast and wear sackcloth. *(7) And he caused it to be proclaimed and published through Nineveh by the decree of the king and his nobles, saying, Let neither man nor beast, herd nor flock, taste anything let them not feed, nor drink water: (8) But let man and beast be covered with sackcloth, and cry mightily unto God yea, let them turn every one from his evil way, and from the violence that is in their hands. (Jonah 3:7-8 KJV)*

The Healing Purr

Dr. Kim Bloomer is a veterinary naturopath and the creator of *Animal Talk Naturally* radio show along with co-host Dr. Jeannie Thomason. She shared a story of how the purr of a cat can heal.

Dr. Bloomer says: I've been doing some reading on the healing behind the cat's purr. I found it so fascinating, I decided to share it.

Growing up we always had cats and dogs. My dad's mom was always fond of Siamese cats so there was always at least one around. I really love hanging around with a cat just listening to it purr and even better, having one sitting on my lap purring. It's no wonder, too, after finding out what the purr is all about. And, it isn't just about contentment. In fact, it's so much more.

A friend in a holistic cat group I belong to sent this article to our group: *Now You Can Take Back One Half the Awful Things You've Said About Cats.*

This article starts off like this: "In the latest issue of *Alternatives for the Health-Conscious Individual* by Dr. David Williams, he talks about some interesting research in vibrations. He says that researchers have found that vibrations or energy currents in the range of 20 to 50 MHz stimulates bone growth. The production of the body's natural anti-inflammatory compounds is increased."

Well, I know a bit about frequencies from aromatherapy and from a great book by Dr. David Stewart, *Healing Oils of the Bible*, which I refer to a lot when I'm doing our weekly online radio show.

For a body to be well and in a state where disease can't touch it, several factors are necessary. One of those is having the body in a proper alkaline/acid balance (80/20 respectively). Another is electrical frequency.

In a human body a healthy person will have a frequency of around 62-320 MHz. The lower it dips, the more serious an illness and/or disease. The essential oils (unadulterated, therapeutic grade) have frequencies of between 50-320 MHz with the rose oil being the highest. I got roses for Valentine's Day and wow, just smelling them is awesome. Now I understand why my grandmother had roses growing everywhere and where she got all her energy!

Back to frequencies and we're getting to the purr in cats in my usual round about way. Optimal frequency for bone stimulation (and healing) is 50 MHz. And you guessed it–a cat's purr frequencies at 25-50 MHz, which just happens to be the best frequency for bone growth and fracture healing!

It's interesting that when a cat is seriously injured and in obvious pain or very ill, they'll purr. They can be a little stray, hungry and not well and they'll be purring when you find them. You thought it was because they were happy to be rescued, huh? Well, I'm sure they are but they are also doing what nature provided for them to help heal themselves—purring for wellness.

I learned that if you have three cats in a room all purring, the frequency is about 120 MHz, so if you want some good healing going on in your home you might want to consider getting a cat or two or ten.

Dr. Kim Bloomer is an expert in the field of health and healing for animals. She implements God's own natural oils, herbs, minerals, vitamins and foods as her basic formula for their long and happy life. I have a word of warning, however. Not all oils are the same and some can be very dangerous. Dr. Bloomer uses only Pure Living Essential Oils as it is an unregulated industry. Other oils can actually be harmful.

I have also learned from some staff and nurses who work in nursing homes something which is quite amazing. "When a person is near death, some dogs and cats living in the nursing homes and allowed to roam free, predict a resident's death. They indicate to the staff and nurses when a person is going to die shortly by lying on the bed of the soon to be departed soul."

CHAPTER 6

Visions of Heaven

A Place Called Heaven
By Dr. Gary Wood

I read ***A Place Called Heaven*** recently by **Dr. Gary Wood.**
It is a true story of **Dr. Gary Woods'** miraculous healing after he
had died from a car accident when he was a young man and went
to Heaven for a period of time. This total healing is so soundly
documented by doctors that there is no doubt that God can heal
completely when it is not humanly possible. I wish to relay the
experience he had concerning animals in Heaven. ***A Place
Called Heaven*** is a book you must read.

Dr. Wood said: I saw a little girl with beautiful long brown hair running
to Jesus. He picked her up and children from all over came running to
him as well. They were all dressed in white robes and while Jesus was
ministering to them, all sorts of animals were with the children. There
was even a fearless lion playing with them and birds were sitting on their
shoulders and the tops of their heads. I saw the grass and flowers so
much alive and many other breathtaking things as well. There is so
much beauty and joy in Heaven. I met my teenage friend who had died
earlier in a car wreck and some of those recorded in the Bible as well. I
saw children playing with Jesus and the animals all around them.

Close Encounters of the God Kind

Evangelist Jesse Duplantis wrote ***Close Encounters of the
God Kind*** about his experience of being caught up in Heaven
for over five hours. Jesse had a praying mother and she wanted
one of her three sons to be a preacher. One day the Lord gave

her the answer, "Jesse." She immediately said, "What? No, not Jesse. It can't be Jesse—he's a heathen!" God does work in mysterious ways and Jesse did become a preacher and famous evangelist.

Jesses Duplantis says: From my trip, I understand Heaven is a truly physical sense. It's a real place. I know that Heaven is a fact. It's beyond a hope; to me it's the reality. But people don't have to believe me. The proof of what I experienced is the fruit in the lives of the people who receive the message.

People have asked me, "Why did the Lord take you to Heaven?" I don't know.

Jesse was in for a surprise as he did not know animals would be in Heaven.

Jesse relates: The first thing I saw was Paradise. It was beautiful with trees lined up alongside the River of Life which flowed through Paradise. There were thousands of people and children. There were horses, dogs, and large cats like lions. I saw the Prophet Jonah and said: ***"Boy, you were in that whale? What was it like to be in that fish?"*** Jonah seemed to hesitate and said: ***"No, I was in disobedience."*** Jonah continued, ***"When I came out of there, I had one thing on my mind, and that was to do what God told me to do."***

I loved the message from the Prophet Jonah to Jesse. Many have said that the story of Jonah is only a story of illustration. It could not be real. However, just before my *Fido* book went to print, I happened to read in the newspaper a true story of a man in Europe who had actually been swallowed by a whale and did live after being in the whale's belly for three days. This evidence is documented by others who saw it all happen.

Visions Beyond the Veil
By H.A. Baker

Reverend Baker and his wife were missionaries to Tibet, now controlled by China, and Formosa. His book documents visions by a most unlikely group of children, orphans and street children who had never known Christ or any Biblical references to Christianity in any way. These young children living in China came to the Adullam Rescue Mission in Yunnanfu, Yunnan Province, China. They became known as the Adullam children.

Visions Beyond the Veil is a book of wonderful visions aligning with Scripture through these young children of China who had never heard of Jesus. They were for the most part, street children without homes, or poor children with one or both parents dead. They were mostly boys ranging in age from six to eighteen without any training in morals and without any education.

The visions and revelations they experienced through prayer and the infilling of the Holy Spirit will come alive to you and increase your understanding of God and His wonderful love of creation and the amazing Heaven that awaits all who will be there. The section revealing visions of heaven and the animal kingdom as seen by the boys is most reassuring.

H.A. Baker says: The Visions by the Adullam Children as recorded are ones beyond anything that could be made up. They would see visions of Heaven for long periods of time, and, at times laugh, other times sob when Jesus told them of his sacrifice so that all man could go to Heaven. Yet, so few were accepting his sacrifice for their soul. They saw visions of hell and the anguish of the lost souls and the devil and his demons who caused such evil. However, they also saw Paradise with trees, delicious fruit, beautiful flowers, and birds singing in the trees. They experienced seeing animals of every size and description from lions to elephants. They saw large and small deer which they rode, and rabbits and all sorts of small friendly pets. They held them in their arms and found a friendly lion to play with. They ran their fingers through the shaggy mane of the lion and brushed his face, and put their hands in his mouth. Then they curled down beside him and just relaxed much like we read in Isaiah 11:6-8. They were led around at times throughout Heaven by angels. The angels were dancing, singing, and praising God. These praises never ceased. One of the young Adullam boys met two Adullam boys who had died and who took him through Paradise and other parts of Heaven.

H.A. Baker says of these visions and the scriptural references concerning the lower creation. Man will be restored to his Eden God and his Eden "park." But man will be restored to more than the primal order. He will be born again into the new spiritual order.

The first order was earthly. The last is spiritual but real. It is similar to the earthly, even as Christ after his resurrection was real and similar, but still spiritual and different from the earthly order. He still could eat and drink with his disciples. He still had flesh and bones that could be felt and hands that could serve fish and bread to his hungry disciples. But in the resurrected order the Lord was not subject to the limitations of the material world of time and space and physical bounds. *Even so the world with its natural order of animal, bird, and plant creation is to be born again into a higher, spiritual order similar to the first creation but also different from it. It will be the real order not again subject to corruption and unreality (Romans 8:20, Weymouth).*

The natural creation is to be born again through the resurrection of Christ. Christ saves more than man. He saved the whole creation that fell into unreality in the fall of man. *"For all creation, gazing eagerly as if with outstretched neck, is waiting and longing to see the manifestation of the sons of God." There was always the hope that, at least, the creation itself would also be set free from the thralldom of decay, so as to enjoy the liberty that will attend the glory of the children of God" (Rom. 8:19-21 Weymouth).*

Perhaps the revelation of such a Paradise in Heaven as the Adullam boy saw will be new to most of the readers as it was to us. "We are so dull of mind and slow of heart to believe all that is written in the scriptures."

H.A. Baker refers to Rev. 21:5, Isaiah 11:6, Col. 1:15, etc. to remind us of some scriptures which reveal this truth.

The children said that Paradise is a "Park" of Plant, Animal, and Regenerated Nature. H.A. Baker said we did not teach these children about Paradise. They taught us. "Paradise" means "Eden."

The Ark had three stories for the animals, Noah and his family. It is a symbolic representative of the trinity which is the three in one, God the father, God the son, and God the Holy Spirit. .

In the book *Heaven and the Angels* by H. A. Baker, Mokiang, Yunnan, China there are many visions by the children of Yunnan as well as others he has written about. Reverend Baker says: Since the land to which we journey should be of greatest concern and interest in this present life, we should find out all we can about the blessed land of Promise. **Reverend Baker quotes from well-known publishers, whose publications in their time were considered orthodox by the churches of their day.** It will be seen, too, that many of the writers from whom I quote were men whose sane views of the things of God and whose spiritual life were not questioned. I hope the reader will accept, as I do, the truth of these revelations as messages of God to men.

The Apostle Paul: "*I know a man in Christ-caught up to the Third Heaven-caught up to Paradise", ***Paul writes.** *"Whether in the body, or out of the body, I cannot tell",* **he further adds.** *"but clearly there is a Paradise in the Third Heaven, and in vision it was as real as life in earth."* **Reverend Baker said:** Cornelius, Peter, Paul and John and others of the Old and New

Testaments have been allowed to be caught up in Paradise and as the Bible says in the last days *(28) And it shall come to pass afterward, (in the last days,) that I will pour out my Spirit upon all flesh: and your sons and your daughters shall prophesy, your old men shall dream dreams, your young men shall see visions; (29) And also upon the servants and upon the handmaidens, in those days will I pour out my Spirit: (Joel 2:28-29 KJV)*

Reverend Baker states: The Adullam Orphanage Chinese children upon whom the Holy Spirit was poured forth as in New Testament days gave them visions of Heaven and the unseen worlds as real as scenes in the present world. Like Paul, they were caught up to Paradise. Whether in the body, or out of the body, like Paul, they could not tell. They thought they left their bodies and went to Heaven. What they saw corresponded with what was seen by others who died and experienced Heaven and came back These children as I have mentioned, were young, had never been exposed to the Bible, to God or to Jesus, were uneducated, poor street children yet they spoke of Heaven and of hell having been revealed through their visions. These visions could not have come from Satan.

Chapter V of *Heaven and the Angels*
Jesus, the Life of the New Jerusalem
"Jesus in Everything"

A direct quote: The highest, or Third Heaven, is the Heaven of the throne of Christ. Of the Son it is written, "Thy throne, O God, is for ever and ever", and "Thou Lord in the beginning hast laid the foundation of the earth; and the Heavens are the work of Thy hands."

Down from this throne in highest Heaven to Bethlehem came the one to be called "Jesus," "the Son of the Highest." He humbled Himself to ride upon an ass and entered the earthly Jerusalem on His way to the deepest humiliation of the cross and the grave. The Holy Spirit inspired multitudes to sing: *"Blessed is He that cometh in the name of the Lord; Hosanna in the highest."*

The wooded hills and verdant valleys; mountains; grand and rolling plains; birds and beasts; fern and flowers; saints and angels in the parks and in the Heavenly air are all a united, harmonious whole; all live in one life of love, the life of Jesus, the All-in-All. Jesus being in the life of all the New Jerusalem from the lowest plain to the highest, and being in every creature from the tiniest bird, or fern, or flower to saints and archangels, all Heaven pulsates with the life of Jesus as one organic whole, one body.

In the Heavenly plains the animal creation, to whom the Lord has given "every herb for food", while grazing in the Heavenly fields, thereby eat and partake of the life of Jesus, the life that comes from pure rivers of water, which water all Paradise.

Corporal Duffy, Our Forever Beagle

Duffy was one of a kind. I told of Duffy's friendship with the neighbor beagle, Linus. Their friendship lasted until Linus went to Heaven. The intelligence of these two beagles was made very evident by a number of family members of Linus as told in *Will I See Fido in Heaven?*

My husband Bob (now in Heaven) and I have two wonderful sons, Eden and Roman. When the boys were little, our younger son Roman, then about six years old, came to us one day with some neighborhood kids carrying a baby beagle puppy. He asked if he could have it and I said no. They said that the owner was going to have it destroyed if they could not find a home for it. They were contacting everyone they could find to see if one of the parents would take it. One of his friends took the other beagle and this was the last one to find a home.

As soon as the boys left, Bob said to me, "Mary, every boy needs a dog in his life," so I agreed. I rushed outside and saw the boys walking sadly down the street with Roman holding on to the little puppy, so dejectedly. I called to him to bring the little beagle back, as he could have it. The little pup's feet hardly touched the ground for several months because we held him constantly. He was the cutest little guy. When he walked his ears touched the ground.

Duffy was, however, a typical beagle hound and would escape at every opportunity. He would run across busy roads in and around our subdivision. He often went to a local store and the employees there would call me to come and get him as he had to cross a very dangerous street to get there. Due to angels I had surrounding him I firmly believed he escaped death several times!

He loved to hide his food. We would find bones buried in our neighbor's garden and all over our house, including under our pillows. Quite often Duffy would get into the cookies we left on the counter, and hide them in the chairs and under the bed covers and other interesting places. One evening our younger son, Roman, who was about ten years old at the time, wanted a cake he saw at the grocery store so we bought it. It had coconut icing and was a very rich cake. We had to go out for just a short time after we brought the groceries in and had left the cake on the table. That turned out to be a big mistake. When we got back the cake had been totally eaten. Not too often did I witness Roman being as mad as when he discovered his delicious cake had been eaten. He had not even had one bite and there was no chance of purchasing another one! Duffy also got into a ham one evening and all night we could hear him drinking water because he was so dehydrated from eating the salty ham.

One night our older son, Eden, had a friend, Steve, who came to visit. I told him to make sure to check under his pillow when he went to bed since Duffy would hide various eatables there without disturbing the bedding. Sure enough, Steve found a peeled boiled egg under his pillow!

Years later, our neighbor, Bob, decided to dig up his garden and discovered numerous bones and items Duffy had buried over the years. Unfortunately for Duffy, when we added two more dogs to the family, his food-hiding days came to an end. The other dogs would find and eat anything he hid.

Duffy lived to be seventeen and a half and was ready to go home when we let him go in 1994. It wasn't until 2002 that I saw Duffy in a vision. He was with my father, even though I couldn't see my father's face clearly. They were standing in a forest clearing, a sort of Paradise and my father was singing the words, "I come to the garden alone." The words are from the opening line of a hymn called "In the Garden."

My father and mother frequently sang "In the Garden" at church and for funerals. When I heard it in my vision, I knew the message was to get alone with God and listen to what He wanted to tell me, to spend more time with Him.

It was my father and my beagle, Duffy, who were chosen by God to deliver the message to me. Dad loved Duffy. The two spent many weeks together during the summer months on dad and mom's farms when we would visit. Duffy loved to chase rabbits there.

Since then my only brother, Mac Allen, has gone on to be with God. One of the songs he requested for his memorial service was "In the Garden." I have been so blessed to have God allow me this wonderful vision.

Here is the message of "In the Garden":

> I come to the garden alone
> While the dew is still on the roses,
> And the voice I hear, falling on my ear,
> The Son of God discloses
> And he walks with me, and He talks with me,
> And He tells me I am His own;
> And the joy we share as we tarry there,
> None other has ever known.

He speaks and the sound of His voice
Is so sweet the birds hush their singing,
And the melody that He gave to me,
Within my heart is ringing
And He walks with me, and He talks with me,
And He tells me I am His own;
And the joy we share as we tarry there,
None other has ever known.

I'd stay in the garden with Him
Tho' the night around me be falling,
But He bids me go; thro' the voice of woe
His voice to me is calling
And he walks with me, and He talks with me,
And He tells me I am His own;
And the joy we share as we tarry there,
None other has ever known.

It is so comforting to sit at sunset and hear the birds singing their praises to God and watch as some of the little animals get ready for night. You can feel God's love and imagine how proud He must be of the majesty of His creation and how much He surely loves every creature He has created.

Visions of the Spiritual World
The Visions of Sadhu Sundar Singh of India
The Reluctant Messenger
Preface by Sundar Singh, original publication 1926

Publishers' preface:
The life of Sadhu Sandar Singh was most remarkable in its Christ-likeness. He was born amidst the depths of Indian culture

and religions, and into a Sikh family. During the early part of his life, Sundar's mother would take him week by week to sit at the feet of the sadhyu, an escetic holy man, who lived some distance away in the rainforest.

But with the death of his beloved mother, when he was fourteen years old, the young Sundar grew increasingly despairing and aggressive. His hatred of the local missionaries and Christians culminated in the public burning of a Bible, which he tore apart page by page and threw into the flames.

Yet, soon Sundar wanted to take his own life. He had arrived at a point of desperation and decided to throw himself under the Ludhiana Express if God did not reveal to him the true way of peace.

At three in the morning he rose from his bed and went out into the moonlit courtyard for the ceremonial bath observed by devout Hindus and Sikhs before worship. He, then, returned to his room and knelt down, bowed his head to the ground, and pleaded that God would reveal himself. Yet, nothing happened. He had not known what to expect: a voice, a vision, and a trance? Still nothing happened. And it was fast approaching the time for the Ludhiana Express.

He lifted his head and opened his eyes and was rather surprised to see a faint cloud of light in the room. It was too early for the dawn. He opened the door and peered out to the courtyard. He saw only darkness. Turning back into the room, he saw that the light in the room was getting brighter. To his sheer amazement, he saw not the face of any of his traditional gods, but of Jesus the Christ.

Jesus Christ was there in the room, shining, radiating an inexpressive joy, peace, and love, looking at him with compassion and asking, "Why do you persecute me? I died for you..."

From then on Sundar Singh became most Christ-like. He traveled India, Tibet, and the rest of the world with the message of Jesus. He visited the United States, Britain, and Australia in 1920 preaching and spreading the good news.

Sundar Singh states: In this book, I have attempted to write about some of the visions which God has given me. Had I considered my own inclinations I would not have published the account of these visions during my life time; but friends, whose judgment I value, have been insistent that, as a spiritual help to others, the publication of the teaching of these visions should not be delayed. In defense of the wishes of these friends, this book is now presented to the public.

At Kotharh, fourteen years ago, while I was praying, my eyes were opened to the Heavenly 'Vision.' So vividly did I see it all that I thought I must have died, and that my soul had passed into the glory of Heaven; but throughout the intervening years, these visions have continued to enrich my life. I cannot call them up at will, but, usually when I am praying or meditating, sometimes as often as eight or ten times in a month, my spiritual eyes are opened to see within the Heavens, and, for an hour or two, I walk in the glory of the Heavenly sphere with Christ Jesus and hold converse with angels and spirits. In the book I speak of good spirits and bad spirits which after death exist in a state intermediate between Heaven and hell and pass on to Heaven or hell.

He states: There is only one source of Life—an Infinite and Almighty Life, whose creative power gave life to all living things. All creatures live in Him and in Him will they remain forever. Again, this Life created innumerable other lives, different in kind, and in the various stages of their progress. Man is one of these, created in God's own image that he might ever remain happy in His Holy presence.

Nothing in this whole universe was ever destroyed, nor can it ever be, because the Creator has never created anything for destruction. If he had wished to destroy it, He would never have created it.

In every part of Heaven, there are superb gardens, which all the time produce every variety of sweet and luscious fruit, and all kinds of sweet scented flowers that never fade. In them, creatures of every kind give praise to God unceasingly. Birds, beautiful in hue, raise their sweet songs of praise, and such as the sweet singing of angels and saints that on hearing their songs a wonderful sense of rapture is experienced.

Sundar was given understanding of man as a free agent. Again I asked, "Would it not have been far better if God had created man and all creation perfect? For then man could neither have committed sin, nor because of sin would there have been so much sorrow and suffering in the world; but now, in a creation made subject to vanity, we have all kinds of suffering to undergo."

An angel who had come from the highest grade of Heaven, and occupied a high position there, replied, "God has not made man like a machine, which would work automatically; nor has He fixed his destiny as in the case of the stars and planets that may not move out of their appointed course, but he has made man in His own image and likeness, a free agent, possessed of understanding, determination, and power to act independently, hence he is superior to all other created things. Had man not been created a free agent he would not have been able to experience the joy of God's presence, nor the joy of Heaven. For he would have been a mere machine that moves without knowing or feeling; or, like the stars that swing unknowingly through infinite space. But man, being a free agent, is by the constitution of his nature, opposed to this kind of soulless perfection—for such a man would have been a mere slave whose very perfection had compelled him to certain acts, and in so doing he could have had no enjoyment because he had no choice of his own. To him there would be no difference between a God and a stone."

Man, and with him all creation, has been subject to vanity but not forever. By his disobedience, man has brought himself and all other creatures into all the ills and suffering of this state of vanity. In this state of spiritual struggle alone can his spiritual powers be fully developed, and only in this struggle can he learn the lesson necessary to his perfection. Therefore, when man, at last, reaches the state of perfection of Heaven, he will thank God for the suffering and struggle of the present world, for then he will fully understand that *"all things work together for good to them that love God"* (Romans 8:28)

And in The Manifestation of God's Love concerning the remainder of Creation another saint told him: "All the inhabitants of Heaven know that God is Love. But, it has been hidden from all eternity that His love is so wonderful that He would become man to save sinners, and for their cleansing would die on the Cross. He suffered thus that He might save men, and all creation which is in subjection to vanity. Thus God in becoming man, has shown His heart to His children. Had any other means been used His infinite love would have remained forever hidden.

Quoted by Sadhu Sundar *"Now the whole creation with earnest expectation, awaits the manifestation of the sons of God when they shall be again restored and glorified. But, at present, they, and all creation, will remain groaning and travailing till this new creation comes to pass. And those who have been born again groan within themselves, waiting for the redemption of the body; and the time approaches when the whole creation, being obedient to God in all things, will be freed from corruption, and from this vanity forever. Then will it remain eternally happy in God, and will fulfill in itself the purpose for which it was created. Then God will be all in all"* (Romans 8:18-23).

⊰{ Janet's Dream }⊱

The following story is a vision my cousin Janet shared. Janet, a former airline stewardess and animal lover, has been involved in saving mules in the west for many years. She had a vision of her father and a familiar friend she so loved on this earth.

My cousin Janet lost her favorite dog and many years later her father went on to Heaven. She said one night about six months after his death she had a vision. It was of her father and some friends sitting at a table in Heaven and with him was her dog. She knew they were fine and together. It gave her such peace.

(21) He will take these weak mortal bodies of ours and change them into glorious bodies like his own using the same mighty power that he will use to conquer everything everywhere. (Philippians 3:21 New Living Bible)

⊰{ The Story of Schona }⊱

A young woman named Jeannie VonHouton called me one day to share the story of her beloved Schoner Madchen VonHouton. She had many questions after she had seen a vision and did not understand it completely. Her story and the experience due to the loss of her beloved pet brought her close to God as well.

Jeannie Says: My dog Schoner Madchen VonHouton, nicknamed Schona, was born 11/21/86 and died 12/16/97. Schona, who had just turned 11 years old, was the most loyal and protective friend a person ever dreamed or hoped to have. Her total dependence on me for her well being aroused a strong sense of obligation to watch over her. Even after her death this obligation remained which made it very important for me to know where Schona went after her death. The following brief overview of Schona's personality should help make it clear why losing such a loved and devoted friend was so extremely difficult for me.

Schona was always extremely happy and had a wonderfully playful nature that brightened up our home. She seemed to understand everything we said to her and she responded to every command, trying her very best to do exactly what was asked. She was also extremely protective of me. Every time I screamed, no matter what the reason, Schona would come running to my rescue. She even protected me from insects. When she was around I felt very safe.

After Schona died, I absolutely had to prove from Scripture what happens to animals after death. The minister of my church said in a sermon that animals, having a soul but not a spirit, returned to dust. I had a hard time believing or accepting that an animal as intelligent, innocent, and pure at heart as Schona would perish.

I began asking Christian acquaintances what they believed happened to animals after death. I always received one of three answers: (1) after death, the animals go back to dust; (2) they hoped that animals go to Heaven after death; or (3) I don't know what happens to animals after death. Hoping to find the answer to this question, I started researching the Bible and going to the library. I located many Scriptures pertaining to animals and from this, decided that animals most certainly do go to Heaven. But, as I felt I had to confirm my conclusion, I continued researching.

I then questioned myself, "Why am I spending so much of my time and energy trying to prove my beloved Schona is in Heaven?" for I had had doubts that Heaven existed. After that I reasoned, "If I am so possessed with trying to prove that Schona is in Heaven, then I must truly believe Heaven exists." I prayed from my heart for the first time without uncertainty, which was a glorious experience. The night of the second day of praying in this manner, I had the most magnificent dream; a figure appeared and instantly it was made known to me that he was a Shepherd and the words were bestowed on me, **"SHE IS**

WITH ME." I knew instantly that this meant my Schona is in Heaven. I did not pay too much attention to the figure in my dream other than to notice that he demonstrated an extreme sense of peace about him. I was searching for my dear Schona, trying to see her with the sheep. After all, he was a Shepherd and she was with him. I never saw her.

The next day I prayed and thanked God for having a dream that gave me such peace because it confirmed that Schona is, indeed, in Heaven. This was the answer I had been seeking since December 16, 1997, the date of my precious Schona's death.

The next day I started thinking about my dream, the Shepherd, and the words given to me, **"SHE IS WITH ME."** I also thought about the fact that I never saw Schona or any sheep. Even though I tried desperately to see them, they just would not appear. I thought to myself, "Why would sheep need to be herded in Heaven?" They would not. At this point, I truly comprehended the ramifications of my dream. A shepherd from Heaven gave me words of comfort. What a glorious experience to behold and what an honor to be bestowed with such a dream, although I do not feel I am worthy. It was given to me and I truly thank and praise God, for this dream has given me such peace. I have no doubts that Schona is in Heaven.

Now, when I start thinking of how much my beloved Schona suffered at the end and how much I miss her, I think of the Shepherd that visited me in my dream and the words of comfort, **"SHE IS WITH ME."** And I know that Schona is out of pain, happy, young again. She is in complete and total peace which is beyond human conception, that only being in God's Light in Heaven can offer.

Schona was my companion and beloved friend. This special bond lead me to search for an answer to where my beloved Schona went after her death. This search not only lead to the answer to my question but also lead to my own salvation. Now, upon my death my beloved Schona and I will be together for eternity. No one could ever receive so much from a friendship.

Recognizing the spiritual world and the symbols God provides for us is so unnatural in this sinful fallen world. We don't really comprehend the eternal world that we will one day see with understanding. 2 Corinthians 4 says the things that are not seen are the eternal part of life, the new birth of purity and joy. *While we look not at the things which are seen, but at the things which are not seen: for the things which are seen are temporal; but the things which are not seen are eternal. (2 Corinthians 4:18 KJV)*

Jeannie called about the confusion of seeing the shepherd in her dream. I asked her if she knew who the shepherd was and she didn't know. I then told her I had no doubt it was Jesus the good shepherd and he was telling her that her beloved Schona was in Heaven with him and with that Jeannie understood the vision.

⊷{ A Vision of Heaven }⊷

Ann Marie's second vision was of a beloved dog she had had in her care and the decision she had to make.

I was driving home from the veterinary office after euthanizing two of my foster dogs that I could not place into adoptive homes. They had both been abused in separate situations and although I had worked with them a great deal, I could not trust that they would be safe dogs to place into homes. They did not have sound temperaments. I do rescue work and have twelve dogs of my own. I cannot keep every dog I foster, and unfortunately, one has to make tough calls in the animal rescue field. Even though I know all the euthanized animals go directly to Heaven, it's still hard to end a life. Because there is such an overpopulation problem with dogs and cats in this country and elsewhere and not enough quality homes for them to go to, logically one knows that some must be euthanized. The only thing that made it easier for me was my faith in God and knowing that He wants the unwanted and He loves the unloved. I know this includes all animals as well as people. I loved Libby, the female Springer, and Logan, my little Rottweiler mix, and knowing what I know about the great God we serve, it's still tough to put an animal to sleep.

As I drove home, I was praying to the Lord to take good care of my little ones and told Him I wanted to see them when I get to Heaven. As I continued driving, I had a vision of Logan and Libby in Heaven! Mere words cannot describe just how beautiful it was! The colors were so much richer than anything on earth—absolutely breathtaking! Logan was sitting on a grassy hill in front of a lake with gorgeous blue mountains in the background and it seemed he was looking directly at me. I knew he was waiting for me to get there, as I was the only home he had known. He seemed happy and peaceful, and sweet. He was truly contented in his surroundings. Libby, the bird dog, was running as fast as she could amongst the lush green grass of the beautiful field in Heaven's country. Her tail was wagging so fast it was just a blur. As dog lovers know, dogs can smile and Logan and Libby both had the biggest smiles I'd ever seen when I saw them in Heaven that day! It was truly glorious!

I began to praise the Lord for his goodness and grace, for loving the animals and for loving me enough to show me a glimpse of what is yet to come. If I had ever doubted that animals do go to Heaven, I would never do so again. This was a true miracle in my life that I will never forget and for which I will always be thankful.

God is so good. *(24)He made the world and everything in it, and since he is Lord of Heaven and earth, he doesn't live in man-made temples; (25) and human hands can't minister to his needs- for he has no needs! He himself gives life and breath to everything, and satisfies every need there is. (Acts 17:24-25 TLB).*

❦ Bobby and Grandpa in Heaven ❦

Ann Marie's third experience reveals the human/animal companionship in Heaven. So many people think that animals go to Heaven but are in a different place. Some say the dogs go to doggie Heaven which is so far from the truth. Those we love on earth, both of our Christian family and the animals, will be with us in Heaven.

Ann Marie says: I had a beautiful, tri-colored cocker spaniel named Bobby. I adopted him from the Humane Society where I worked after a heartless woman dumped him there. She had gotten him as a gift from her husband whom she had recently divorced and she said that the dog reminded her of him. Bobby was three years old. The poor little dog was terrified and he grabbed on to her leg and held on for dear life as a scared little child would hold on to its mother. I had to peel him off of her as she looked down in disgust. She turned her back on him and walked out, never saying goodbye and never looking back. Bobby never stopped looking for her. He began to whine pitifully. He was very depressed and would not eat for three days. I knew I had to take him home for fear he would wither away at the shelter. I was always thankful that God gave me compassion for His animals while I always had to pray for patience to deal with people.

Bobby had a wonderful life with my family and me. He adjusted well and was a sweet and happy dog. No one could ask for a more faithful and well-mannered little guy. He could even sing! We were blessed with Bobby and loved him dearly. He went everywhere with me. When I wasn't home he would lay up on my bed waiting for my return. My grandmother always said that my grandfather, who had passed on years before, would have loved Bobby. We had Bobby until he was nineteen years old and his body just gave out. I believe he is with my grandfather now in Heaven. Grandpa was a Christian man, a doctor, and big dog lover.

The day I took poor old Bobby to the vet to be euthanized, it broke my heart. I was not ready to let him go, but I knew I had to for his sake. I did not want him to suffer. I prayed that God would take him and give him a lap to sit on. He loved to sit on my lap. I had a dream that night that was as real as it could be. I know God gave me this dream. In it I saw my grandfather who looked younger than he did when he died. He was holding Bobby on his lap and Bobby was licking his face and wagging his tail with a joy that dogs get from being with ones they love. God had answered my prayer.

1 Corinthians 15 speaks about the dead being brought back to life again. This includes both man and the non-human creation. *(35) But someone may ask, "How will the dead be brought back to life again? What kind of bodies will they have?" (36) What a foolish question! You will find the answer in your own garden! When you put a seed into the ground it doesn't grow into a plant unless it "dies" first. (37) And when the green shoot comes up out of the seed, it is very different from the seed you first planted. For all you put into the ground is a dry little seed of wheat, or whatever it is you are planting, (38) then God gives it a beautiful new body-just the kind he wants it to have; a different kind of plant grows from each kind of seed. (39) And just as there are different kinds of seeds and plants, so also there are different kinds of flesh. Humans, animals, fish, and birds are all different. (40) The angels in Heaven have bodies far different from ours, and the beauty and the glory of their bodies is different from the beauty and glory of ours. (41) The sun has one kind of glory while the moon and stars have another kind. And the stars differ from each other in their beauty and brightness. (42) In the same way, our earthly bodies which die and decay are different from the bodies we shall have when we come back to life again, for they will never die. (43) The bodies we have now embarrass us for they become sick and die; but they will be full of glory when we come back to life again. Yes, they are weak, dying bodies now, but when we live again they will be full of strength. (1 Corinthians 15:35-43 TLB)*

⊰{ Dear Old Sport }⊱

Mrs. Rebecca Springer was born in 1832. She was a nineteenth-century American author who wrote *Intra Muros*. She was unconscious for a number of days and had a vision of Heaven which, in her vision, spanned a period of years. She saw animals in Heaven. Many have used parts of her story but they bear repeating. This is the story of Old Sport, the dog, and Mae, her young niece who had died.

In her vision she reports: I saw the mansions of family members, visited with them and worked with them in Heaven. I went to the River of Life, saw Jesus, saw children playing and heard and saw the birds in the trees. The birds were of all colors and kinds. The flowers were all beautiful as were the trees. The flowers sprang back up when walked on. Heaven was far more beautiful than she had imagined but it is a duplicate or glorification of earth. What is on earth is also in Heaven. I saw many animals in Heaven also.

The following is a passage from her original book, *Intra Muros*. While in Heaven she says: Not far from our Heavenly home we saw a group of children playing upon the grass, and in their midst was a beautiful great dog, over which they were rolling and tumbling with the greatest freedom. As we approached, he broke away from them and came bounding to meet us, and crouched and fawned at my very feet with every gesture of glad welcome. "Do you not know him, auntie?" Mae (my niece who had died very young) asked me brightly. "It is dear old Sport!" He responded to my caresses with every expression of delight, and Mae laughed aloud at our mutual joy. **She goes on to say:** I had so hoped that I would find him in Heaven as he was far more intelligent and faithful than many mortal human beings. Sport had saved the life of little Will but sacrificed his own life instead. Will was crossing the track in front of an approaching train. Sport ran between Will and the train keeping Will from coming onto the tracks.

Rebecca and her niece then went on to say to Sport: "Dear, dear old Sport, you shall never leave me again!" caressing him fondly. Sport then jumped to his feet and barked joyously running and frolicking before us the remainder of my stay.

Revelation 21 tells of the new world which the apostle John referred to as the New Jerusalem, the Holy city, coming down out of Heaven. *(3) Then I heard a loud voice call from the throne, 'Look, here God lives among human beings. He will make* his home among them; they will be his people *and he will be their God,* God-with them. *(4) He will wipe away all tears from their eyes; there will be no more death, and no more mourning or sadness or pain. The world of the past has gone.' (5) Then the One sitting on the throne spoke, 'Look, I am making the whole of creation new. Write this," What I am saying is trustworthy and will come true."(Revelation 21:3-5 NJB)*

⊰ A Tribute to Babe ⊱

Nora Templeton shared this story about her wonderful and faithful English Setter. Nora had times in her life when giving up seemed to be the easiest thing to do, but a loving God knew the remedy she needed. It was her beloved Babe that encouraged and nudged her on. This is the vision Nora experienced as she read her tribute at the gravesite of Babe.

Nora states: God showed me in an open vision that Babe and the others that had passed on before were reunited, running free in Heaven—no more pain—just doing what English Setters do. This was wonderful of the Lord, but the sorrow and grief I felt at the time was a bit overwhelming. However, today, I rejoice in the mercy of God to have shown this to me.

You are worthy, our Lord and God, to receive glory and honor and power, for You created all things, and by Your will they were created and have their being., (Revelation 4:11 NIV)

⊰ My Beloved Bruno ⊱

Gina Warrington shared the story of her faithful dog Bruno. It is an incredible story unlike any I have ever heard. It is a lesson I believe, that God wants each of us to understand: dying is not the end of life, but really the beginning. If animals were in the wild they would be able to have gone on to Heaven. However, often we hold our pets captive in a domesticated state with us even though they are suffering and need to be released from this earthly state.

Gina Warrington says: I lost my beloved Bruno on Christmas Eve after a very short battle with lymphoma. He was a boxer whom I had for five years. He was my best friend and protector. I was heartbroken. *The Lord spoke to me through the whole incident. He took him from my arms as if He were picking up a newborn baby. Lifting his head first then his body, He took him out of my arms so very gently. I hung on pretty tight!* The devil kept putting pictures of him rotting in the grave in my mind. I saw pictures of the sadness and death. He was lying to me as is his character. I screamed and cried in desperation to think that! It took me some time to understand the truth of it all...I do now praise God, thanks to your books, Mary, and God's word!

As I went through the flu bug yesterday not being able to keep anything on my stomach and feeling desperately ill, I TOTALLY understood why God was screaming at me... *Release him to Me! He needed to go home!* He was sick. God told me to *"Trust me now in this. I will open up the windows of Heaven. I will bring peace to his body."* I believe He did. Bruno is now romping around playing chase with the other precious creatures and enjoying the love and care of the Master's presence and His Heaven. I am so very blessed. I do not feel desperate at all. I know he is happy and feels wonderful! I know he is thinking of me sweetly and with God-given intelligence! He knows my care for him and appreciates it and awaits me to be with him. That is what matters. I now am only more anxious to be at "home"! There is no telling how precious and wonderful and exciting a life we have waiting for us.

When God said He would open the windows of Heaven, I believe that is just what He did. He sent a wonderful next door neighbor to minister to me during the two and a half week illness. She is a strong Christian and prayer warrior. As she was praying for me after I had put Bruno to sleep, she saw a vision from God. She said that Bruno was in Heaven, he was the same size, very large, but puppy-like. Jesus was waiting and all the animals were arriving from all over. Still coming, she said, he was just looking around at the animals and Jesus was standing there. It was as if he had just arrived. God had told me the night before not to give him any more medicine, just release Bruno to Him. That He would give peace to his body. I really struggled with it but now I understand why I was not to give him the medicine. It would have made him feel worse. I put him to sleep on Christmas Eve. I hurt very badly but it is SUCH a comfort to believe my friend's vision to be true and I know God's word is true. I will see Bruno in Heaven. Death truly has no victory! Even over the creation!

For everything comes from him; everything exists by his power and is intended for his glory. To him be glory evermore. Amen. (Roman 11:36 New Living Bible)

❧ The Angora Kitten ❧

In the book *Intra Muros (Within the Gates)*, Mrs. Springer writes about a little girl and her Angora kitten in one of her visits to Heaven during her illness.

Mrs. Springer stated that during one of her Heavenly visits she witnessed a little girl come to Heaven. She was from a large, affectionate family. Mrs. Springer saw the little girl sitting in the arms of Jesus and while he was holding her and talking to her, a beautiful Angora kitten came to her. The kitten was one the child had been very fond of on earth. It had become sick and died some weeks before the little girl died, to her great sorrow. It came running across the grass and sprang directly into her arms and lay down in complete contentment. The little girl, with great joy as can only be seen in Heaven, hugged and kissed the kitten.

⁂ Otis and Me ⁂

Denise McKay sent this inspiring story of Jesus and her dog, Otis. Denise loves animals and works for Second Chance Animal Rescue Society.

Denise says: Otis died in my arms at the hands of my veterinarian. I prayed fervently and pleaded with God to be reunited with him when I leave this world. Since then, I have had a recurring dream that I am walking in the most beautiful garden, barefoot. I can feel the grass between my toes. I cannot see who is walking beside me, only His feet, but I know it is Jesus. I can feel Him talking to me. The only words I hear Him say are, **"*I have something to show you.*"** When I look up, my beloved Otis is running toward me. He is full size, not stunted as he was in life, and he climbs up my legs and into my arms. I always awake with the feeling that he was resting on my cheek and the side of my nose, as he always did.

Ecclesiasticus 41 says we are not to dread death. It is really only the beginning of life and dying does not mean any innocent life, man or animal, is going to hell. Physical death is the will of God so we can be made perfect. *(3) Do not dread death's sentences; remember those who came before you and those who will come after.(4) This is the sentence passed on all living creatures by the Lord, so why object to what seems good to the Most High? Whether your life lasts ten or a hundred or a thousand years, its length will not be held against you in Sheol.(Ecclesiasticus 41:3-4 NJB)* **The New English Bible says "in the grave."**

General William Booth's Vision of Heaven

General William Booth was the founder of The Salvation Army. He tells of his amazing vision of Heaven in London, England in 1906.

No human eyes ever beheld such perfection, such beauty. No earthly ear ever heard such music. No human heart ever experienced such ecstasy as it was my privilege to see, hear, and feel in the celestial country. Around me was an atmosphere so balmy that it made my whole frame vibrate with pleasure. The bank of roses on which I found myself reposing had, flowing by it, the waters of the clearest, purest river that seemed to dance with delight to its own murmurings.

The trees that grew upon the banks were covered with the greenest foliage and laden with delicious fruit-sweet beyond all earthly sweetness—and by lifting my hand I could pluck and taste; while in every direction above and around me the whole air seemed to be laden with sweet odors coming from the fairest flowers.

The blue skies, the towering mountains, the green valleys, the shady groves, the luxuriant vineyards, the charming flowers, the flowing rivers —were all exquisitely beautiful beyond the power of language to describe.

Then in, about, and indeed everywhere, were the loveliest birds and the most graceful of animals. I was enraptured with the scene. I was certainly a little surprised to find these living creatures here, having been always skeptical as to the resurrection of the animal world. There, however, they certainly were.

But as it is written, Eye hath not seen, nor ear heard, neither have entered into the heart of man, the things that God has prepared for them that love him." (1 Corinthians 2:9 KJV)

CHAPTER 7

Angels in Creation

❧ Angel and the Angel Fish ☙

This incredible story was sent to me from Pat Rason of Tonawanda, NY. She had lost a dog, cat and discovered her other cat had Feline Immunodeficiency Virus within the span of two weeks. She told me of a wonderful revelation from God through the eyes and mouth of her three-year-old daughter, Jacquie. You will never forget this story.

Pat states: When my little girl, Jacquie, was about three, she would quite often tell me about seeing angels in her room. She would be very excited and describe them quite well for a three-year-old. I would frequently ask her if they spoke anything or carried anything. Once she said yes, one has a book, and one has a sword. This surely got my full attention. One night after she had gone to bed I was downstairs and I happened to look in the fish tank. To my surprise, her favorite fish, that had been swimming around just fine when we said goodnight to him a few hours earlier, was not alive on the bottom of the tank. Ironically, it was a big angel fish. Well, the next morning I went to Jacquie's room and we had our usual conversation. I asked if she saw any angels. She told me she had, and the angel was carrying something in her hand. I asked her what it was and she told me it was her fish! I told her the fish had died, and she very matter of factually said, "No, mamma, angel took fishy to Heaven!"

Needless to say, I then knew God had some plans for his creation. Jan went on to say: "Mary, as I talked to you on the phone the Lord kept reminding me to read about Noah and the ark. I couldn't quite figure out why until I read a Charles Spurgeon book about Biblical types of Jesus Christ, and where he was showing how Christ brought the righteous unto Himself, and the ark was a type of salvation. I started thinking that if Jesus brought the righteous Noah and his family into the ark, he most certainly is, bringing the animals." In Genesis 7:7-9 Noah and his family entered the ark and Noah brought in pairs of all animals to be saved as well. In Romans 8 it describes man's redemption or salvation first, then the reconciliation of the animals back to God. So just as man and the animals walked into the ark we can better understand the ark as the first biblical symbol of salvation. I also checked Matthew Henry's commentaries and he briefly said the same thing.

(3) The creation shall be liberated from its bondage and brought into the glorious freedom of the children of God (v.21)-they shall no more be subject to vanity and corruption. The lower world shall be renewed when there will be new Heavens there will be a new earth. (4) the creation does therefore earnestly expect the sons of God to be revealed, (v.19) (Romans 8:19-21Matthew Henry's Commentary)

Romans 8:19-22 in the 1557 Geneva Bible says: *(19) For the fervent desire of the creature abydeth, lokyng when the sonnes of God shal appear. (21)Because the same creature also, shal be delyuered from the bondage of corruption, into the glorious libertie of the sonnes of God. (22) For we knowe that euery creature groaneth with vs also, and trauayleth in payne euen vnto this tyme. (Romans 8:21-22 The Geneva Bible 1557)*

The (v) in the Geneva Bible is our (u) and the (u) is a (v). Some of the words are spelled as they sound and not as we spell them today.

The only reason Noah and his family was allowed to live was because they were righteous before God. The animals also were righteous, innocent creatures, created to be preserved and to multiply for the pleasure and benefits of God's divine plan. We would not need animals to live. We had all kinds of grain, fruit and all the food God designed our bodies to eat in the first place. And man could plant his own food, harvest it; he could grow cotton to make clothes, etc. So, in all reality, there would have been no need to keep anything else alive if God loved only man and wanted to preserve him alone.

When we read the Ten Commandments there are two commandments that include animals. The fourth which says that all are to rest on the Sabbath even the animals and the 10th commandment which says one is not to covet one's neighbor's animals either. I interpret the scripture as illustrating the point that there is "good news" for all the creation! And we are to share that good news with all of mankind.

❦ Queenie and the Angels ❧
From the book *Angels On Assignment*
by Charles and Frances Hunter

Reverend Buck speaks about his dog, Queenie, and Gabriel and Chrioni, the angels who came often to visit. The angel Michael also appeared to Reverend Buck on one of the 26 angelic visits. If you have not read this book, I would say it is a must-read. You can download this book free on the internet.

Reverend Buck was a minister in Utah who has now gone to be with the Lord. Reverend Buck started having visitations from Angels. He was thrilled to be so privileged but could not understand why God had chosen him. No doubt God knew what He was doing as Reverend Buck had such a humble spirit and was such an honest and Godly man. The angels told him much of what God wants all who will come to Him to learn about His love for us and truths we need to know.

Each time the angels came they told Reverend Buck more about Heaven, God, and what their lives were like and how they were helping God's people on earth. Reverend Buck and his wife were devoted Christians with a faithful church congregation. They never felt that they were special so they didn't understand why

God chose Reverend Buck to reveal such wonderful things about angels, Heaven, the earth and things we all need to know about the present and the future.

The angels would come in the middle of the night. Reverend Buck thought the angels would wake up his wife when they came but she never awakened. However, there was one member of the family who did know when the angels were coming and knew before Reverend Buck. It was his dog, Queenie.

Reverend Buck said: On the night of June 18, 1978, I went to bed at my usual time with no advance notice that something was about to happen which would change my entire life!

About three o'clock in the morning, I was abruptly awakened when someone grasped my arms and sat me right up in bed! The room was dark because the shades were pulled, but there was just enough light from outside so I could detect the outline of a huge being.

To say the least, I was frightened because he was so strong I couldn't free myself from his grip. My fear didn't last, however, because I quickly became aware of a supernatural presence, and it didn't take me long to realize that this Heavenly being was an angel from God. He confirmed this, turned loose of my shoulders, and told me not to be afraid! Then he told me that God had sent him because the prayers of God's people had been heard, and he was to deliver the message that their prayers had not only been heard, but had been answered! Hallelujah! I wasn't dreaming, it wasn't a vision, it was something very, very real!

As we continued talking, he spoke so loudly I was sure he was going to wake up my wife who was asleep next to me. He didn't, but I wish he had!

My dog, Queenie, comes into our room once in while when she gets lonesome, and sleeps beside the bed. She was there that night and was interested in everything the angel had to say. She was right beside me and I could feel her head turning every which way against my leg as first the angel spoke and then I answered! It was an unusual visit!

This unique conversation lasted for two solid hours as the angel shared magnificent truths from the Word of God with me. He discussed the unfolding plan of God for the entire world and brought me warm feelings from God's own heart as to the concern He has for His people. His love for people is so great, He is a lot more interested in them then He is in procedure! He loves people!

As the angel was speaking to me on another occasion he told me his name was Gabriel! I was stunned! Then he introduced me to the second angel, whose name was Chroni!

As Gabriel was talking with me, Chroni, the other angel, was playing with Queenie, tickling her ears, getting her on her back and having fun with her. Queenie lapped it up! I wish she could talk because I would like to know what her impressions were. She has had a rare experience for a dog, and acted as though she thought it was really great!

Upon another angelic visit, Queenie, our purebred Great Dane, quietly "woofed' as she pressed her wet nose against my face. The time was about 2 a.m. I knew what was up by now. This is the way she rouses me when she becomes aware that angelic visitors are in the house.

Reverend Buck said of the angels, no two are alike. Chroni was very tall, seven feet or so high, and probably would weigh about 400 pounds in a fleshly earthly form. They dressed differently from each other and wore their hair differently. Chroni looked more casual.

Reverend Buck said: Chroni often wears a brown pullover shirt and is casually but neatly dressed in loose-fitting trousers. His shirt laces at the top with what looks like a shoelace. Gabriel is taller and usually appears in a shimmering white tunic with a radiant gold belt about five inches wide, white trousers and highly polished, bronze-colored shoes. His hair is the color of gold!

The Man Who Talked With Angels

The story of Reverend Buck's life by his daughter Sharon White says of Queenie: If only Queenie could talk, imagine the things she could tell us! She is a beautiful Great Dane. She was with daddy during most of his meetings with the angels. She has been privileged to have her ears scratched by these Heavenly beings.

Queenie was to be a birthday present to Mrs. Buck, but Queenie became Reverend Buck's constant companion. Sharon says: Queenie spent many hours in daddy's office as he prayed with people and counseled with them. When some people would be fearful of the big Dane, we staff members would smile and tell them not to be because, "Queenie is a Christian, and helps pastor pray with people!"

When daddy was out of town, Queenie would mournfully come to my office to lay in the sun.

She is very gentle and loves children. When Maranatha School came into existence through Central Assembly Church, Queenie no doubt felt like she was in Heaven with all the children to play with. She became the school mascot, and the team name became the "Great Danes." Queenie even received her own activity card with her picture on it, entitling her to free access into all the school activities.

When my father went to be with the Lord, we all expected Queenie to quit eating and mourn until she died, because she loved her master so much. But perhaps the Father, who hears even the soft sound of a tiny little sparrow falling to the earth, whispered into her ear that it was okay: "Her master is with God!" Queenie did not really mourn. Prior to his death, when daddy would be gone, Queenie wouldn't eat well. But this time, she continued to eat, and although it took her a little while to be frisky, I really believe Queenie knows where her master is.

The wonderful revelations Reverend Buck shares with the Hunters, who published *Angels On Assignment*, were so numerous and so inspirational.

He spoke of how the angels circle those we want to come to Jesus and just keep circling until it happens. His experience with the angels and being in Heaven is an amazing story and one you will know is true.

(6) Seek the LORD while He may be found, Call ye upon Him while He is near; (7) Let the wicked forsake his way, And the man of iniquity his thoughts; And let him return unto the LORD, and He will have compassion upon him, And to our God, for He will abundantly pardon. (8) For My thoughts are not your thoughts, Neither are your ways My ways, saith the LORD (9) For as the Heavens are higher than the earth, So are My ways higher than your ways, And My thoughts then your thoughts. (Isaiah 55:6-13 Jewish Holy Scriptures)

⊰{ JoJo and the Angels }⊱

Arthur Hernandez and Fred Sober have been friends since 1994, when Arthur moved to Reno, Nevada, after retiring from the U.S. Navy. They have shared their Christian faith and their love for Arthur's dog, JoJo, for many years.

Arthur says: On December 23, 2009, JoJo, my beloved Border Collie, started having strokes. All I could do was clean the saliva out of her mouth, pet and talk to her. I called Fred and he immediately came over to say his goodbyes. We took turns trying to comfort JoJo while the other prayed. After about five hours, JoJo passed on. My other dog, Nightly, started to cry (howl), just as Fred and I were crying. Nightly definitely knew that JoJo had left this earth.

After some time, both Fred and I got our composure back. Fred told me that he saw angels around JoJo, and then she appeared on the spirit side with the angels. He said she first looked around, and then followed in the midst of the angels, heading off into the distance.

Praise ye him, all his angels; praise ye him, all his host (Psalm 148:2 KJV).

Angels for the Sacrificial Animal

Diane Havek, who had discovered the meanings of the word "Fido," wrote me about another revelation she had concerning the sacrifice of animals. We know that because they were and are sinless creatures, God chose some of the non-meat, non scavenger animals to be the sacrificial animals to cover the sins of man until Jesus came to, once and for all, take away our sins. I have heard people say they have seen Jesus on Heavenly trips and that you can see his scars, the nail holes in his hands but that they are really beautiful. Diane had a similar revelation from God.

God did require some sacrifice of animals to cover the sins of man until Jesus came but He did not want the sacrifice of animals without true repentance. God said that it was the sacrifice of praise and obedience to Him He sought, not the blood of the animals except upon certain occasions. Diane found in her observation and meditation concerning the spirit and soul of the sacrificial animal that the angel came for the animal upon its sacrifice for the sins of man.

Diane quotes Revelation 19 *"And I saw Heaven opened, and behold a white horse and he that sat upon him was called Faithful and True". (Revelation 19:11 KJV)*

And Judges 13. *"Manoah took a kid with a meat offering and offered it...it came to pass, when the flame went up toward Heaven from off the alter, that the angel of the Lord ascended in the flame of the alter."(Judges 13:19 KJV)*

Diane says: It is my belief that God reveals here that animals' souls (sacrificial animals) were made sin and had to be cleansed by fire before the animals' souls could be admitted to Heaven. I believe that the angel was ascending to the Lord with the spirit of the animal who had been baptized by the fire of God. I don't believe that the angel was just showing off—he ascended in the flame of a sweet-smelling sacrifice, and I believe the angel took the animal with him. *"O Lamb of God who taketh away the sins of the world."* That prayer is true about the lambs of the Old Testament who were made sin to reclaim men from the evil one.

(Re: Manoah) Notice that the animal was sacrificed and cleansed by fire before the angel ascended (or at the same time.)

Could this be possible? The story of Stephen when he was stoned suggests through scripture that his spirit had already left before he was stoned to death.

Tobias, His Dog, and Raphael the Angel

The Book of Tobit is found in the original Hebrew Scriptures and fragments are found in the Dead Sea Scrolls are evidence of their authenticity. I quote from the 1611 King James Bible version, The New English Bible, New Jerusalem Bible and the 1609 Douay Rheims version. However, the 1611 King James Bible is far more detailed yet harder to read.

This is the story of a young man, an angel and a dog who went together to recover the family fortune from Israel, the family's home land. Tobit, his wife Anna and their son Tobias, along with the other Jewish people were exiled to Nineveh in the days of Shalmaneser king of Assyria, from their home in Thisbe, which is south of Kedesh-Naphtali in Upper Galilee around 200 B.C.

Tobit had been honest and upright all of his life and had given much to others when he was young living in the land of Israel. Each year he would go to Jerusalem with the first yield of fruits, and beasts, the tithe of cattle and the sheep's first shearings. They would be given to the priest, the sons of Aaron, for the alter. When the banishment into Assyria came, he was taken away and went to Nineveh. When Shalmaneser died, his son succeeded him and the roads to and from Media were barred. Tobit could no longer get to his home. Because many of his people were killed, he buried them and that was against the law. The king found out and took all of Tobit's earthly goods and he was hunted to be put to death. Tobit had nothing but his wife, Anna, and his son, Tobias. Then the king was murdered. His son, Esarhaddon, succeeded him. Tobit's nephew became chancellor, allowing his return to Nineveh. There a relative was murdered and Tobit buried him. He took a bath and went to sleep by the courtyard wall where birds often perched. Their droppings fell in his eyes, causing blindness.

Tobit's wife, Anna, had to work spinning wool to make clothes to provide for them after her husband became blind. The time came when Tobias, the son, would have to go back to their home country to retrieve the family wealth. He was the only child and his parents were greatly concerned for his safety but there was no one else to go so he was told to find a trustworthy man to accompany him on his trip. *Tobias went out to find a man who knew the way and would accompany him to Media, and found himself face to face with the angel Raphael. Not knowing he was an angel of God, he questioned him: 'Where do you come from, young man?' 'I am an Israelite,' he replied, 'one of your fellow countrymen, and I have come here to find work.' Tobias asked, 'Do you know the road to Media?' 'Yes,' he said, 'I have often been there: I have often traveled to Media and used to lodge with Gabael one of our kinsmen.''* (*Tobit 5: 4-6 NEB*) Tobias told the angel that if he would go with him his father would pay him. The angel agreed to go. Tobias went to tell his parents. After goodbyes, *Tobias left accompanied by the angel. His dog followed behind. (Tobit 6:11 NEB)* **The 1611 King James Bible says**: *"they went forth and the young man's dogge with them"* (6:11 *The 1611 King James Bible*)

The Angel instructs Tobias on the cure for his father's eyes.

On their way, a large fish jumped up out of the river where Tobias had gone to bathe. The angel told Tobias to kill it and remove the heart, liver, and gall. *The gall is for anointing a man's eye when white patches have spread over them, or for blowing on the white patches in the eyes; the eyes will then recover.'* The heart and the liver are a cure for driving away evil spirits. *Raphael said: 'Take the fish-gall in your hand.' The dog went with the angel and Tobias, following at their heels. (Tobit 6:1-6,8 NJB).*

The story continues: Tobias asked the angel who he was and he said: *"My name is Azarias"*, but he was really Raphael the angel. The angel told Tobias to stay with his kinsman, Raguel. Raguel had a daughter called Sara, often spelled Sarah, but apart from Sara he had no other sons or daughters. The angel said: *You are the next of kin; she belongs to you before anyone else and you may claim her father's inheritance. She is a thoughtful, courageous and very lovely girl, and her father loves her dearly. You have the right to marry her. (Tobit 6: 12 NJB)*

The story goes on. That seems all well and good until Tobias found out that Sara had already been given in marriage seven times. Each of her bridegrooms had died in the bridal room on the night of their wedding. He heard people say it was a demon that killed them and this made Tobias quite concerned for his own well being. The angel said: *To her the demon does no harm because he loves her, but as soon as a man tries to approach her, he dies.(Tobit 6:15 NJB)* **Tobias let it be known that he was his father's only son, and had no desire to die. However, the angel told him not to worry about the demon; that Sara this very evening would be given to Tobias for his wife. Raphael told Tobias:** *"Once you are in the bridal room, take the heart and liver of the fish and lay a little of it on the burning incense. The reek will rise, the demon will smell it and flee, and there is no danger that he will ever be found near the girl again. Then before you sleep together, first, stand up both of you and pray. Ask the Lord of Heaven to grant you his grace and protection. Do not be afraid; she was destined for you from the beginning; and you are the one to save her." (Tobit 6:17-18 NJB)*

Tobias falls in love with Sara and agrees to marry her. Sara's father, Raguel, was joyous that his daughter would be married to one of his kinsmen and he praised God. *Then Raguel praised God, and said, O God, thou art worthy to be praised with all pure and holy saints: therefore let thy Saints praise thee with all thy creatures, and let all thine Angels and thine elect praise thee for ever. (Tobit 8:15 the 1611 King James Bible)*

After the wedding and the wedding feast, Tobias recovered the family treasures to take back to his father. Tobias, Raphael, the dog and his new wife, Sara, prepared for the long trip back to Nineveh.

The next morning Tobias told Sara to rise and prepare for the journey to his home. *'Get up, my love let us pray and beseech our Lord to show us mercy and keep us safe.' She got up and they began to pray that they might be kept safe. Tobias said: We praise thee, O God of our fathers, we praise thy name for ever and ever. Let the Heavens and all thy creation praise thee for ever. (Tobit 8:5 NEB)*

Raphael told Tobias they should go on ahead of Sara, her handmaidens and the herdsmen with the animals given by her father so they could prepare the house for the new bride. *(2) Then Raphael said to Tobias thou knowest brother, how thou didst leave thy father (3) Let us haste before thy wife, and prepare the house (4) and take in thy hand the gall of the fish: so they went their way and the dog went after them. (Tobit 11:2-4 the 1611 King James Bible).*

Tobias blessed his father with the return of the family fortune, his new wife from their own kinsmen, and a cure to restore his father's eyesight.

Upon their return, Tobias, as instructed by the angel, put the oil from the fishes' gall on his father's eyes and Tobit's eyesight was restored. [The footnotes in the New American Bible say that Tobias put the oil on his father in front of all who had witnessed his blindness, including the dog.]

(11)Tobias went up to him with the fish-gall in his hand and blew it into his father's eyes, and took him by the arm and said: 'It will be all right father.' (14)Tobit flung his arms round him and burst into tears. 'I can see you, my son, the light of my eyes! He cried 'Praise be to God, and praise to his great name, and to all his holy angels. May his great name rest upon us. (Tobit 11:11,14 NEB).

When it was time to pay the man who had traveled with Tobias to his homeland, the angel told Tobit: *(12) When you and Sarah prayed, it was*

I who brought your prayers into the glorious presence of the Lord; and so too whenever you buried the dead. (13) That day when you got up from your dinner without hesitation to go and bury the corpse, (14) I was sent to test you; and again God sent me to cure both you and Sarah your daughter-in-law at the same time. (15) 'I am Raphael, one of the seven angels who stand in attendance on the Lord and enter his glorious presence. (18) It is no thanks to me that I have been with you' it was the will of God. Worship him all your life long, sing his praise. (19) Take note that I ate no food; what appeared to you was a vision. (20) And now praise the Lord, give thanks to God here on earth; I am ascending to him who sent me. Write down all these things that have happened to you.' (21) He then ascended and when they rose to their feet, he was no longer to be seen. (22) They sang hymns of praise to God, giving him thanks for these great deeds he had done when the angel appeared to them. (Tobit 12:12-15, 18-22 NJB)

(1) Praise to the ever-living God and to his kingdom (4) Exalt him in the sight of every living creature for he is our Lord and God; he is our Father and our God for ever. (Tobit 13:1, 4 NJB)

(1) Tobit died peacefully at the age of one hundred and twelve and received an honorable burial in Nineveh. (2) He was sixty-two years old when he lost his eye sight, and after he recovered it he lived in prosperity, giving alms and continually blessing God and praising the divine Majesty. (Tobit 14:1-2 The New American Bible)

Sometimes we may encounter angels disguised as humans and not know it. It is a scene somewhat like we might see today if only we could see into the spirit world.

Balaam's Donkey and the Angel of the Lord

I believe almost everyone is familiar with Balaam and the donkey mentioned in the Book of Numbers. When the Israelites were entering the land of Canaan, Balak, the Moabite king, feared the Israelites and called for the soothsayer Balaam to put a curse on them. God told Balaam not to curse the Israelites but Balak's offer was more then Balaam could refuse. God allowed Balaam to be disobedient to teach him a lesson. It was Balaam's donkey and God's mercy which saved him from being killed. As Balaam, riding his ass, and his two servants went forth, the ass saw the angel of the Lord which stood in her path. *(23) "And the ass saw the angel of the Lord standing in the way, and his sword drawn in his hand: and the ass turned aside out of the way, and went into the field: and Balaam smote the ass, to turn her into the way.(24) But the angel of the Lord stood in a path of the vineyards, a wall being on this side, and a wall on that side. (25)And when the ass saw the angel of the Lord, she thrust herself unto the wall, and crushed Balaam's foot against the wall: and he smote her again. (26) And the angel of the Lord went further, and stood in a narrow place, where was no way to turn either to the right hand or to the left. (27)And when the ass saw the angel of the Lord, she fell down under Balaam: and Balaam's anger was kindled, and he smote the ass with a staff. (28)And the Lord opened the mouth of the ass, and she said unto Balaam. What have I done unto thee, that thou hast smitten me these three times?(29) And Balaam said unto the ass, Because thou has mocked me: I would there were a sword in mine hand, for now would I kill thee. (30)And the ass said unto Balaam, Am not I thine ass upon which thou hast ridden ever since I was thine unto this day? Was I ever wont to do unto thee? And he said, Nay. (31) Then the Lord opened the eyes of Balaam, and he saw the angel of the Lord standing in the way, and his sword drawn in his hand: and he bowed down his head, and fell flat on his face. (32) And the angel of the Lord said unto him, Wherefore hast thou smitten thine ass these three times? Behold, I went out to withstand thee, because thy way is perverse before me. (33) And the ass saw me, and turned from me these three times: unless she had turned from me, surely now also I had slain thee, and saved her alive (Numbers 22:23-33 KJV)*

It is the most interesting example of how God can communicate with and through animals.

Pastor Ron Tucker's Convincing Surprises

Dr. Ladenius, the Angels and his Cat

In 1989, I was one of two non-clergy writers to address animals going to Heaven. I wanted confirmation from my pastor that the book was of God, but he didn't have an opinion on the subject matter at first. A few incidents happened within the month, however, to convince him that animals must have eternal life.

The first was a lady who had just become a Christian and who came into his office weeping because she didn't know if her pet would be in Heaven. Pastor Ron had no real answer for her—and then the very next week, my husband and I came into his office with the manuscript of *Will I See Fido in Heaven?*

Pastor Ron later wrote a wonderful letter to me concerning the scriptural revelation found in the book, as did the associate pastor, Rev. Smith, now retired. Another associate pastor at the church who also read the manuscript had two personal visions that led her to believe animals are in Heaven. They are included in the book.

Another bit of wisdom came through a story told by a visiting preacher, Dr. Fred Ladenius.

Dr. Ladenius was a writer for the Vatican for 18 years. He came to Grace Church in St. Louis to speak about his encounter with angels, his life as a writer and about becoming a born-again Christian after meeting with Billy Graham, who had come to speak with the Pope. However, he stopped in the middle of his sermon to tell us about his cat that had died, an interesting interlude, which, I believe, was as much for Pastor Ron's benefit as anyone else in the congregation.

One day as he sat in his garden (with his cat, Tabea) reading the Bible, a company of angels appeared to him. They were dressed in pure white, a white he had never seen before. Some were sitting on the fence, some were laying on the ground. The entire scene was peaceful and natural and both Fred and Tabea were enjoying their presence.

At this point in his story, Fred took off in a different direction and started talking about Tabea, announcing that the cat now was in Heaven. With the mention that Tabea was in Heaven you could hear a slightly embarrassed laugh from Pastor Ron, but that did not slow Dr. Ladenius down one bit. He started talking about how Tabea was not interested in associating with the non-Christians of humanity. However, when the Full Gospel Businessmen who met at the Ladenius' house were due to arrive, Tabea would sit waiting anxiously.

It was at this time in the discussion that Pastor Ron tried to get back on the topic of angels by saying, "I don't know where our theology is going here." Dr. Ladenius, however, kept right on with his revelation concerning his cat and the remainder of the animal kingdom. He stated: "But, God, after the flood, made a covenant with Noah and the animals and stated that God would not make a covenant with those who are not able to understand – so animals have a soul."

Pastor Ron eventually was able to bring the conversation back to angels. Dr. Ladenius found he was able to speak with his Heavenly visitors. They told him his garden was full of angels who protected humans and who were angelic heads of the villages, states and areas surrounding his home in Switzerland. He never asked why they were there nor did he think to ask. He only knew that he had been thinking how nice it would be to see angels and now he was!

He went on to say that because angels are messengers of God charged with helping us, we can expect them to do things for us. However, we are never, never to pray to angels.

ᶓ The Angel and the Cross ᶔ

This story is from Betty D. Allen. It is a most amazing story about a mysterious visitor who came to Betty's room and changed her life forever.

I became a Christian thirty-plus years ago. I always believed in God, but you can believe and still not be a Christian. Over thirty years ago I worked in a factory and had been working a lot of overtime with no day off.

One night, I decided, again, to work over and I fell to the floor. My co-worker was an EMT and he would not let me get up and go home as that was my intention. I told him not to worry for I lived only 20 miles down the road. He would not leave my side and had someone call for the ambulance and off I went to the hospital to the ICU unit. They stated that I had a heart attack and I was going to stay for a while. I became very afraid and started crying. My husband was called to the hospital. I told him not to worry and to go home to get some rest for he had to go to work. I was really trying to be brave and not let my family think it could be serious.

Soon after he left I became frightened and felt very alone. I wondered what would happen to my children, my family, and my beloved pets that I felt only I could love and care for. How could I leave them all at such an early age? (I was in my thirties.) I felt I was not ready to go yet. I had graduation-weddings-college-grandkids and so much to be a part of. I closed my eyes and prayed in silence. I must have been really tired and had fallen asleep when I felt someone tapping on my arm. He said *"Don't worry for everything will be all right. Just don't lose your faith in God."* I opened my eyes and a man was standing near my bed and he asked me to open my hand. He said, *"I'll give you strength and a promise."* I opened my hand and he placed an old cross in it. I closed my hand so tightly it was as if it was my life line, the most treasured gift one could ever receive. I must have fallen asleep again and when I awakened I thought it must have been a dream until I opened my hand and there was the old cross.

I asked the ICU nurse who the man was who had come into my room. The nurse said; "Betty, no one has been in your room. Why?"

she asked. I said yes, there was and he left me this cross and I want to thank him. She asked me again, "Where did you get the cross?" I said again "From the man that came into my room." She gave me a strange look, shook her head, and walked away. I held the cross tight in my hand this time and prayed out loud. I said: "God, if you give me one more chance my life and soul are yours forever." That day I knew I became a Christian because I felt different inside.

I never told my story because I believed people might have thought I was nuts or the story is just too unbelievable. You know, you really don't have to go to church every Sunday with all your fancy clothes because God is everywhere. I learned that God will not give you more in life then you can handle. Sometimes, we do wonder why we have to go through heartaches, pain, money issues and so on but this is a fallen world due to the sins of man. No doubt, however, these trials test our faith. If we put our faith totally in God everything seems to work out the way that is best for us in the end.

Don't ever be ashamed of telling people you are a Christian. Some day they may face a challenge and they will know where to turn to find help through God and the salvation He offers. God gives us the right to choose Him and His son Jesus. If we do not choose God, our life, our soul will never have contentment. We will never receive peace and happiness because there is no second chance, no turning back after death. There is no other opportunity to enter the wondrous Heaven God has prepared for us and for all of the animal creation He created for His pleasure and for us to care for on earth. Keep God in your heart as He is the Greatest.

That if thou shall confess with thy mouth the Lord Jesus, and shall believe in thine heart that God hath raised him from the dead, thou shall be saved. (Romans 10:9 KJV)

CHAPTER 8

The Miracles of Fido

Understanding My God-given Mission

I believe each of us has a purpose to fulfill in this life. If we're open to God's leading, He'll reveal our mission and be with us to see it through. It's up to us to follow and complete it. If we do, we will feel fulfilled in ways beyond our wildest dreams.

My primary God-given mission in life began in 1989 when I started writing my first book, *Will I See Fido in Heaven?* However, prior to my understanding that this was my mission, God had to prepare me to pursue it. Jesus did that by revealing to me, in a dream, a personal fault I needed to recognize. There have been two times during the writing of the *Fido* book in which I had messages delivered by God or his son Jesus, in a way that I knew it was them personally. I have been so blessed that if nothing in my life ever happened in the form of a blessing or miracle these two experiences have been more then any blessings I would ever hope for. They changed my life forever. I know how much my Heavenly father loves me and though I have been through many types of trials I know they have all been learning experiences to become more spiritually mature in being the person God wants me to be. I fall far short every day but I know He is still there picking me up and carrying me when I fall.

The Meaning of Fido

I had never known why I felt the need to have the word "Fido" in the title of my first book *Will I See Fido in Heaven?* but I did feel that the ending of the book, "Will Fido See *You* in Heaven?" was to be important.

I had been awakened two times about 3:00 in the morning with God speaking to me about the book and He always called it *"Fido"* each time. I would hear the Holy Spirit in a form of a mental imprint quote Scripture or a specific message and end by saying,*" It concerns Fido."* The message I remember the clearest came one night about a year before "Will I See Fido in Heaven" was published. I had prayed God would let me see Heaven like others I had read about but that was not His plan. The truth is I was afraid to have *Will I See Fido In Heaven?* published because I thought people, especially clergy, would say I was some crazy misguided lady who didn't know what she was talking about. I was the first woman other then Frances Svedbeck to write on this topic in the United States in the past 100 years covering the entire Bible on a subject that seemed forbidden in the pulpit. I prayed for over an hour on my knees to see if God would let me view Heaven some way but got so tired I crawled into bed and went to sleep. Suddenly sometime after 3:00 in the morning the Holy Spirit spoke to me saying: *"No weapon that is formed against thee shall prosper"* and then the words *"It concerns Fido."* That was Isaiah 54:17 which I had never memorized. The remainder of that scripture given to me the next day by my dear friend Debbie is: *"and every tongue that shall rise against thee in judgment thou shall condemn. This is the heritage of the servants of the LORD, and their righteousness is of me, saith the LORD.* I took God at His word and was no longer afraid to have it published.

I had received some criticism as some thought, by the title, that it must be a children's book or some simple nonsense book, so I decided possibly I needed to change the title for the second edition to "Will I See My Pet in Heaven?" I felt a need to pray with my friend Debbie. I took the book over and I asked if she would pray with me concerning its title. We prayed for a short while in the spirit and suddenly the Holy Spirit spoke to Debbie saying *"It is written in Heaven."* From then on I knew that the paperback book should retain the title *Will I*

See Fido in Heaven? even though the book was about all animals, not just dogs, and thought it might possibly limit the readers, other than dog lovers. That question was to be answered one day when the phone rang and Diane Jevak, an English teacher from Woodbridge, Virginia, called me about the meaning of "Fido."

⊷⊰{ My Beloved Beowulf }⊱⊶

Diane's dog Beowulf had gone to Heaven and she had read *Will I See Fido in Heaven?* giving her comfort but she was puzzled about the title. I told her God gave me the title and suddenly she realized what the word "Fido" meant. She became most excited and was celebrating the knowledge God had revealed to her what "Fido" meant. I had to wait until she calmed down to explain it to me. I was absolutely shocked and thrilled with what she had found out as the book had been published for about six years by then. In her story "My Beloved Beowulf" she reveals the two meanings of "Fido."

Diane states: On May 26, 2001, I brought my dog, Beowulf, to the vet for his most important visit. It was the hardest thing I have ever done. I couldn't let Beowulf suffer any longer. His eyes that Saturday morning told me all that I didn't want to know. He was asking me to let him go, and I loved him so much I needed to find the courage. I know that the Lord was with me every step of the way because there was a peace and serenity present in spite of the turmoil I felt. No one else was in the doctor's office, and I did not have to wait.

My last words to Beowulf were taken from *Hamlet*: "Good night, sweet prince, and flights of angels sing thee to thy rest."

That day I went home and put Beowulf's pictures and little red bandanna on my coffee table so I would feel close to him. I started reading the Bible again, and committed myself to a closer walk with the Lord.

At school I searched the Internet for support from Scripture that my beloved companion was in Heaven. When I saw the title of the book, *Will I See Fido in Heaven?* I knew I needed to purchase a copy right away. Before the book arrived, I thought about the title and decided I didn't like the word "Fido" in the title because it sounded too generic— like the equivalent of a "Jane Doe." But I was determined to read the book and check out the Scriptural references because I didn't want to get any "false hopes" about my pet's destiny.

When I had come home from putting my dog to sleep, I opened my Bible to Ecclesiastes 3, and God began taking me through the Bible, showing me that my beloved baby was in Heaven with Him. Many of the references that God showed me were also the same references contained in Mary's book, so it was confirmation that what I was learning was indeed true.

I kept on thinking about the title. I had phoned Mary and spoken with her and she said that God had given her the title. All of a sudden I remembered my Latin. "Semper Fidelis," the Marine motto, came to mind. I remembered *Fidelis* meant "faithful, loyal and true." To confirm this, at school the next day, I asked the Latin teacher the meaning of the word "Fidelis." She told me that "Fidelis" meant "faithful and loyal." The word "faithful and true" kept going through my mind. By now I knew for certain that "Fido" was not the name of a generic dog; "Fido" was related to the Latin word "Fidelis." (After all, is there anything more "faithful and true" than our beloved companions?)

Little by little, God revealed to me the wonderful meaning of the title of the book. One sentence in Mary's book really spoke to me. The sentence about the more important question is not "Will I See Fido in Heaven?" but "Will Fido See *Me* in Heaven?" Using the meaning for "Fidelis" I substituted "faithful and true" for "Fido" in two of the key sentences of Mary's book. Now the sentence read, "Will I See Faithful and True in Heaven?" Will I see my "Faithful and True" Friend, my Beowulf in Heaven? Translating again, will my "Faithful and True" Friend, my Beowulf, see ME in Heaven?

But the most important revelation of all came when I heard a small voice whisper to me, *"And what is MY name?"* With tears in my eyes I replied, "O Lord, Your name IS "Faithful and True." Now the title of the book became: Will I See "Faithful and True," The Lord, in Heaven? Will "Faithful and True," the Lord, see ME in Heaven?" I knew that Mary had indeed been given the title of her book by God, and I knew that "Fido" meant "faithful and true" in reference to the Lord, the King of Kings Himself! Jesus. The Lord gave us "Faithful and True" friends to be companions to us on earth just as He is always a "Faithful and True" companion to us.

I turned in the Bible to Revelation and knew that if the title of Mary's book was intended to be taken on many levels that I would find references to support "Faithful and True" being the Lord's name. I found the following references,

Revelation, Chapter 3, verse 14 (KJV): *"And unto the angel of the church of the Laodicea's write; These things saith* **the Amen, the Faithful and True witness, the beginning of the Creation of God.**"

Revelation Chapter 22, verse 6 (KJV) *"And he said unto me, These sayings are Faithful and True: and the Lord God...sent his angel to shew unto his servants the things which shortly must be done."*

Revelation 19:11 (KJV) *"And I saw Heaven opened and behold a white horse And he that sat upon him was called Faithful and True"*

The Lord also showed me that my last words to my dog were based in Scripture. In the Bible the souls of the just were taken by angels to Abraham's bosom. I smiled as I imagined Beowulf on the ride of his life.

After Beowulf went to God I looked closely at his little red bandanna. There were chubby yellow M&M candies wearing what looked like angel wings and the candies were smiling and waving goodbye. Surrounding the candies were red hearts. I knew that Beowulf had sent me a message through his bandanna, telling me that he was happy and that everything was all right.

Beowulf had worn that bandanna for months and I never really "saw" it until the time came when I needed comfort the most.

Even after all the Scripture, even after reading Mary's book, a portion of my heart did not believe. But when I searched the internet under "Fido" and found that "Fido" is Latin for "I believe," I no longer doubted that Beowulf is waiting for me. I thank Mary for her precious book, and I thank God for gently reproving me when I thought that the title for the book was too elementary and generic.

I Met Jesus

In this dream, I was sitting in a large room at a social gathering and started talking to a seemingly average yet, very charismatic man with shoulder-length medium brown hair. He was sitting to my right on a footstool and appeared to be in his early thirties. His voice was gentle; his eyes were warm, yet they seemed to penetrate my very soul.

As we talked, I turned my head to look straight at him and suddenly realized I was talking to Jesus. I jumped up off the divan and began singing to him. I sang a song that sounded similar to "How Great Thou Art," but it was something I had made up.

At that point, I awoke from my dream, grabbed a pencil and paper and ran into the family room to write down the words to the song I had sung in my dream. I wrote and wrote and when the wonderful song of love to my Lord and Savior was all written down I went back to bed.

As soon as I awakened the next morning I ran to see what I had written. The only words on the page were "I love you Lord" repeated over and over from the top of the page to the bottom. I was so upset that this was all I had written. I had felt sure God had given me a magnificent Christian song that would be a blessing to many.

The next evening at work I shared the experience with my friend, Carol Smith. With her spiritual wisdom she said, "Mary, that song was only to be shared with Jesus." It was then I remembered that in the vision, Jesus stood up facing me, and without saying a word, spoke to me mentally without his lips moving. He told me I had a problem with false pride. He showed me when he sat on a footstool which was lower than me on the divan that I needed to become humble, a servant to others as he has been for my salvation and for that of all mankind.

God has revealed so many things to me while I was writing *Will I See Fido in Heaven?* I want to share some of the experiences with you. There were so many miracles and so many revelations from God that I became accustomed to His responses. When the book was complete the visions ceased for a while.

I am still amazed at God's faithfulness when we set about to accomplish His purpose for our lives. I hope that by sharing miracles I experienced, others will be encouraged in the mission or missions God has given them.

Miracles Early-on

My Covenant with God

In the spring of 1989, I pleaded with God to allow the animals to be in Heaven. I have a deep, lifelong love for animals and remember that even as a little girl I hoped my dog, Tipsy, who was allowed to go with me to church, would go to Heaven. That feeling never left me and as an adult I was still hoping the same. That day in 1989, I told God I was willing to do anything He asked of me if only animals could have everlasting life with believers in Heaven.

I was later to realize that I had made a covenant with God that day. The things that were to happen later also made me realize that one does not break a covenant with God and still expect God to continually bless them. Three months after my plea, I found that animals do, indeed, go to Heaven and the news was contained within the Holy Bible itself. I was to learn what had not been taught for over 200 years in the church.

I also realized that God did have a purpose for putting such great love for animals in my heart. And I learned that He didn't need any sacrifice from me for animals to be in Heaven. What He did want was for me to preach the Word, and the avenue for that was through talking about animals in Heaven.

I began to tell some of my Christian friends about the Scriptures God had led me to and they began finding resource books for me to review. Two found a scripture for me to add about animals resting on the seventh day just as man was told to do. Before I knew it, I was searching through the original Greek and Hebrew translations to make sure no Scripture would be misunderstood as many Scriptures are symbolic and don't mean what they appear to mean. And for back up, others were reviewing my material to make sure I had not misunderstood or misinterpreted any scriptures in the book. It was most exciting and there was mounting evidence of many similarities in God's plan between man and animals, facts I had no idea of.

Yet I had not taken my covenant with God too seriously and periodically over the next five years I would stop working on the book for several weeks at a time. I noticed a pattern emerging in my life whenever I didn't work on the book faithfully. Turmoil would come into my life. We would lose money, family problems would emerge, our pets would get sick, and on and on.

I knew I was to get the word out and knew that the writing of the book would lead many to the Lord. But, I was fearful (even though many people encouraged me to write the book) to give the world knowledge that God does have eternal plans for all His non-human creatures.

Finally, one day in church the pastor talked about covenants and that when the people in the Old Testament disobeyed, God would remove His blessings on them. It occurred to me that turmoil in my life was His way of getting my attention to complete the book. But still I procrastinated.

God's Message Isaiah 54:17: "It Concerns Fido"

One night I knelt down by my bed in prayer and asked God for something to help my faith. I knew of people who proclaimed they'd been given a glimpse of Heaven, such as Robert Lairdon, who wrote *I Saw Heaven*, and Reverend Buck, whose similar experiences were recorded in *Angels on Assignment*. My prayer that night was to also be given a glimpse and to actually see animals in Heaven. Then, I felt I would have the courage to finish the book. I prayed for over an hour and then sleepily crawled into bed.

About 3 a.m. I was suddenly awakened with these words in my head: **No weapon formed against you will prosper. It concerns Fido.** After the Holy Spirit spoke these words to me I sat up in bed and said: "God, that is not what I asked you for. I don't understand why you gave me this message." Then I lay down and went back to sleep.

"No weapon formed against you will prosper" is from Isaiah 54:17. When I awakened, I pondered this Scripture and the message came to me that it was fear of criticism that kept me from publishing *Will I See Fido in Heaven?* I realized I didn't need more evidence that animals went to Heaven – God had already given me all the evidence I needed that animals do have immortality. How could one doubt with over 275 Scriptures from 31 Books of the Bible that together make it so very clear? Either, I believed the Bible, or I did not. Besides, my saying I'd gone to Heaven and had seen animals there would convince some that I was simply crazy and would discredit the Word of God on the subject.

God was reassuring me through Scripture that He would protect me, so I need not worry about what others might say. I felt that even more strongly when, later that day, a friend gave me the remainder of Isaiah 54:17: *and every tongue that shall rise against thee in judgment thou shall condemn. This is the heritage of the servants of the LORD, and their righteousness is of me, saith the LORD.*

The same day in church, the pastor focused on Isaiah 54:17. Later in the week a radio minister did the same. I have often asked God to confirm things for me in threes and he continually does because He knows I am such a doubting Thomas! After receiving three of the same message, I knew I had to finish writing the book and trust God to make the arrangements to get it published.

I did not have the money to publish *Will I See Fido In Heaven?* I also did not have all the research completed for details I felt I needed to address in the book. I prayed for another Christian to help with both, and God provided Roger Fritz, a brilliant thinker and strategist who was in demand as a consultant for leading companies. Roger attended my church and was also a consultant to the music education company we have operated for many years. In fact, that was why I had gone to see him that day—to discuss the music education business. He made the mistake of asking me what else I was doing and I told him about the book. I mentioned that I needed help and being a kind Christian man, he volunteered.

Roger and I were able to pull together a simplified explanation of body, soul, and spirit for the proper understanding of information within the book.

No Money to Publish *Fido*

Finally, the book was completed, but I had no money to publish. One Sunday, as my husband and I were walking in the front door of church, we saw Roger. Our church was so large it was rare to run into him. He stopped me and told me not to worry about the cost for publishing the book, because he would take care of that. I couldn't believe my ears. I praised God and cried with joy throughout the sermon.

Am I Alone in This?

It was important to me to discover whether noted theologians had ever written on animals in Heaven. I'd found commentary by one, but I was still a coward and thought if I could just include a short statement and scriptural references from three other theologians it would help my credibility, especially among clergy.

Two days after I sent the manuscript for its final editing I found another theologian's affirmation on the subject. Soon after that I found more when a lady from our church brought me a book. I hurriedly received permission to add a few sentences to my book on what I'd found.

I used several translations of the Bible beyond the King James Bible. For example, God planned for me to use the Catholic Bible. Many are unaware that the original King James Version and other Protestant Bibles contained all of the Apocrypha books found in the modern day Catholic Bible until 1885. I didn't even know that I had The New Jerusalem Bible, a Catholic version in my library until God brought it to my attention during my research. And, another strange thing happened. My friend Debbie and I went to pray with Tony Rhodes, a Catholic and friend of my husband, who was dying of cancer. He had bought the Douay Rheims Bible which I knew nothing about and it was lying on his coffee table. I picked it up and noticed the date of publication in the 1600s. I immediately looked up Genesis 9:8-18. I was thrilled to see this early translation. Knowing that I was excited about it Tony insisted I keep it. It has been a precious gift from Tony who is now in Heaven. It has been an invaluable part of my biblical research material ever since.

Time and time again, books came to me from very unusual sources and led me to more revelations concerning the immortality of animals.

Dad's Old *Reader's Digest* Surprise

Another story was brought to me in an unusual way while sorting through many old books belonging to my parents after they passed away.

Both were Christians and Dad took a number of subscriptions of various Christian magazines. As I was going through them, I happened to pick up a book published by *Reader's Digest* that included a 1957 article reprinted from *Guideposts* magazine. It was called "A Child Blessed," and was purported to have originated with the Apostle John. This touching story reveals how animals do know things beyond this world. It made immediate sense. The Apostle John was the most beloved of Jesus' Apostles and it is believed was probably observing our Lord as he gave comfort to a little boy who had just lost his dog. The Apostle John died of old age and not from martyrdom as most of the Apostles were, giving him time to recall and to write things he witnessed about Jesus. Some of the things and experiences he observed when he was with Jesus are recorded in the Bible and some, like the story "A Child Blessed" were not included in the Bible.

I called both *Guideposts* and *Reader's Digest* hoping to verify that the story was truly from the Apostle John. Both stated that they believed it to be the truth since it had run in two Christian publications and was found in some of the ancient manuscripts. They gave permission for me to reprint it in my book

Dad loved animals very much and because of him, a very special story believed to have been told by our loving Savior Jesus and passed on to us by his beloved Apostle John had found its way into my book. Dad was chosen by God to help with this book to glorify Him. What joy I have when I think of both my earthly and my Heavenly Father.

God Sends Miracle Stories

Although many of the stories in *Will I See Fido In Heaven?* were personal experiences, eight of them were told to me through complete providence. "A Dog named Ricky" was from our accountant Vi. "Merrylegs had a Foal" and "Rawhide Saves a Friend" were two stories from the Jensens whom I met by accident trying to find land for the new Pets and People Village. "Butchie" and "Tribute to Theresa and Cotton" were from a minister at Grace Church. "Heidi" was a dear friend and professional pianist who arranged some of the music for our Land of Music© education company. "Puppy Love" came from a newspaper article I had been given and asked to contact the owners to interview. "The Wren Family" was from my cousin Marilyn in northern Missouri. "Beagle to Beagle" was told to me by my dear friends the Jaziorskis, whom my beagle, Duffy, visited on a daily basis. I did not seek out any of these stories. They all came to me without knowing how valuable they would be in the understanding of the immortality of animals as they pertained to the various categories of scripture such as the praise of animals to God, the soul and spirit of animals, the eternal covenant God made with man and animals, and many more.

Who Will Publish *Fido?*

I did have an offer from a Christian publishing company to publish the book, but I decided against working with them when they wanted to change things I felt were important to leave as is. However, during our correspondence the editor brought up two questions concerning two Scriptures. Because of his questions, I addressed the subject of symbolic language in the book, a discussion important for understanding many of the verses referenced.

When I later learned that others had the same questions, I realized the contact made with this company, even though the publishing arrangement didn't work out, resulted in more clarity for people reading the book.

An Attorney and Fido—Isaiah 11:6-9

The next step was to find a Christian company to properly edit the book for publication. That information came without searching also. They eventually contacted me with an offer to publish the book. However, they changed their mind and broke the contract as I learned they did with other clients. But that was also part of God's plan.

That experience led me to seek a Christian attorney to review their contract. Our church recommended someone. In the process of contacting him, I received another confirmation. I had asked God for more evidence that Isaiah 11:6-9 actually meant animals also, as it is symbolic Scripture. The answer came when I contacted the attorney. I told him that I was a born-again Christian but that he might not agree with the subject I was writing on and could think I was somewhat unusual.

When I told him the book was about the immortality of animals from a biblical perspective he said, "I have no problem with that as I definitely believe animals go to Heaven." He then asked if he could share a story of his own experience concerning Scripture, the Holy Spirit and his dog. The Scripture he shared was Isaiah 11:6-9 and I knew without a doubt that what I had placed in the book was truly correct. He gave me permission to include it in *Fido*. That was a blessing.

A team of Christian scholars spent hours in research to verify that the Scriptures I had included within the book could be accurately confirmed through the original Greek and Hebrew study guides, affirming my interpretation was correct and the meaning of such words as "creatures" were used properly in my commentary.

All in all, five people helped in the research and some of them took the book to clergy, both Protestant and Catholic, to get their opinions of the validity of my interpretation of Scriptures concerning the animals. All agreed with it. Some were Baptist, one was a Catholic priest, and some were non-denominational ministers. Since that time many clergy of almost all Christian denominations and churches have begun to speak out in accordance with Scripture affirming animals do go to Heaven.

I asked God for three Scriptures concerning every subject addressed within the book and God provided them. When someone would tell me something, I would have two more confirmations. This happened with such frequency that I became accustomed to God's guidance in this manner.

Confirmation from the Editor

I had one more concern and that was that the man who was editing the book, Lloyd Hildebrand, chosen by the Christian publishing house, Destiny Image, Inc., would be in agreement with my interpretation of Scriptures and God's love for all creation. As he was finishing editing, he sent a message saying the family dog had passed away and the book was of great comfort to him.

Though I certainly did not want to hear such sad news, I knew God in His perfect timing had given us both comfort and the message we needed at exactly the right time.

God, What About *Fido?*

Next, my husband and I took the book to some dear Christian friends and decided to pray over it. As we prayed, the Holy Spirit spoke to my friend Debbie saying, *"I am well pleased.."* I was so full of joy at this confirmation that I was not being misled in any way.

The Apocrypha Books and the Truth Behind Them

God led me to use two of the Apocrypha books found now mainly in the Catholic Bible in the writing of *Will I See Fido In Heaven?* The Apocrypha books of the Bible were canonized in 406 by the Council of Carthage. They were part of the original Hebrew Scriptures. As a Protestant, I knew there had been disagreement over whether these books were of God. However, being obedient to the leading of the Holy Spirit I included them. Later I discovered that there is absolute proof that they were and are of God as revealed in the research of the Protestant minister and researcher, Dr. Craig Lampe.

Dreams, Visions and Messages from God
Preparing Me for writing *Will I See Fido in Heaven?*

The visions and dreams that occurred during the writing of *Will I See Fido in Heaven?* including the message through the Holy Spirit concerning Isaiah 54:17, continue to motivate me. To this day I do not understand the total significance of each but I do know God has unlimited love for all His creation, especially Man.

Native American Indians

The first vision occurred when I was visiting my son Eden and his family in Texas.

One early morning between 2 and 3 AM (which is the time most of my visions occurred), I saw myself standing on a hill with a Native American Indian standing beside me. Down at the bottom of the hill were many, many Native American Indians and they were looking up at us. We were all praising God that all the animals were to be in Heaven. I was very puzzled as to what the message meant and why I would have such a vision.

Soon after I returned to my home my husband and I went to see some very good friends of ours, Carol and Jerry Smith. Jerry has studied Native American Indians and has a deep love for them. When I revealed my vision, Jerry explained that it has always been the custom of the native American Indians to thank God for their meat, and to ask the animal to forgive them before they killed it for food. I was shocked that God would reveal such a custom.

Television and the White Buffalo Calf

Shortly after that I was sitting in my family room one morning reading the Bible when I felt an urgency to turn on the television. I had not watched television in the morning hours since the shuttle Challenger blew up almost eight years earlier, but I turned it on this day.

On the screen I saw an early morning talk show host interviewing an Indian in one of the northern states who was talking about a white buffalo calf just born. The Indian explained that according to a story passed on through the ages, when a white buffalo calf was born it was the sign that the end times were near. The interviewer asked what that might mean for Christians and the Indian said, "The return of Jesus."

God Spoke to Me about Love

My next vision was most unusual. I was floating above the earth near the ocean and I looked down to see a bull near the edge of the water. He was down on his knees, dying.

As I witnessed this bull, a voice spoke to me saying, ***"Mary, take the bull back to its owner."*** Though I don't remember actually taking the bull back, I do know I obeyed and it was in a Far Eastern country. The man was dark-skinned and seemed to be of Arabian, or Indian descent.

Some time seemed to pass and I was again floating above the earth in the same place. The ocean was on the eastern side of the land. Again I saw the same bull at the edge of the water, dying.

Again, I heard a voice say, ***"Mary, take the bull back to its owner."*** I immediately said, "But God, that man does not like people and he doesn't like you very much, either.."

As I stood there arguing with my Heavenly father, He said only, ***"Mary, love."*** Then His presence was gone and although I continued to argue, there was no one to listen.

Of the visions I have had, hearing the voice of God speak to me was the most breathtaking experience I have ever had. I heard our Lord say my name firmly, fatherly, yet lovingly. The word *love* was spoken with limitless compassion, yet it had a quality of reprimand. It allowed me to know that I don't begin to understand His love for every single person and the animals. I am to obey His commands

just as any child should obey a parent. And, most of all, I am to love unconditionally to reflect the love God has for each of us and even the animals.

I heard two more messages on God's love the same week. How fitting. I also understood the vision to mean that the message within *Will I See Fido In Heaven?* is to be taken throughout the world to tell people everywhere that God does truly love all creation – men and women from every walk of life and the non-human creatures as well. We are to reach out in love to all people and become the vessels through which God can bring the lost to eternal life in Heaven through His son Jesus.

Angels Watching Over Me

My last vision concerning the book occurred in 1994 and was one that was at first most frightening.

In my vision I was a teenager walking down a dark dirt road in the country with very tall trees on both sides. I appeared to be walking north. As I walked along, a black car appeared to the left of me with four men in it. The car stopped and the two men in the back seat got out of the car. One started coming toward me while the other stood there watching. I knew instantly that they were going to rape and kill me.

Just as the man got near me, a huge, bright bubble appeared, forming a dome-like room made of glass that I perceived to be a restaurant. It appeared on the right side of the road and as I looked inside this unusual structure I saw many people sitting watching the men. One large woman sitting closest to where I stood seemed most protective of me.

As the people inside just stared at these men, the two who were going to capture me jumped back in the car and they all sped off. I stood there for a moment terrified concerning what almost happened to me. Then, I heard a voice say, *"It concerns Fido."* I knew it was the Holy Spirit speaking to me again. I finally went back to sleep, though for a time I was physically and mentally shaken.

The next morning I could not understand what the vision meant. I first thought four men will try to destroy and discredit the book. But later on in the day as I was praying, asking God for revelation, I was instantly reminded that during my pre-teen and early-teen years of life, starting in seventh grade, I had been attacked and raped by an older teenage boy from town who threatened my life if I told anyone. I also was repeatedly molested by a teacher in front of an entire class of students for three years, and a neighbor man attacked me during junior high. Another man stalked me later in life.

This vision reminded me that my life had been in danger a number of times. God was showing me that He had saved my life from four men in all who were controlled by four evil spirits. I then understood that the words, "It concerns Fido," as spoken by the Holy Spirit, meant that God had saved my life to write *Will I See Fido In Heaven?* I knew instantly that that was my main mission in life.

I also kept thinking of the large lady in the dream who seemed protective of me. She seemed like an angel but her face looked like a schoolmate of mine named Lila (though Lila was not in any way large). It was then I remembered that Lila had protected me many times from the male teacher who had molested me. This teacher would arrange for me to ride in his car on all of our basketball games out of town. When he did, Lila would always get in the car and sit between us.

I never told my parents what happened to me during those years. The teacher was eventually fired after allegations of molestation were made. My father heard about it at a school board meeting but my name was never mentioned to him. He couldn't believe the allegations. When he asked me if they were true, I said yes, but was too afraid and ashamed to admit I was a victim. Dad probably could not have dealt well with that revelation. He was very strict and this was the 1950s. Sex was never spoken about among my family or friends.

Likewise, Lila and I never said a word to each other about it, but praise God she was there on every basketball trip going and coming.

When I speak to people and work with them, now, I often see them through different eyes. I know that God sometimes has people interceding as angels to protect us and quite often He uses His non-human creatures as well.

Revelations of Divine Love

I had given a book signing at the Vivia Book store in San Antonio, Texas. After the book signing and lecture was over a young lady who worked there handed me *Revelations of Divine Love* and said, "I think you will want this book and I feel led to give it to you." I was most humbled that she would be so thoughtful. After I got back to St. Louis I started reading it and found that it contained wonderful revelations I knew had to be of God.

There are two versions of the book held today in the British Museum. I am taking excerpts from the longer version.

Julian of Norwich was born in the fourteenth century. She was of the Catholic faith. Julian had a burning desire to know God and His son Jesus as intimately as possible and she prayed for this for years. Her prayers were that she could be like Jesus. She was not learned by her own account and she did not have scriptural references other than those possibly quoted by the priests of that time. During that period in history, the Bible was not read by the Catholic congregations, and even the priests would not always have a Bible to reference. Martin Luther who became the youngest Catholic priest in the early 1500s had never read or had access to the Bible for several years. When he did, he discovered through the Bible that we are saved by grace and not by good works. (Martin Luther is now known as the founder of the Lutheran Church. After his death, his followers chose to name their Christian doctrine after him.) Due to the inaccessibility of Bibles at that time it would be probable that Julian too, would not have access to a Bible. She never mentioned any scriptures as one familiar with scriptures would easily relate to. Many of her visions have specific scriptural references.

Dame Julian lived from 1342-1416. She was a recluse who lived in Norwich. She became very ill and was near death when the visions occurred.

The Revelation of Divine Love by Julian of Norwich was recognized from the first to have more than a private and personal value, a judgment that each reader may test for himself if he will read her vivid and strangely moving record. Her visions have never strayed away from the Biblical truths. Julian questions her visions herself and had to come to the terms that God was truly revealing truths to her that needed to be shared. I will cover some that pertain to creation including the animal world.

She writes that the revelations were given in May 1373, when she was thirty and a half years old.

Julian's mother was in attendance, together with other companions, at the illness from which she nearly died, and which, was the context of her revelations. She could have been a deeply religious woman living at home. No one knows what her position in life was. The parish priest who came to administer the last rites was accompanied by a child. However, we do not know who the child was or why a child would be at such a serious and sad event.

The "showings" or revelations came to Julian in three ways.

All the blessed teaching of our Lord God was shown by three parts; that is to say:

1. By bodily sight, For the "bodily sight" I had said as I saw, as truly as I can.

2. By word formed in my understanding, And for the "word," I have said them right as our Lord showed them to me.

3. By ghostly sight. And for the "ghostly sight," I have said some deal (a great deal), but I may never fully tell it.

God showed Julian that sin is more vile and painful than hell; it hurts nature but grace rescues nature (creation) and destroys sin.

Julian says: The spiritual martyrdom of Mary and others of Christ's followers; all things suffered with Him, good and bad alike were revealed to me.

Here, too, I saw a close affinity between Christ and ourselves—at least, so I thought—for when He suffered, we suffered. All creatures capable of suffering pain suffered with Him; I mean all creatures that God has made for our use. Even Heaven and earth languished for grief in their own peculiar way when Christ died. It is their nature to know Him to be their God, from whom they drew all their powers. When He failed, then needs must be that they too most properly should fail to the limit of their ability, grieving for His pains. So, too, His friends suffered pain because they loved Him.

Julian states: Thus our good Lord answered all the question, and doubts that I could produce. Most reassuringly, he said, "I may make everything all right; I am able to; I intend to, and I shall. You will see for yourself that every sort of thing will be all right."

When he says "I may," I understand it to refer to the Father; when he says "I am able to," to the Son; when he says "I intend to," it is the Holy Spirit; when he says "I shall," it means the blessed Trinity in Unity—three Persons and one truth.

Everything will be well, and Scripture fulfilled; it is the will of Christ that we keep ourselves steadfastly in the Faith of the Holy Church.

On one occasion the good Lord said, "Everything is going to be all right." On another, "You will see for yourself that every sort of thing will be all right." In these two sayings the soul discerns various meanings. One is that he wants us to know that not only does he care for great and noble things, but equally for little and small, lowly and simple things as well. This is his meaning: "Everything will be all right." We are to know that the least thing will not be forgotten. God said everything will be all right. The fullness of joy is to see God in all things. To see the same blessed power, wisdom, and love by which He made them are all things being continually led, and our Lord, Himself will bring them there. In due time, we shall see.

Julian was well aware of hell and that many would go there along with the fallen angels and Satan as she spoke of in her understanding. No doubt she was concerned about the creation below man as she saw man as wicked, sinful and the destroyer of creation. So the revelation that all creation below man, from the largest to the smallest, the most insignificant is going to continue on was a great comfort to her.

The thirteenth revelation; God's will is that we should greatly value all His works; the noble nature of all creation; sin is known by suffering. This revelation declares the will of God to be that we should greatly value all His works: the noble nature of all creation, the Excellency of Man's creation, the supremest (supremacy) of His (God's) works, and the precious atonement He has made for man's sin, turning our blame into eternal Splendour.

Jesus, who in this vision informed me of all I needed, answered, "Sin was necessary – but it is all right; it is all going to be all right; everything is going to be all right." In this simple word *sin*, our Lord reminded me in a general sort of way of all that is not good: the despicable shame and utter self-denial he endured for us, both in his life and in his dying, and all the suffering and pain of his creation, both spiritual and physical. Adam's was the greatest sin; its repartition (the making of amends for wrongs or injuries done) is more pleasing to God than even the sin was harmful.

The glorious city of the soul: made so nobly, it cannot be better made. The Trinity rejoices over it eternally. The soul finds rest in none but God, whose seat is in the soul, and who rules all things.

We have need of love, longing, and pity. God's longing takes three forms, and so does ours. On the Day of Judgment the joy of the blessed will be increased as they see the true reason for all that God has done. They will tremble and fear, rejoice and be thankful. They will marvel at the greatness of God, the completion of his creation.

Julian was given many visions and God showed Julian that not all will go to Heaven. Concerning people, we are saved by grace and we must be born again as the Gospel of John 3:1-16 says. The Catholic version, Douay Rheims Bible says in Chapter 3 of the Gospel of John verse 3, 5, and 7 you must be born again. That is consistent with the King James version as well.

Julian states: "The foundation of the Christian Faith is the redemption of mankind effected by Christ's death. This is not only the logical and necessary means of universal salvation, but something which has to be personally appropriated by each individual. Julian sees first of all the love of God revealed in the death of Christ. The whole Trinity is involved in this love, and each Person plays his part."

Julian said: I was puzzled by sin, the darkness of hell and the fiend, the many creatures (people) that shall be damned; as angels that fell out of Heaven for pride, which be now fiends. **(A fiend is an evil spirit or demon; Satan, a wicked and cruel person.)**

Julian wrote her visions down but did not have the one answer she was still looking for until fifteen years later. The following is the answer:

The good Lord showed that He wants us to pray thus for His work: thanking, trusting, and enjoying Him. He gave this revelation because He wants it to be known; in such knowledge He will give us grace to love Him; after fifteen years the answer was given: the reason for this whole revelation was **love.** May Jesus grant us this love! Amen.

There are numerous scriptures whose meanings are found in some of the revelations our Lord gave Julian centuries ago concerning both man and all of creation below man. Romans 8:18-20. *For the earnest expectation of the creature waiteth for the manifestation of the sons of God. For (even the whole) creation (all nature) waits expectantly and longs earnestly for God's sons to be made known-waits for the revealing, the disclosing of their sonship. For creation (nature) was subjected to frailty-to futility, condemned to frustration-not because of some intentional fault on its part, but by the will of Him Who so subjected it. {Yet} with the hope* (Romans 8:19-20 AMP)

Nature, all living things under man was corrupted due to Man's sins and Man's sins continue to destroy creation until a time when God will right every wrong through His son Jesus. Romans 8:21-22 says: *Nature (creation) itself will be set free from its bondage to decay and corruption [and gain an entrance] into the glorious freedom of God's children. We know that the whole creation (of irrational creatures) has been moaning together in the pains of labor until now. Referencing Ecclesiastes 1:2 KJV Vanity of vanities; saith the Preacher, vanity of vanities; all is vanity.(Romans 8:21-22 AMP)*

Matthew Henry's Commentary explains Ecclesiastes 1:2. *That they are all meaningless v.2. Everything is meaningless, not only in the abuse of it, when it is perverted by the sin of man, but even in the use of it. It is expressed here very emphatically; not only, All is vain, but in the abstract, All is meaningless; as if meaninglessness were the proprium quarto modo property in the fourth mode, of the things of this world, that which enters into the nature of them. They are not* *only meaningless but utterly meaningless, meaningless in the highest degree. Many speak contemptuously of the world because they are hermits, and know it not, or beggars, and have it not; but Solomon knew it. He had dived into nature's depths (1 Kings 4. 33), and he had it, more of it perhaps than ever any man had. He spoke deliberately, and laid it down as a fundamental principle, on which he grounded the necessity of being religious. One main thing he intended was to show that the everlasting throne and kingdom must be of another world; for all things in this world are subject to meaninglessness, and therefore have not in them sufficient to answer the extent of that promise. Matthew Henry's Commentary explains Ecclesiastes1:2)*

All creation was therefore hopeless, subject to the sins of man until Jesus came to deliver creation back to God. All creation awaits this great event.

The book of Revelation Chapter 5 says: *And every creature which is in Heaven, and on the earth, and under the earth, and such as are in the sea and all that are in them, heard I saying, Blessing, and honour, and glory, and power, be unto him that sitteth upon the throne, and unto the Lamb for ever and ever. (Revelation 5:13 KJV)*

And He that overcometh shall inherit all things; and I will be his God, and he shall be my son (Revelation 21:7 KJV).

The Book of Isaiah speaks of the future in Heaven and on earth.

Isaiah 11:6-9 says that the wolf shall dwell with the lamb and the leopard shall lie down with the kid. Man and animals shall live in harmony in the new Heaven and the new earth. Heaven and earth restored to its original state.

Remember the Bible says: *For every beast of the forest is mine, and the cattle on a thousand hills, I know all the fowls of the mountains; and the wild beasts of the field are mine. (Psalm 50:10-11 KJV)*

CHAPTER 9

A Tribute to My Babies in Heaven

I want to give tribute to three wonderful pets that have been part of my life and went to Heaven in recent years. Praise God, I will be with them again, and next time it will be forever.

❧ Angel and Lindy Together Forever ❧

For three years we had to keep our beautiful white/golden English cocker spaniel in a harness to walk her and let her go to the bathroom. She was attacked by our two big dogs two times and our German shepherd once after that. Angel was really not very nice to the other dogs and she would snarl at them. We had spoiled her so. She was rescued by some college students in Texas who witnessed her being kicked and abused by her owner. She was only two months old at the time. She was beautiful as a puppy and adult dog but the spoiling did not allow her to take the position in the pack she should have with our other dogs. For three years, I would get up in the middle of the night (often several times) and take her out to go to the bathroom.

It was about two weeks before Christmas and she was to the point of walking all night long, falling, unable to get up. I knew she was in extreme pain. At the same time, our very handsome little Sheltie, Lindy, was also suffering. He had been thrown out of a car in the woods and picked up by our daughter and her husband when he was only about two months old. They were about the same age and size, slept together and were almost inseparable. Lindy has always been a very loving little guy and never had a problem with anyone or any dog. He loved to carry the newspaper in from the front yard and I know he is carrying important things around for Jesus in Heaven. Lindy was almost blind and could not hear, plus his back legs had been giving out on him and he could not get up on his own much of the time. I decided to let them go on to Heaven together but I put it off week after week and month after month. The last two weeks I became so exhausted trying to walk them day and night and I know they both were in such pain that it was selfish for me to allow them to suffer any more. My husband and I were with them when Dr. Steinberg came to let them go on to Heaven. Releasing them from our home made it more peaceful for them and for us.

I do praise God we could give them all a wonderful life.. I have peace that I will be with them in Heaven. *(19) The Lord hath prepared his throne in Heaven: and his kingdom shall rule over all. (20) Bless the Lord, all ye his angels: you that are mighty in strength, and execute his word, hearkening to the voice of his orders. (21) Bless the Lord, all ye his hosts: you ministers of his that do his will. (22) Bless the Lord, all his works: in every place of his dominion, O my soul, bless thou the Lord. (Psalm 102:19-22 Douay Rheims1609 Bible)*

⸙{ Saving Lucy }⸙

Our wonderful black lab/chow mix Lucy has now joined my other beloved pets in Heaven. The family, (mother, father and three children) who had her had raised her from a puppy to age two but the mother no longer wanted her. I had heard about Lucy at a meeting at the non-kill shelter I worked with in Illinois. I told them to please contact the family immediately to tell them I would take her as the mother was going to have her put to sleep the next day. The father loved her and had notified one of the people attending the meeting to see if someone would take her because his wife would not take her to a shelter. She believed it was better to put her to sleep than to have her in a shelter where she might not get adopted. The husband was overjoyed when they called him that night to tell him that someone who loves animals would take her. The next day he and their three children brought her to us with tears in his eyes thanking us for saving her life. We shared her life for seven more years before she died, suddenly, of cancer. She was so loved. Lucy loved to play with our German shepherd mix, Sally. They spent most of their life together.

I read the promise God made in Ephesians 1. God has predestined all things to come back to Him, all creation below man and all of mankind who have accepted Jesus as their Lord and Savior. *(11) In whom also we have obtained an inheritance, being predestined according to the purpose of him who worketh all things after the counsel of his own will (Ephesians 1:11 KJV)*

❧ Dedicated to My Beloved Sally ❧

Sally, our truly beloved German Shepherd, came to us a lost young puppy about six months old. She had rope about six feet long tied around her neck and was wandering up a country road searching for a home. She found her way to the home of our friends, Bob and Dr. Lana Richard, but they could not keep her; thus she became ours to love and care for.

On November 20, 2009, I had to let my beautiful, soccer-ball-playing and fun-loving German Shepherd, Sally, go to Heaven. She was fourteen and had huge lumps all over her neck, under her neck and in every lymph node in her body. She had had a couple of lumps for years but they were benign. However, in the last three months, more appeared. Within the next month, it was obvious that there were a great deal more lumps. I started treating them with all of the known cancer-preventing medications and health foods I could find but it became a hopeless situation. The last month I noticed that she seemed in great pain and our walks were very slow; and then, she would not go for a walk at all. I had to face the fact that the lumps were surely cancer and were destroying her body causing her great pain.

God gives us charge over the animal kingdom but He also assures us of two things: one is that the animals belong to Him and their spirits go directly to Heaven to be with Him when their bodies die, just as all Christians who physically die. There is another charge we have over creation, which is the responsibility of letting them go back to the God who created them when they are suffering with no hope of recovery. Our selfish souls want to hold on to them even when they are in horrible pain. We keep them in a kind of prison so they cannot escape to Heaven and be with God and His son Jesus.

My problem was, how did I really know when it was time to let Sally go? I prayed for several weeks but the Wednesday night before, I simply asked God if He would somehow give me a sign to let me know when it was her time to go. And, as He did with my husband, Bob, two years before he died, God answered my prayer, but this time it was by using others to bring me the news.

A group of my friends meet on Thursdays to pray for our country and our families. This Thursday they prayed for Sally and they prayed for me to let her go.

A member of our prayer team, Sandy, called first thing Friday morning and said she had had a vision early that morning and it was wonderful. It was the answer to the prayer I prayed Wednesday night asking God to please give me a sign just to let me know I was doing the right thing by releasing Sally back to Him.

Sandy said: ***This morning I was still asleep when my daughter called to give me instructions for the day on packing to leave on our trip. As I was hanging up the phone I just started praying for you and Sally. I saw Sally healed and running down the streets of gold—so happy! I said: "Jesus, is she looking for Mary?" I felt such joy and had to tell you that she will be so happy when she gets home.***

Now, this is not all of the story. Please understand that Sandy is a born-again, spirit-filled woman of great faith who spends a great deal of time in intercessory prayer and I have no doubt she hears from God. And, as I said, there is actually more to this story and it comes from a different person in a different state who does not know Sandy at all.

I called Ron Friday morning, who was at the cabin in Missouri, and told him that I had made the decision to let Sally go home to be with God today. I immediately noticed a choking in his voice and I asked what was wrong. His reply was, *"How strange,"* and there was silence on the other end of the line. He then started talking again and said he had had a dream about her the previous night. He said he was so shocked that she was going to be going to Heaven today and he seemed confused because of what happened in his dream. If you remember the story of Pepi, the Friday night after we had let her go, all night I felt she was cold and Ron dreamed that she was lost and he told her to go toward the light. He didn't have any idea what I was thinking and feeling that night after she was put to sleep. Something similar happened this time; however, this was a prophecy or vision of the future because he saw what was yet to happen. Remember, Ron is at the cabin in Missouri and I am living in Wichita Falls, Texas, with Sally.

Ron said: *In my dream, I saw Sally prancing down the street and thought she must have gotten out of the house somehow. I called her and she came to me and talked, or at least, I knew what she was thinking/saying. She said she was very happy and she was going to play with Pepi, Angel, and Lindy* (Sally's canine pals now in Heaven)*, and then she just ran off into the light down the street. I could tell she was no longer in pain by the way she ran, kind of like a happy puppy. Then, I woke up.*

I tried to remember everything. I found myself thinking, "Why is she going to Heaven now?" as she was alive and in pain at Mary's. Yet, I could see she was happy and not in pain in my dream. I thought I would tell Mary about the dream the next time we spoke. I remember feeling guilty about having the dream because Sally was still alive. I understood how much pain she must be in and did not want what happened to our dog Mr. Blue to happen to her. We kept him alive when he should have been allowed to cross over. Faithfully, he endured what must have been awful pain trying to please us as he always had. I did not want this to happen ever again.

So to understand God's message to me, who was Sally looking for in Sandy's vision? Was she was looking for Pepi, Angel, Lindy, or possibly her pal, Lucy, as revealed in Ron's dream? After all, she knew where she was going and she knew they were there.

There is even more, however, and that came from a wonderful friend, V.J. whose life story I am writing. I called V.J. to tell her that we could not meet Friday because I had to let Sally go to Heaven. I started crying because Sally was still able to walk, and for some reason, I felt that because she could still get around it was not time for her to leave. V.J. prayed for me and for Sally and then she said: **"I believe Sally wants to walk into the animal hospital to show you that she is going to walk right into Heaven."** After I had received the visions from Sandy and Ron, and V.J.'s comment, everything fit together so I could get through letting her go. It had to have been orchestrated by God to receive what was brought to me as all three, Sally, Ron and V.J. together gave me complete peace.

There is a question one might ask concerning Sally. Did she know I was going to let her go that day? Did she know ahead of time or did

God give those visions to Sandy and Ron to give me comfort? I don't really know. Both may be true. Let me give you my reasons.

I believe God gave me the confirmations that I needed ahead of time through Sandy, V.J., and Ron to let Sally go on to Heaven. I remember that God gave me three visions and spoke to me that my first husband, Bob, would be in Heaven two years before he suddenly died of a heart attack. My son, Eden, wanted to make sure his dad was saved as he had been having some health issues so God's messages gave us great comfort. God answered that question very dramatically in three separate visions and the words He spoke to me while driving home from Bob's after Christmas about six months before he died. So, is it possible that God reveals things ahead of time concerning both our loved ones and our pets? It does appear that way.

Another reason I believe the signs they gave me could be true is found in my book, *Will I See Fido in Heaven?* which contains the story "A Child Blessed," as told by the beloved Apostle John, about a little boy whose dog had died. Jesus was giving comfort and understanding to the little boy revealing to him that animals see beyond this world. They understand the things of God man does not because they are sinless creatures spiritually connected with God. They apparently know life continues beyond this world. John wrote the story, which if in the Bible would be considered scripture, just as the story of Jonah and Balaam's donkey. Volumes and volumes of writings by the Old and New Testament writers are not found in the Bible, but are wonderful and credible stories and scriptures nonetheless. I also believe there are stories within *Animal Miracles of the God Kind* and some wonderful true-life animal stories in *Will I See Fido In Heaven?* to support my belief that not only does God give us warnings of things to come but also that animals do understand beyond this sin-laden world which has blinded man because of his sinful nature.

Scripture says, *"To be absent from the body is to be present with the Lord,"* should anyone question where the soul and spirit of the saved person and the animals go. The Book of Revelation 20:4 says: *"There are no more tears, sorrow, death, or pain in Heaven."* Those in Heaven, both man and animals, do not see our pain or sorrow on earth. They have complete joy. My Sally is not sitting at some rainbow bridge waiting for me to come. She is running free, playing with all of our other pets and my family. I have no doubt, however, that she will be there to greet me when my time comes and I can meet my Savior face to face.

I also received a wonderful e-mail Friday evening from another dear friend, Bishop and Evangelical minister, Dr. Debra Schmidt, when she wrote: ***"I understand how hard it was for you, Mary, but I also know in my heart that Sally knew it was her time to go to be with our Lord and you helped her out of your love for her. Just imagine how beautiful your homecoming will be the day you sit with Jesus as He smiles at you and all of your four-legged friends that await you. I can see His smile right now as I write this, my sister."***

Now, my friends, as I close the messages of and from God concerning His love for both man and animals, know that I have to be the most blessed person on earth to have such a wonderful family and fantastic friends such as I have. Another dear Christian friend, Barbara Grazdan, edited this book so you could make sense of it. That only proves how good God has been to me. What more could anyone ask from life in this world?

The Souls of Pets
by Robert Clark
Poet and Research specialist

Did my guardian angel see another angel there watching over me,
lying there beside my bed, my slippers as a pillow for your head.
And though I'm a pauper one would have thought
you guarded a prince's sleep with all the love you have brought.
Now has the Lord taken your soul
or is it as I seem to recall?
Someone once said you have no soul at all.

Not all souls included, all pets excluded.
Is that how the sign over Heaven's gates read?
Does that sound like Jesus, loving creator, sustainer and Lord,
Or even remotely resemble something He would have decreed?

Little one, does the Rock of Ages hold no place for you?
Is there nothing beyond these things man proclaims as true?
When God sees each sparrow that falls from the sky
How is it you would be excluded from the sweet bye and bye?

Not all souls included, all pets excluded.
Is that how the sign over Heaven's gates read?
Does that sound like Jesus, loving creator, sustainer and Lord,
Or even remotely resemble something He would have decreed?

And now that we've said goodbye these thoughts come to mind
For all those He created after their kind.
God said the souls of all living things
and the breath of all mankind was right there in His hands.
So no doubt you'll be included in His eternal plans.

Closing Prayer
For all who have special pet companions in Heaven

Cheryl Beaverson loves Guinea pigs and has written a tribute dedicated to each of them. They have filled her life with love and companionship and when they go on to Heaven, a great void is left.

I rejoice in the Lord because He is a God of love. I give Him praise that my pets are now free of the burdens and suffering of life here on this earth and are now in the presence of their Creator. My tribute is dedicated to each of them:

Gracious and Precious Father:

Thank you Lord for all that you have created. You are the sustainer of all life and continue to always provide for the needs of all that you have created. Thank you for the pets that you have placed in our care. Remind us always that they belong to you and that you give them to us to take care of and to learn from them your unconditional love.

Lord, we bring you our grief in the loss of our pet. We bring you thanks for those that live among us and have given freely of their love. We commit our friend and companion into your hands and return their soul back to you Beloved Father.

My precious friend, be one with God, be one with Christ and be one with the Holy Spirit. May Jesus greet you at the gates of Heaven where you will live forever and we will rejoice when once again we will be together.

In Jesus' Precious and Holy name,

Amen!

Appendices

Appendix 1:
Words and their various meanings

There are words in the Bible that may mean one thing in specific scriptures and something else in others. The following words are some examples which can help you in understanding more clearly what scriptures mean depending on the subject. Often there are scriptures that use symbolic language illustrating animals and trees, tribes and human beings to mean other than what the literal words say.

1. **Beast**— can mean man and or animals or the devil.

2. **Trees**— historic locations, tribes of people, types of trees.

3. **Creatures**— can refer to man, animals, angels, all, one or two of them. In the New Testament it says *go throughout the world and preach the gospel to every creature.* This means to preach to Jews and Gentiles. Isaiah 65:26 speaks of the lamb and the wolf feeding together. That refers to men who are enemies on earth but will be friends in Heaven.

4. **Perish**— does not mean that something is lost forever, or disappears forever. It does not indicate that the person or animal goes to hell. It means that it is forgotten or dies. The dictionary says disappears or dies. One good example is when the Disciples were in the boat and they thought they were going to sink and they cried out to Jesus, "Save us, lest we perish."

5. **Works**— can mean all creation.. However the word "works" can mean what God does in creating and continuing His work in creation. It can also mean what man does to live a Godly life such as sacrificing for others or to live in a way that is of no blessing or benefit to anyone but him or herself.

6. **Breath of Life**— means the spirit. Some scriptures say the breath of the spirit of life. God breathes His spirit into all living beings.

7. **Life blood**— means the living flowing spirit within the blood which takes the oxygen/breath throughout the body. As long as the blood is flowing in the body the person or animals is still breathing which is their breath of life. When the blood stops flowing, the spirit leaves, thus the breath of life goes back to the creator or to hell depending on the person's relationship with God. Animals' spirits go back to God.

8. **Being**— means soul, living being or living soul.

9. **Host**— refers to all kinds of beings in creation including the stars and other planetary objects in the Heavens as well. Hosts help; thus, it is presumed that angels, people, animals all who help God in some way in creation at times can be implied.

10. **World**— can mean all creation, man, animals, earth sky, stars, plant life. However when scripture says the world is righteous, the reference is all creation outside of man. Man is judged separately from the world according to scripture. The world is pure and innocent. The world is righteous. Man is sinful.

11. **Righteous**—Those of the human race who are in right standing with God and all creation below man.

12. The original translation of the word "servant" is actually "slave" When one becomes a Christian they become a slave (owned by God and His son Jesus). A servant is one who has freedom to work for others and themselves. A slave has to work for his master as he belongs to that master.

Other books, DVDs and Music CDs
by Mary Buddemeyer-Porter

Will I See Fido in Heaven? Amazon Christian bestseller paperback book

Will I See My Pet in Heaven? book on CD

Animals, Immortal Beings paperback book

All Creation Praise The Lord music CD with narration album and booklet

All Creation Rejoice music DVD

I'll See You In Heaven My Friend pet loss DVD

I'll See You In Heaven My Friend music DVD

Animals in Paradise documentary

Recommended Books and DVDs by Other Authors

Angels on Assignment
by Charles and Francis Hunter
(download on internet)

A Place Called Heaven
by Dr. Gary Wood

Close Encounters of the God Kind
by Jesse Duplantis

The Man Who Talked With Angels
by Sharon White

Recommended Pet Book Authors

All Creatures of Our God and King
by Teri Wilson

The Immortality of Animals
by Dr. Elijah Buckner

Animal Gospel
by Dr. Andrew Linzey

Animals Have Souls and Do Go To Heaven
by Bill LaSalle

I'll See You Again My Friend
by Skip Daniels

End Notes

Angels
By Charles Capps © 1954-1958
Published by Harrison House, Inc.
P.O. Box 35035
Tulsa, OK 74153

Angels On Assignment
by Charles and Frances Hunter
(Now downloadable on the internet)

A Place Called Heaven
by Dr. Gary Wood
Published by Gary Wood Ministries
3506 Highway 6 South #33
Sugarland, TX 77478
(Used by Permission)

Close Encounters of The God Kind
by Jesse Duplantis
Harrison House Publications
P.O. Box 35035
Tulsa, OK 74153
(Used by Permission)

Do Animals Go To Heaven?
By Frances Svedbeck
F. Svedbeck Publishing, 1994
2865 Dole Road
Myrtle Creek, OR 97457

Animals Taught Me That: A Faith-Based Journey
A. Kim Bloomer, V.N.D.
Crossbooks Publishing
Dr. Bloomer is co-host of "Animal Talk Naturally" radio show,
www.AnimalTalkNaturally.com
(Used by Permission)

Heaven and The Angels
By H.A. Baker, Mokiang, Yunnan, China
Distributed by
The Christ Mission
330 East Boardman St.,
Youngstown 3, Ohio, U.S.A.

Intra Muros
by Rebecca Ruther Springer [1832-1904]
A David C. Cook Publication
Elgin, IL 1898

General William Booth's Vision of Heaven
General William Booth
Founder of The Salvation Army
London, England 1906

John Wesley, An On-line Exhibition:
The John Ryland's University Library of Manchester:
http://rylibweb.man.ac.uk/data1/dg/methodist/jwol1.html

Mysteries of the Bible Now Revealed
Reverend David Allen Lewis
New Leaf Press, Inc. © 1999

Revelations of Divine Love
Julian of Norwich
Printed by the Penguin Group
Penguin Books U.S.A. Inc. 375 Hudson Street
New York, NY 10014
Copyright © Clifton Wolters, 1966
All Rights Reserved

The Forbidden Book
by Dr. Craig Lampe © 2003 All rights Reserved.
WWW.GREATSITE.COM.

The Man Who Talked With Angels
by Sharon White Copyright ©1982
Healing Stream Ministries
Pastor Ted Buck
Central Assembly 12000 Fairview Avenue
Boise, Idaho 83813

The Visions of Sadhu Sundar Singh of India, 1926
Published By Noah's Ark,
P.O. Box 607, Armidale,
NSW, 2350, Australia, 1996
E-mail: noah@northnet.com.au
http://reluctant-messenger.com/sadhu-sundar-singh.htm

Visions Beyond the Veil
by H.A. Baker
Published by Osterhus Publishing House 4500 W. Broadway
Minneapolis, Minn. 55422, USA. 12th English Edition
Biblical Publication Information

Biblical Publication Information

Authorized 1611 Version of the King James Bible
Lazarus Ministry Press © 2000 by Greyden Press.
Columbus, Ohio 43204 All rights reserved.

Douay-Rheims Bible, Old Testament 1609, New Testament 1582,
Printed by Tan Books and Publishers, Inc., Rockford, Illinois 61105

Good News Bible Today's English Version
ABS American Bible Society, New York © 1976, 1966, 1971

Holy Bible, New Living Translation
© 1997 Tyndale House Publishers, Inc, Wheaton, Illinois

Holy Bible Unauthorized King James Version (KJV), 1943

Matthew Henry's Commentary
The NIV Matthew Henry Commentary in One Volume
Zondervan Publishing House Grand Rapids, Michigan
A Division of Harper Collins Publishers
© 1992 by Harper Collins Publishers Ltd.

New American Bible
St. Joseph Medium Size Edition
Catholic Book Publishing Co. New York
© 1992, 1987, 1980, 1970

New International Version The Student Bible,
Zondervan Bible Publishers, Grand Rapids, Michigan
1986, 1973, 1978

New Jerusalem Bible (NJB),
Barton, Longman & Todd, Ltd. and Doubleday, a Division of
Bantam Doubleday Dell Publishing Group, Inc., 1985)

NKJV New King James Version The Maxwell Leadership Bible
Thomas Nelson Bible, A Division of Thomas Nelson, Inc.
The New Maxwell Leadership Bible
© 2002 by Maxwell Motivation, Inc.

The Bible in Today's English Version (The Good News Bible)
(TEV), Zondervan Bible Publishers © 1973, 1978, 1984.

The Dead Sea Scrolls, Uncovered
Text copyright by Robert Eisenman and Michael Wise,
Element Books Limited, 1992, 1994.

The Geneva Edition 1st Printing, 1st Edition: 1560
Published by Lazarus Ministry Press © 1998 All Rights Reserved
Vintage Archives 2020 Builders Place Columbus, OH 43204

The Holy Bible, New King James Version
© 1982 by Thomas Nelson, Inc.

The Holy Scriptures Jewish Publication Society of America 1917
Printed by the Jewish Publication Society of America Philadelphia
Forty-first Impression, September 1958 781st Thousand

The Living Bible paraphrased (TLB)
Tyndale House Publishers, Inc, ©1971)
Used by permission. All rights reserved.

The New English Bible with Apocrypha – Oxford Study Edition
Oxford University Press New York © 1976

The New Testament in Modern English Student Edition
J.B. Phillips by MacMillan Publishing Company New York

The Open Bible the Authorized King James Version
Copyright © 1975 by Thomas Nelson Inc. Publishers
Nashville, Tennessee

The New Oxford Annotated Bible New Revised Standard Version
Oxford University Press New York © 1991, 1994

About the Author

Dr. Mary Buddemeyer-Porter is the author of Amazon Christian Bestseller *Will I See Fido In Heaven?* and of *Animals, Immortal Beings*.

She is also a Regional Emmy®-nominated songwriter and television producer.

Mary appears in "Animals In Paradise," the heart-warming documentary featuring Jack Hanna, Jackie Zieman, Reverend Lawrence Bishop and other noted personalities. There are many wonderful true-life stories demonstrating God's love and eternal plans for animals as well as man. The documentary is based on her books and features her music as well.

Mary has appeared on national television in the United States and Europe, and has granted numerous radio interviews, all on the biblical proof of animal immortality. She speaks in churches and for various animal associations speaking on this very subject. Mary donates much of her time in grief counseling and the rescue of many homeless animals.

Mary Buddemeyer-Porter received her formal biblical studies at Missouri Baptist University and Maryville University in St. Louis MO. She has a BA in Music Education with a minor in Science and Dance. She has a Master of Arts in Teaching from Webster University, Webster Groves, MO. She received her Ph.D. in Creation Theology at Crossroads Bible College and Theological Seminary and is currently developing a student study guide and course on Creation Theology for the Institute.

Mary has taught music, science, and movement/choreography in elementary, junior high, high school and college.

Mary is a member of ASCAP and has produced two children's cable television series, "Movin' On" and "Wild Workout," for which she was nominated for a Regional Emmy®, both as a producer and songwriter.

Mary is co-author of the popular music education system "The Land of Music®," published by Note Family, Inc. Mary has won awards for her work in the music education industry. She has given seminars throughout much of the United States for the Land of Music® curriculum she helped create and has appeared on television as an advocate for music education.

Mary has two sons, one daughter-in-law, four grandchildren and numerous pets. She is an evangelical Christian, a member of Wesley United Methodist Church and various Christian organizations.